THE
LAST
FALLEN
REALM

Also by Graci Kim

The Last Fallen Star
The Last Fallen Moon

THE
LAST
FALLEN
REALM

A Gifted Clans Novel

BOOK THREE

by GRACI KIM

RICK RIORDAN PRESENTS

Disney • HYPERION   LOS ANGELES NEW YORK

*All Korean words used in this book have been transliterated
according to the Revised Romanization of Korean system.*

Copyright © 2023 by Graci Kim

All rights reserved. Published by Disney • Hyperion, an imprint of Buena
Vista Books, Inc. No part of this book may be reproduced or transmitted
in any form or by any means, electronic or mechanical, including
photocopying, recording, or by any information storage and retrieval system,
without written permission from the publisher. For information address
Disney • Hyperion, 77 West 66th Street, New York, New York 10023.

First Edition, June 2023
1 3 5 7 9 10 8 6 4 2
FAC-004510-23103
Printed in the United States of America

This book is set in Corton, Goudy Trajan Pro Medium,
Goudy Old Style/Fontspring
Stock images: watercolor 61613686, sun 89398255,
moon 1471622636/Shutterstock
Designed by Joann Hill

Library of Congress Control Number: 2022048890
ISBN 978-1-368-07316-5
Reinforced binding

Follow @ReadRiordan

Visit www.DisneyBooks.com

Logo Applies to Text Stock Only

For Halmeoni the sun, and Halmeoni the moon—
two of the mightiest women to ever have shined

Contents

Mago Halmi

They say being a mother is the most challenging job in the world. You love your children more than life itself. But to be a good mother, sometimes you have to sit back and do the hard thing. That is, to say, do nothing.

At times, you must endure in silence as they commit grave mistakes, hoping they learn from their actions. Hoping you have instilled in them sufficient humility to see them through. Hoping they will do better next time. If there *is* a next time.

It may be difficult to believe, but my six divine children were once young, too. Innocent, ignorant, and unadulterated by the ravages of time. Ah. Indeed. Those were, as they say, the good days of old.

My eldest, Gom, borne of the cave bear. A dutiful girl. She used to spend her days outside, tending to injured birds with broken wings, long until the sun disappeared over the horizon and her stomach ached for nourishment. Service and sacrifice came as naturally to her as her ability to mend flesh and bone.

My second, Horangi, borne of the mountain tiger. A studious girl. She would spend her days inside reading, devouring words like they were morning dewdrops after a drought, shedding light on the darkest crevasses of the mind. Knowledge and truth was her sustenance, of which she never tired of consuming.

It was just Gom and Horangi for some years, blissful in their respective quests for mastery. A quiet life, but peaceful and filled with purpose. Until the triplets arrived, bringing with them a cocktail of chaos and renaissance.

The first of the triplets, Samjogo, borne of the three-legged crow. A commanding girl. She was proficient in the art of authority, leading our busy household with precision and efficiency, despite the persistent pleas of her sisters for leniency. For she saw wisdom in such leadership, and took pride in her role as such.

The second of the triplets, Gumiho, borne of the nine-tailed fox. A beautiful girl. Many an hour she would spend preening herself in the mirror, reigning dominion over the washroom. But one must not underestimate the power of beauty, for it can also wield influence, and of this she was very accomplished.

The last of the triplets, Tokki, borne of the moon rabbit. A skillful girl. No one dared challenge her in her domain of the scullery, where she experimented and perfected divine morsels for our consumptive enjoyment. With her quiet heart, she was marked by obedience—a trait that guaranteed adoration by her older sisters.

The triplets did all things as one body, led by Samjogo at their helm. And as they grew, the trio began to outsmart their older two siblings with their fast wits and quick strategies. A formidable team they made, leaving Gom and Horangi in the dust, scratching their heads.

But there was one thing all five sisters underestimated. One goddess, in particular. Their youngest sibling, Miru, borne of the water dragon. A special girl. Unlike the others in many ways, but especially so in her disinterest of her older sisters' games of strategy and competition. Always at my side, she desired nothing more than to help provide and protect our family. With her emotions as voluptuous as the falling rains, she dreamed of nothing more than to be like me.

A *mother.*

Sometimes, I look back and wonder if I could have done things differently. Or perhaps I would do it exactly as I did. One cannot be sure. However, there is one thing I do know. They were right.

Being a mother is the most challenging job there is.

And I would know.

After all, I created the world.

1.
What Happens in Vegas,
Stays in Vegas

"HEY, KID, DID YOU KNOW LAS Vegas is Spanish for 'The Meadows'?" Dahl, my soul twin, asks, glancing up excitedly from his phone. He runs his palm down the side of his moon-colored hair, and his eyes sparkle as if they're housing teeny fairy lights. "Can you believe that in the 1800s, this place was just an expanse of wild grass? And to think it's now the neon capital of the world!"

Areum, my domesticated bird-woman, shrunken to dove size, cocks her head politely. "That is quite an interesting fact, Dahl Oh," she responds, addressing him with his full name now that my parents have officially adopted him into our family. Areum is sitting next to Dahl on one of the faux leather fold-out seats of the Galaxy Convention Center, which is teeming with witches who have traveled from all across the country to be here.

"Yeah, that's pretty cool," I respond, only half listening. I'm too busy watching a video that my sister, Hattie, just sent me, while simultaneously feeding a willow leaf to the furry brown caterpillar on my shoulder.

In the video, Hattie's introducing her imugis to an obstacle course in the Spiritrealm's Central Park this morning. Since deciding to stay down in the underworld to solve the mystery of her unending coma in the Mortalrealm, Hattie has really leaned into her new responsibility as guardian of the hell-beasts. It's like she was born to be an imugi charmer.

As for my own caterpillar-charming skills, I first encountered the little creature at the Memory Archives down in the Spiritrealm, but they secretly tagged along with me all the way to the land of the living. Hence why I've named them Taggy.

"And to think we've been in this glorious city a week already and all we've seen is the inside of stuffy convention centers," Dahl says. He looks longingly at his Top Things I Must Do in Sin City list on his Notes app. (Spoiler alert: It's basically a compilation of every *single* thing you can do in Vegas.)

"We can see the Luxor Hotel pyramid from here," I remind him.

"Sure, but we haven't actually *been* there or checked out the sky beam, have we?" Dahl points out.

Areum squawks. "And we also passed the Eiffel Tower replica yesterday, Dahl Oh."

"And let's not forget when you were *desperate* to try the toilet for the first time," I remind my recently-turned-mortal brother, referring to only six months ago when he crossed over from the Spiritrealm into the Mortalrealm with a bucket list that had *using a toilet* as his #1 activity. "I believe your exact words were *Is it normal for my butt to feel like it's burning? Because I think we need to call the fire service.* I'd be more choosy with the bucket-list items, if I were you."

Dahl leans back in his chair and pops up the collar on his black leather jacket, completely unfazed by my teasing. "But, guys, there's an M&M's World here. That's all I'm saying."

Satisfied that Taggy is demolishing the juicy leaf, I turn my attention to the hustle and bustle around us. "Besides, we're not here to sightsee. We have a job to do."

As if on cue, Sora and Austin, my Horangi guardians, jump up on stage to address the crowds of witches mingling in the large auditorium.

Austin grabs one of the two mics. "All right, everyone. Hope that icebreaker gave you an opportunity to mingle and get to know one another. It's almost lunchtime, so let's get straight into it. But first, has anyone not received their bio-chip yet?"

He points offstage to his left, where Taeyo, my Horangi friend (and Dahl's new BFF), is manning a small table. He's wearing a bright orange bow tie over a purple striped shirt, and a handful of people are lined up waiting to have the scholar clan's tiny invention inserted into their wrists, allowing them to awaken their inner elemental powers. He waves earnestly as people turn their attention to him.

A few hands rise up from the sea of heads.

"Only a few of you, now." Austin nods. "Great. Please join the line so we can get started with the training module."

As the remaining stragglers queue up at Taeyo's station, Sora picks up the second mic. "As you all know, for the past six months, the Horangi clan has been working around the clock to get as many members of the gifted clans armed and trained with our proprietary elemental biochip technology. The abandonment of the goddesses was a shock to us all, leaving the Tokki, Samjogo, Gumiho, and Miru clans without their gifts. And now we know that a war is on the horizon. These are unprecedented times, indeed."

She holds up her Gi-less wrist, as if to make a point. "But that's why we're doing this. We scholars know that there is hope *and* magic beyond the goddesses' divine power. We are proof that witches do not need patron goddesses to thrive. That's why we have been working closely with the Council of Elders at each of the clan chapters around the world to ensure that *all* witches have the means to protect themselves, and one another, in these trying times to come."

Nervous murmurs spread through the auditorium, and I push down an errant hiccup trying to escape my throat. *Trying* is an understatement if there ever was one. Ever since the Haetae told me and Dahl that the goddesses were planning a war against the Mortalrealm, and that my brother and I had to lead the gifted clans into the Age of the Final Eclipse (the *wah?*), I have been nothing but a bundle of nerves. I mean, first of all, we're *thirteen years old*, for crying out loud. We can't even drive yet, let alone lead an army of witches. And secondly, the Haetae said it himself, but Dahl and I have yet to unlock our "true potential." We may be the last fallen star and the last fallen moon, but if the goddesses attacked right now, there is nothing we could do to protect the world from five vengeful goddesses who want revenge for their slain sister.

Sora stands tall on the stage, radiating calmness and commanding respect. "We are therefore incredibly grateful for you all, taking the time to travel across the country to attend these training modules. As you may be aware, this is a global rollout, and we understand all of South Korea, New Zealand, and Brazil have already upskilled their gifted populations. We here in the US are almost there. This week is one of the biggest rollout events we've organized, and as you can imagine, we are ecstatic with the turnout."

The crowd nods in approval, and I think of my parents and Auntie Okja, currently stationed at the nearby Presley Convention Center. They've set up healing hubs all around the city so if any witches get injured during training they can get help without having to go to a saram hospital. When you're learning to wield the five sacred elements of water, wood, fire, metal, and earth, accidents are bound to happen. Luckily, that's one good thing that has come out of the past half year. My trip down to the Spiritrealm resulted in Saint Heo Jun becoming the new patron god of the Gom clan, which means my parents, along with every other healing witch, have reacquired their ability to heal. YUS!

Sora looks down at me sitting in the front row and smiles proudly. "Now, before Austin and Taeyo give us a demo of their respective metal and water affinities, I'd like to invite our leaders—Riley Oh and Dahl Oh—to come and say a few words."

My entire body freezes up. No matter how many times I hear it, the word *leader* put in the same sentence as my name makes me feel queasy. Adults have been looking to us as if we're some kind of divine saviors who will lead the clans to victory in the impending war. But like I mentioned before, *cough cough*, we are just two kids who can sometimes (read: *once*) manage to talk telepathically. That's officially the extent of our superpowers.

I chew my lip and nod my head toward Dahl. "I'm not feeling too hot. You okay to go up alone?"

"Am I ever!" he responds. "I've got this, kid. You sit back and relax, and let me handle things. Bada bing, bada boom!"

He strides up to the stage with his head held high, and after palming his overpomaded elephant-trunk hair from front to back, he launches into his well-rehearsed speech to the audience. I've heard it a million times already—him sharing the tale of how we met, our discovery of the key of all keys using our teardrop stones and Mago Halmi's binyeo, our alliance with Mayor Yeomra down in the Spiritrealm, and how we must work together for the sake of the world to win against the evil wrath of the goddesses. He then launches into the climax of his rousing speech by sharing the prophecy as the Haetae shared it with him:

"'When the dark sun and moon are united once more,
Together they'll unlock the key of all keys.
That opens the door to the dawn of an era,
Of which they'll call the Age of the Final Eclipse.'"

I have to hand it to him. He's a natural. For Dahl, this is all a great big adventure, where nothing is too big or daunting. Whereas for me, it feels like the weight of the three realms is on my shoulders. I don't have Dahl's swagger. I don't have Hattie's conviction. I definitely don't have Sora's poise or command, nor do I share Taeyo's brilliant mind. I can't even use elemental magic like the rest of the witches because of a deal I made with a dokkaebi goblin last summer.

The truth is, I wasn't born to be a hero. It's as simple as that.

Taggy tickles the side of my neck with their little fuzzy legs, as if to say, *But you're really good at caring for me. That counts for something!*

A little bit of weight drops from my shoulders and melts into my shoes. I mean, I'll admit—my wakerpillar is thriving in the land of the living. In fact, they've gotten so plump, it's a wonder their little legs aren't crumpling underneath their weight.

People are oohing and aahing at something Dahl just said, when I spot a group of kids who look about ten years old, wearing matching RILOH STAN tops and approaching me way too eagerly. They all have identical ripped jeans and necklaces in the shape of hearts. One of them even has a plushie of an inmyeonjo on her shoulder.

Oh no. I know these young witches. They're the ones that have been badgering me on social media for months, begging me to endorse their RilOh fan account and inviting me to give a series of "motivational talks" to the fan club's membership. I squirm in my seat, and all my insecurities tumble over me like a box of Legos. Everyone is wanting something from me that I can't give them.

Acting on instinct, I grab my bag and make a run for it. Luckily, Dahl's now got to what I call the "cheerleading section" of his speech, where he gets everyone to stand and chant

"*We. Can. Do. This! WE. CAN. DO. THIS!*" over and over at the top of their lungs. There's enough of a commotion that even the RilOh stans lose me in the mass of stomping, clapping witches.

When I get to the lobby, I take out Dahl's mun-pen and our key of all keys from my bag. With practiced ease, I draw a door in the air using the pen that Mayor Yeomra gifted my twin, the entire time picturing the imugi obstacle course at Central Park in the Spiritrealm. Hopefully, Hattie's still there with the imugis.

A mahogany door appears in front of me, as solid as the ground I'm on, and I place the key of all keys into the perfectly shaped groove on its surface. A bright red light explodes behind the door, and even before it's finished glowing, I've opened the door and stepped through the threshold.

"Rye! Hey! Didn't know you were coming." My sister, Hattie, rushes over from a seesaw-looking portion of the hellbeasts' agility course to wrap me in one of her tight bear hugs. She pulls away and studies my face. "You okay? You look a little pale."

"I'm fine." I shake my head, taking in the lush greenery of the afterlife's Central Park. The afterlife seems extra serene and peaceful today. "Just needed to, you know, get away."

She yawns. "I get that. Just don't tell the old fuddy-duds you used the mun-pen again." She laughs. "Or else they might burst another hernia."

The gifted council elders have been on my case about visiting Hattie too often in the Spiritrealm. Something about it being unnatural to use such a shortcut between the living and the dead, and the risk that poses for the structural fabric between the realms or something. Hattie and I were worried for the first few weeks, but it's been six months of regular use and it's been absolutely fine.

Hattie yawns again, and Namjoon, her favorite part-snake, part-yong creature, comes to rub his head in her side, vying for one of the dried squid snacks in Hattie's pocket.

"Dude, that's the second yawn in less than a minute. You not sleeping well?" I ask.

She shakes her head. "It's just that weird dream I've been having."

"The one with the sad song?"

Ever since Hattie moved to the Spiritrealm, she's been having this recurring dream where she's being cradled like a baby and she wakes up humming this eerie lullaby that we haven't been able to find anywhere online.

"Yup, but now there's another one I keep having, too." She frowns. "I'm at a fountain, it's *pouring* with rain, and this huge dragon comes out of the water wearing a crown. Its hands explode into purple fire. And I feel sad and relieved and grateful all at the same time. The next thing I know, I'm rising out of the water myself."

"Weird," I agree. "Maybe it's some sort of clue to waking you up in the Mortalrealm. You know, like how the Samjogo clan used to be able to get dream premonitions."

She shrugs. "Maybe." She pauses. "You *did* take my body with you to Vegas, right?"

I put my hands on my hips. "Duh! As if we'd leave your body at home alone."

She grins. "Good. Hope the digs are nice."

Ha. I don't tell her that we're staying at a two-star motel that smells like cigarettes with a drained pool that's growing a weird bed of funky grass. "We did bring your favorite pillow," I say.

Satisfied, my sister makes Namjoon do a run of the agility course, as if he's some kind of prized show dog. He's really good—fast, nimble, and graceful. I'm thinking how much Mong, our Samoyed back home, and Yeowu, the fox-red Labrador puppy I met in the underworld, would love this course, too, when my phone goes off. It's a text on KakaoTalk from an unknown contact.

RilOh!! We need your help. Come back please!

I thumb back a response.

Who is this??

But when I realize they wrote my name as RilOh, my heart sinks. The young witches somehow got ahold of my number.

How did you get my number?? I demand.

Oh, um . . . yeah . . . sorry about the stalkerness. My name's Phoebe, the leader of the RilOh Fan Club. But trust us, you need to get back right away!! WE NEED YOU!

Hattie peeks over my shoulder, just as messages start exploding on our friend chat group.

What's going on?! Is anyone else seeing this??

Umm what's happening to the sun?

WHY IS THE SKY FLICKERING?

OMG there's a purple fire on the Luxor pyramid . . .

Guys . . . do you think the WAR is finally here?!

Hattie and I exchange a nervous look.

"I think you better go," she says quietly but firmly.

I bite my lip. "What if this *is* war?" I whisper. "What if the goddesses have made their first move?"

She squeezes my hand. "Then we'll deal with it together, as a family. As a team. And as an alliance. This is what we've been preparing for."

I nod, but my nerves are playing jitterbugs and the mun-pen shakes in my hand as I try to draw a door. It comes out all wobbly and uneven, and Hattie ends up drawing it for me.

Hattie pulls me into a quick hug, careful not to squash Taggy on my neck. "Keep me updated, sis. I'll go let Mayor Yeomra know, and we'll be expecting news from you soon." She pushes me through the door. "Be safe!"

I step through and into the parking lot outside the Galaxy Convention Center. For a moment, I'm disoriented. All the witches from the training module are crowded in the parking lot, gaping upward, staring at the strobe light in the sky. The sun is flashing on and off like a manic neon lightbulb, making it feel like the world is a few palpitations away from a heart attack. A full-on external rupture.

"There you are!" Dahl cries, almost bowling into me. He's accompanied by Areum and Taeyo. They all look panicked. "Thank Mago we found you!"

"Wha—what's going on?" I manage.

Taeyo nervously fiddles with his bow tie, and uses his other hand to point to the voracious purple fire burning on the peak of Luxor Hotel's pyramid across the road. "The sun started flickering, so we all came out, and we saw *that*." A gigantic creature the shape of an oversize dog covered in orange flames is flying circles around the violet bonfire, and it barks so loud, the ground beneath us trembles.

"Um, is that humongous dog on *fire?*" I exclaim.

"It's a bulgae," Areum explains, leaping onto my other shoulder to where Taggy is almost permanently attached.

"*Bool-geh?*" I sound out. "As in *fire dog?*"

"Indeed. The dogs of the Godrealm," my inmyeonjo answers. "Extremely intelligent but notoriously difficult to train. They only ever want to play."

"But why is it *here?*" I ask. "What is a divine fire dog doing in the *Mortal*realm?"

"And *how* is it here?" Dahl adds, shaking his leg nervously.

Areum *caw-caws*. "I do not know, Riley Oh and Dahl Oh. But I fear it has much to do with the goddesses and their plan for war." She opens her wings and prepares to fly. "Allow me to investigate. I will return soon."

"Be careful up there, Areum!" I order.

More people from nearby buildings have started to gather outside, gazing up at the bulgae and pulsating sky with disbelief and shock. How are we going to explain this to the saram? We don't even have the Tokki clans' Memoryhaze potion to wipe their memories anymore.

"Wow, they've gone all out with the special effects!" a saram bystander comments.

"This *is* Sin City, after all," the bystander's friend agrees. "This must be part of some big light show. Can't believe we timed our visit so well!"

Relief washes over me to have one less thing to worry about. There are upsides to being in Vegas. But the feeling is short-lived because the bulgae has now started to howl so loud I have to block my ears. The creature continues to fly anxious circles around the purple fire, which is now burning so fiercely that it looks like it might devour the entire pyramid. The sun is flickering even faster now, too, making it hard to focus on anything.

"Do you feel that, kid?" Dahl asks, wincing.

"Ugh." I clutch my stomach and nod. I feel it deep inside me, as if it's happening to my own body. The onset of darkness. The eve of the end.

Suddenly, the purple flames explode out of the pyramid like an erupting volcano, making the bulgae yelp and scamper away into the sky. We all shield our eyes from the burn, the sheer brilliance of the fire stealing the air from our lungs.

"Guys, it's gone..." Dahl mutters in disbelief.

I assume he's talking about the bulgae. Or the fire. But when I finally find my wits and open my eyes again, I realize those are not the only things that have disappeared.

It should be around midday right now, with the full glare of the sun. But there is nothing left in the sky. The sun is gone.

I wait for the moon to illuminate in the absence of light. For the twinkle of the stars. But there is nothing but an empty void. The world is completely and utterly dark.

In fact, if it wasn't for the cascading neon lights of the hotels and casinos slowly switching on across the city, I wouldn't even be able to see my own hands.

"Oh my Mago," I breathe. "The sky has fallen."

2.
Why Is Orange Chicken
So Delicious?

 CONSIDERING THE SUN JUST literally disappeared from the sky, the saram bystanders out on the streets of Vegas are surprisingly calm.

"Unbelievable!" one woman nearby exclaims, shaking her head in amazement as she glances up at the dark and empty void. "How did they do that?! Must be some kind of promo stunt for a new show, eh?"

The man standing next to her nods, impressed. "Must be a huge network to fund such a large-scale production. I can't wait to tell my grandson about it!"

The gifted witches on the other hand, are well and truly freaking out.

"It's the goddesses," a woman I recognize from the training module hisses, pulling her hands down her face. "It has to be! They're flexing their muscles. Taunting us. Proving we're no match for them!"

Nervous whispers spread through the group of witches, and

I even hear one person crying. Austin quickly steps in, trying to cajole the group before chaos takes over.

Sora pulls me aside, calm and steady. "We'll keep things under control here. You and Dahl go find your parents and come up with a plan of attack. We need to understand how widespread this is." She pauses. "If this is the goddesses' first move, we need to be united in how we respond."

I bite my lip and look over at Dahl, who is working with Taeyo to break up a bunch of witches who—by the looks of the blood gushing out of one of their noses—have already engaged in some fisticuffs. Fear brings out the worst in people.

"But I'm just... I'm not..." I trail off, feeling anxious tears building behind my eyes. "We haven't unlocked our true potential yet," I finally whisper. "We're not ready. *I'm* not ready."

"Yes, you are," Sora assures me, squeezing my shoulder. "You just have to believe in yourself the way we all believe in you. Let yourself be the hero you already are inside."

And with that, she pushes me toward Dahl. "Keep us updated."

I start to argue back, because I'd rather do *anything* than be at the helm of this war. Honestly, I'd rather be eating busloads of fried car tires at the Hell of Boiling Oil than be taking on this responsibility. But Dahl is already pulling me away from the crowd.

"Did you see the messages on our family group chat, kid?"

I shake my head and reach into my pocket for my phone. Before I can read it, Dahl catches me up.

"We're meeting at the Panda Express in the Miracle Mile Shops. You know the one, inside Planet Hollywood."

"Panda Express?" I ask, momentarily confused. "Why there?"

He smiles sheepishly. "I *need* to try their orange chicken, okay? Besides, there's no reason we can't kill two birds with one stone. It's within walking distance for all of us."

I shrug, too overcome by nerves to school him about his bucket-list obsession again.

"Eomma and Appa are going to meet us there," he continues, "so we can figure out our next steps."

I nod meekly. "I'll message the others."

Dahl opens Google Maps and directs us northward up the Strip, which is the main road running through the city. As he strides forward, I send a quick message to our friends on KaTalk, letting them know the plan. They're all stationed at different training locations around the city, and they've got to be experiencing the same chaotic situation as us.

David and I are gonna stay back and help here, but keep us updated, Jennie Byun, a Samjogo and my ex-archnemesis turned friend, texts back immediately. *I don't need my seeing abilities to know things are about to get SERIOUS around here.*

Things are going feral here, too, so Noah and I'll stay and do as much crowd control as we can, Cosette Chung, our beautiful Gumiho friend, responds. *Let us know when the plan shapes up. We'll follow your lead.*

Then:

Me and Boris are close by. We'll meet you there ASAP.

That last text is from my best friend, Emmett Harrison.

A jittery feeling tickles me from inside my rib cage, and I don't know if it's just from anxiety . . . or something else. If I'm being honest, things between me and Emmett have gotten a bit strange since his memories were restored. But now's not the time to worry about that. I shrug it off and quickly chase behind Dahl, who is already speeding off.

Dahl assures me the walk won't take more than twenty minutes—less if we power walk. But it feels a lot longer. Why? Because the city has become . . . *different* since the fire exploded out of the pyramid. Of course, all the lights in the sky are off, which makes the whole place feel eerie, like we're inside a video game set in an alien apocalypse. But it's more than that. There is something *off* about the city.

For example, we walk past a replica of the Statue of Liberty (which Dahl is *very* excited about, because it reminds him of the Statue of Eternity back home) and at first it looks just like the New York landmark, albeit only a third of the size. But as we keep walking and we look at it from a different angle, the statue changes. Suddenly, it's a gigantic stone butterfly that honestly is so beautiful it makes me want to cry. When we walk a few more steps and look back, it's returned to being Lady Liberty. I glance back at the Luxor pyramid, and that seems to be flickering into the form of a mountain every once in a while. Every few buildings, something like this happens, and it reminds me of those holographic cards that you move from side to side to reveal a different image.

But that's not the end of it. We're about ten minutes from

Panda Express (according to Dahl's Google Maps) when it starts raining. And when I say rain, I mean it starts POURING. It's like someone turned the shower on full blast, and the empty night sky is suddenly zero to hero in a matter of seconds. Lightning streaks across the empty vastness, followed by deep rumbles of thunder, and the water pressure is so intense it's a physical barrier masking my vision.

Then, as quickly as it began, it stops. The sky dries up in an instant, and it's as if we totally imagined the freak storm. Not a single drop of moisture. A minute later, the downpour is back with a vengeance.

"I think the city is having an identity crisis," Dahl whines, wringing water out of his drenched (and no longer perfectly styled) white hair.

"And the weather, too," I respond, squeezing the ends of my wet sweater.

He nods glumly. "Doesn't it know how long it takes to get my hair looking this good?"

"I do." I put a stopwatch on him this morning as he got ready. "If I remember correctly, it took exactly forty-four min—"

The flapping of large, powerful wings interrupts me, and I freeze mid-step.

"Did you hear that?" I ask. I know the sound of Areum's wings in flight. And this is *way* louder. As if there are *many* more wings.

"It sounded like—"

"There!" I point where the outlines of five winged horses fly by over our heads, illuminated from beneath by the lights of the hotels and casinos.

A choir of unbridled neighs sound as they pass, and I gape at my soul twin. "There are *cheollimas* here. On the Strip. In Las Vegas. In the *Mortalrealm*!"

His eyebrows furrow, and he takes my hand. "Come on, let's hurry."

The Miracle Mile Shops are in a huge, LA-themed indoor mall that has a domed ceiling painted with an uber-realistic blue sky. No matter what time of day it is outside, it looks like it's twilight indoors, and the effect is jarring as we leave Vegas Alien Apocalypse behind for California Strip Mall.

Our parents are already waiting at the entrance of Panda Express, and they run over when they see us.

"Oh, thank Mago you're both okay!" Eomma cries, squeezing us hard.

"That's weird," I muse, glancing up quizzically at the restaurant's logo. It says *Bonghwang Express*, and there's a bird on it instead of a panda. "When did they rebrand?"

"What's a bonghwang?" Dahl asks.

"A bonghwang is a Korean phoenix," Appa responds. "A benevolent creature from the Godrealm. And, unfortunately, we're as perplexed as you are about the sudden change in logo. Come on in—let's sit first, then talk."

They usher us inside the restaurant, and I'm relieved to find that, despite the altered sign outside, the interior has remained the familiar cheerful version of the Panda Express chain I know and love. It houses the same too-bright lights, the same fast-food-style menu displayed above the counter, and the same sweet, fried waft of orange chicken.

"Whoa, that smells incredible," Dahl breathes, his eyes a little gooey.

"Let's get you some to try," Eomma suggests, eager for her newfound son to experience as many mortal delicacies as he can.

Appa nods. "We can't fight a war hungry now, can we?"

They take Dahl to check out the precooked options, and I find us a seat at the largest table near the window. I've just sat down when a familiar face walks up to the restaurant. He has Boris the dragon-on-wheels tucked neatly under his arm.

Emmett's eyes meet mine, and immediately, I feel a weird tingle in my toes. I mentioned this briefly before, but things have gotten . . . *strange* between me and my baking-obsessed, dog-loving, used-to-be-allergic-to-emotions-but-now-oddly-open BFF. At first, when his memory of me was restored six months ago, it was like all my birthdays had come at once. I'd finally gotten my best friend back. Hurray!

But then things started to change. I mean, sure, he still wears black from head to toe, and he can still frown anyone under the table. But he's also *different*.

For one, he shot up like a mung bean sprout. I used to be taller than him, but now he's got half a head on me, and it's unsettling to look up at him. Sometimes he studies me with this funny expression on his face that makes me feel like someone dropped a bowl of Skittles inside my stomach. When he looks at me that way, I feel the intense need to run away from him but also toward him at the same time . . . which makes absolutely *zero* sense. Oh yeah, his voice has also dropped, and now when he says "Hey," my face goes bright red and I can't keep eye contact if my life depended on it.

"Hey," Emmett says, taking the seat opposite me.

My face goes bright red, and I quickly avert my eyes. (See?!)

"Do we think this is it? The goddesses' first move?" Emmett asks.

Dahl and our parents return with two trays of food and hands everyone a pair of chopsticks.

"I'm afraid it seems that way," Appa answers solemnly, taking a seat next to Eomma, his face grim. "With the sun disappearing and divine creatures suddenly appearing in the city, I can't think who else might be behind this."

Eomma tenses. "It appears the war has finally begun."

We all go silent, because even though that's what we're all thinking, it's sobering to hear it be said aloud.

"We've been running training modules for months now. As a community, we're as prepared as we can be," Dahl says between mouthfuls of chicken and fried rice. Ever the optimist.

"But *we're* not prepared," I remind him, pointing between him and me. I tap my foot nervously on the shiny floors of the restaurant. "We haven't unlocked our powers yet, Dahl. We're not *ready*. This can't be happening yet."

A foot reaches out under the table to calm mine, and when I glance up, Emmett gives me a small nod as if to say, *You've got this, just breathe.* When it dawns on me that it's *Emmett's* foot that's touching mine under the table, my leg flings back so fast that my heel whacks into the wall behind me. *Ow!*

Luckily, before anyone asks why I'm acting so jumpy, two things happen at the same time.

Areum lands on the ground outside the window, shrinks into dove size, and flies into the restaurant toward us. She lands on my shoulder and coos a greeting into my ear.

Also, my phone rings with a video call from Hattie.

"Rye, I heard what happened!" my sister calls out as soon as I accept the Soom call (which is like Zoom, but the Spiritrealm version). "Is everyone okay?"

She's standing in a familiar-looking forest, gazing up at us, which makes me think she must be Sooming from the mayor's banquet forest in the underworld's H-Mart (aka the best snacks bar ever created). Namjoon, her imugi, is standing proud by her side. And next to them is Mayor Yeomra, dressed in his royal red-and-gold hanbok, looking as regal as ever.

I prop my phone up against the napkin dispenser so everyone can see one another. "Yeah, we're okay, Hat. So far, anyway."

"Hello, sweetheart!" Eomma and Appa call out in unison, waving to the screen. "Hope the mayor is feeding you well down there?"

"I absolutely am, Mr. and Mrs. Oh," Mayor Yeomra responds with a warm smile, cupping his hands demurely behind his back. "Your daughter is a huge asset down in this realm. I don't know what I'd do without her, really."

One of the worst things about Hattie deciding to stay down in the Spiritrealm was explaining to my parents that their daughter had decided to reside in the land of the dead. But over time, they've come to appreciate how healthy and happy she is down there, and that this is all temporary until we figure out how to fix Hattie's mysterious coma.

"It's gotta be them," Hattie says, having drawn her own conclusions. "Who else would have the power to break the sky?"

The mayor's face tightens, but he looks determined. "I agree with Hattie that it must be the goddesses. But we have the element of surprise on our side. They don't know our two realms have an alliance. Whatever they have in store for us, we will work together to ensure our citizens remain safe."

"If only we knew what they were planning," I murmur. "If we could figure that out, then we—"

"There is a more pressing situation we must first contend with," Areum interrupts, ruffling her feathers from her perch on my shoulder.

"What did you find out on your recon mission to the Godrealm?" I press. "Did you find out what the bulgae was doing down here in our realm?"

Dahl swallows a big chunk of oily chicken. "Did the goddesses send it down?"

Areum squawks a few times as if to clear her throat. "It appears this was not the goddesses' doing at all."

Eomma frowns. "If not them, then who?"

"I appears there is a tear in the fabric between the Mortalrealm and the Godrealm, allowing divine creatures to fall through the holes and into this world."

The table gasps audibly.

"And I am afraid the tear is only getting larger as we speak," Areum concludes.

My rib cage fills with guilt. "So the elders were right?" I whisper. "The sky fell because I used the mun-pen and Key too often?"

"It can't just be that," Eomma consoles me across the table, "Surely, the goddesses were involved."

Appa nods in support, but it's no consolation. The elders had schooled me about the risks of overuse on the structural fabric between the realms, but I hadn't listened. The bulgae and the cheollimas we saw earlier—they're here because of *me*.

Hattie's voice cracks through the speakers on my phone. "It's not true. It can't be."

"Do you think that's got something to do with the city's identity crisis?" Dahl asks quietly. "Panda Express turning into Bonghwang Express, the Statue of Liberty being a butterfly, the pyramid turning into a mountain..."

Areum tightens her grip on my shoulder before responding, as if preparing me for what she's about to say. "You are correct, Dahl Oh. The double-ups are being caused by the tear. It appears pockets of the Godrealm are leaking down onto Las Vegas, superimposing themselves over our realm. It's making our two worlds merge in an unnatural manner."

"Like when you put frosting on a cake before the cake's cooled down," Emmett muses. "It melts down into the cake, making it all soggy and gross."

Areum nods her avian head. "And the tear will eventually reach beyond Las Vegas. Soon, the Godrealm will be leaking over the entire Mortalrealm."

"Which means the goddesses will be able to roam the Mortalrealm freely," I conclude darkly. After all, the Cave Bear Goddess tried to destroy the last fallen star—tried to destroy *me*—so that she could roam the land of the living at will. By going to visit Hattie too often, I've basically given them exactly what they wanted.

Ugh. Facepalm.

"And since the three realms exist on top of one another, it will only be a matter of time before the leak also seeps down into the Spiritrealm," Mayor Yeomra states solemnly. "If I were to borrow Mr. Harrison's analogy, it appears the land of the dead will also become quote unquote 'soggy and gross.'"

An earsplintering bolt of thunder cracks somewhere in the sky, and we almost jump out of our skins. Namjoon whimpers from my phone's screen, and Taggy rubs their little wakerpillar legs on the side of my neck, making a shiver run down my spine.

"And then there's this weird, wild weather to add to all our problems," I lament. "As if we don't already have a billion things to worry about!"

"Don't forget the purple exploding light from the pyramid," Dahl adds unhelpfully. "Oh, and how the world just got plunged into complete darkness." He looks at me, and I know he's thinking about that deep-seated dread we both felt when the sun got extinguished from the sky. It had felt like . . . like *doom*.

The mayor speaks up from my phone. "For now, we need to focus on fixing the leaks. We need to cover up the tears."

We all nod, unanimous.

"But *how?*" I manage.

The silence feels much too heavy.

Hattie's the one to finally break it. "*No. Freaking. Way.*" She puts her hands on her hips in the Spiritrealm's food forest and looks like she's just made a huge discovery. "I've been having this weird recurring dream, and I just figured out why. I know *exactly* what we need to do!"

Those of us sitting inside Panda/Bonghwang Express huddle closer around my small phone screen.

"Are you talking about the sad lullaby dream?" I ask. "Or the new dragon one?"

"The new one," she confirms. "You guys need to find Yongwang."

"*Yongwang?*" Dahl echoes. "The ruler of the Spiritrealm's underwater borough who no one's seen in hundreds of years?"

Emmett frowns up a storm. "No offense, Hat. But what does the Dragon King have to do with anything?"

"This is going to sound bizarro, but hear me out, okay?" Hattie licks her lips and launches into her dream for the second time today. "In my dream, there's this fountain—one of those super-old ones that look like it's from ancient Rome or something. Anyway, I'm standing there, and it's raining. Not just a sun shower, but, like, a full-on *wall* of rain, and this huge dragon comes out of the water wearing a crown. Its hands explode into purple fire. Then, the next thing I know, I'm rising from the fountain, as if I just woke up or something."

I exhale sharply, finally catching on. "A purple fire . . . just like the one at Luxor's pyramid. It *must've* been a premonition!"

She nods. "And I'm certain the dragon with the crown is

the Dragon King. I think Yongwang sent me a message so we'd find him. Because he can *help* us."

Eomma leans into the small screen, her voice wanting. "And it ends with you rising from the water, sweetheart. So you'll be waking up from your coma soon, too."

"Maybe," Hattie says tentatively. "But the Dragon King *has* to be connected somehow. I'm sure of it."

"The fountain from your dream," Dahl says, holding up his phone. It's opened to his Notes app with the screeds of places he wants to visit in Vegas. "You said it looked like it belonged in ancient Rome?"

Hattie nods. "Kind of like the Trevi Fountain. You know, that famous one that people throw coins into."

He scrolls down on his phone. "The Trevi Fountain you say. . . ."

Dahl finds whatever he was looking for. "Bada bing, bada boom, kid! Caesars Palace! It has an exact replica of the Trevi Fountain. And it's just off the Strip!"

He grins excitedly and pops the collar on his leather jacket. "That's gotta be the place in Hattie's dream. *That's* where we need to go!"

Areum squawks in approval, as Namjoon shakes his scaly hips on the screen.

Filled with hope, I grin. I smile harder than I've smiled in *months*, and I look over triumphantly at Emmett . . . who is staring at me in that funny way again. My face goes hot, and I quickly divert my gaze to my phone, just in time to see Hattie fist-pump the air.

"I don't know how and I don't know why," she starts, "but I

have a feeling that Yongwang will have the answers we need." She pauses. "Maybe even for my coma."

Eomma's and Appa's eyes well up as they pretend to be busy clearing the trays of food.

"Well then," I conclude, making for the door, "the last one to Rome is a rotten egg."

3.
Vegas Wasn't Built in a Day

On the walk to the Trevi Fountain replica, I message my Horangi fam and our friend group chat to let them know our plan and where we're headed. Then I ask Areum to do a quick flyover of the Strip and the main training module locations around the city, to make sure nothing terrible is happening that we need to know about. By the time we get to Caesars Palace, Taeyo has come to join us.

"Taeyo, my man!" Dahl calls out, offering out his palm in greeting. "So pumped you're joining us."

Taeyo takes Dahl's hand, and they do their little broshake, which ends with the finger-pointing, leg-shaking dance move from Dahl's favorite movie, *Grease*.

"Happy to be here! Hopefully I'll be useful," Taeyo says cheerfully, waving his biochipped wrist.

Dahl had decided Taeyo's water-manipulation skills might be helpful at the fountain. But honestly, I suspect Taeyo and

Dahl's budding bromance had something to do with it, too. Since Dahl joined us Mortalrealm-side, the two of them have been thick as thieves. There's something about Taeyo's earnestness and Dahl's enthusiasm that just work together, like peanut butter and jelly. Or tteokbokki and cheese.

"So this is it, huh?" I say, turning our attention to the beautiful marble water feature. It's being illuminated by upward lighting, and it's complete with a half-naked-man sculpture standing proudly in the middle.

It turns out the Trevi Fountain replica is not actually inside Caesars Palace, but rather right outside the hotel and casino's shopping complex. Yes, that's right—yet another mall. If Vegas was a human, the hotels and casinos would be its bones, and shopping centers its joints.

A handful of tourists are also here, and if any of them are freaking about the blacked-out sky, they're doing a good job of hiding it. Some whisper about how exciting it is to be part of TV history in the making, while others marvel at how avant-garde and ambitious the entire PR stunt is. My parents loiter around them, pretending to be tourists, too, adding a little "Oh, Vegas is amazing, right?" at opportune moments.

"So is it everything you'd hoped for and more?" I ask Dahl teasingly. "Would you recommend others include the Trevi replica on their Vegas bucket lists, too?"

"It's a bit smaller than I expected, but it's just as amazing." He considers the feature carefully, and if he's heard my sarcasm, he's choosing to ignore it. "Did you know that the strapping dude in the middle there, behind the winged horses, is Oceanus, the Titan god of the river from Greek mythology?"

"So, essentially the equivalent of our Dragon King," Taeyo adds, adjusting his bow tie and looking fascinated. "Maybe that's why Hattie's dream pointed us here. That would make sense."

Emmett comes to join Dahl and Taeyo, and he studies the fountain, too. He points to the woman on the left of Oceanus, who's spilling water from an urn, and then to the man on the right, who's holding a cup. "Who are those two flanking him?"

"I believe the woman is Abundance," Taeyo responds. "As in she's the personification of all that is plentiful. And the man is Salubrity. It means healthiness."

When we look at him in surprise, he blushes. "What? I'm a Horangi—of course I looked it up. *Knowledge and Truth*, right?"

I consider the snake that's drinking out of the cup in the man's hand, and I shudder. It reminds me of the salmosa that poisoned the Spring of Eternal Life in the Spiritrealm, and it's hard to equate any snakes near water to healthiness.

"So what now?" Emmett asks, unfolding Boris and tickling behind the dragon scooter's ears. "We just wait around until the Dragon King eventually—*hopefully*—turns up?"

"That's a good point, Emmett. We need to let him know that Hattie sent us," Taeyo says. He looks curiously over at Boris, whose tail is now wagging happily from side to side. "If only I had enough time to reprogram Ghostr. Boris is a dragon scooter, so theoretically, I could do a cell biopsy and use it to program a beaconing device, reformat the GPS radius, and use the app to track any other creatures in the vicinity who share similar DNA. It's a long shot, but it *might* work."

Emmett frowns. "Let's not get too hasty now." He hugs

Boris protectively to his chest. "Do we even know the dude has scales?"

"Well, he *is* a yong," Dahl confirms. "And the ineo twins we met in the Spiritrealm were descendants of Yongwang, and even they had beautiful tails covered in scales."

Taggy snuggles into the crook of my neck, using my sweater as a blanket, as if snuggling in to enjoy the show. I let the boys hash their theories out with each other, and walk up to the edge of the fountain. It's surprisingly deep, but definitely not deep enough that an actual dragon could live inside—not that I've ever seen one in real life. I chew my lip. Surely, Hattie wasn't wrong. She was so sure about what she'd experienced in her dream. If Yongwang isn't here, there *must* be a clue some-where near this fountain that will lead us to him.

"Hey, Eomma, Appa," I call out, looking over my shoulder for my parents. "Do you think that—"

My parents look . . . off somehow. They're standing together with their heads raised to the sky, staring at the empty expanse. I follow their gaze upward, but there's nothing there but the hazy shadow of clouds being illuminated by the lights of the city.

"What are you guys looking at?" I call out.

They don't answer. They don't move an inch. When I get closer, I realize they're not even blinking. They're standing dead still, like statues.

"Eomma, Appa," I say louder this time, shaking them by the shoulders. "Snap out of it!" I motion the boys over. "Guys, something's wrong."

As Dahl, Taeyo, and Emmett hurry over, my parents remain

solid and lifeless. I shake my eomma even harder, but she's frozen so rigidly that I almost knock her over like a bowling pin.

Just then, Eomma stirs, her eyes blinking and warmth returning to her face. "Riley, honey, did you hear that?"

I whine in relief as Appa shakes his head and wakes up from the stunned reverie, too.

"Hear what?" Dahl demands.

They both crease their foreheads, trying to remember.

"I . . . I heard . . . I don't know," Appa breathes, rubbing his head. "It was right there at the tip of my tongue, and now for the life of me, I can't recall what I was about to say."

We lead them to some seats in the far edge of the monument. "Just sit and relax for a bit, okay?" I say.

Dahl nods. "Maybe it's delayed shock from everything that's happened today."

Our parents look dazed and confused, but don't argue about taking a breather. They sit close, holding each other's hands.

"Don't worry about us," Appa assures us, though his voice is a little shaky. "We'll be fine. Just give us a minute."

The boys are sharing looks of concern, having a conversation just with their eyebrows, when I hear it.

Riley, Riley.

Someone is calling my name. It's faint, as if floating on the breeze from miles away. I look to the boys, but they're not showing any signs of having heard it.

Riley, Riley, Rileyyy.

It's coming from the fountain.

Unable to resist the strange pull of the voice, I follow it toward the edge of the monument. The voice abruptly stops.

But not before I notice something has changed. The water in the Trevi has become more choppy and wild—as if it's in the middle of the ocean rather than a man-made fountain.

"Something's changed," I call out to the boys. "The water looks like it's—"

There's a sudden flurry of movement as a small crowd of tourists gather around the fountain, disorienting me. For a moment, there are too many things passing by my vision—a tourist's fanny pack, a snippet of Taeyo's bright orange bow tie, the hood of Emmett's black sweater, a sleek woman with heavy cat-eye makeup in a fox-red fur coat.

Something careens into me—some*one*?—and suddenly, my center of gravity is off and I'm keeling. My arms flail about in front of me, but there's nothing to grab hold of. It's only when my head comes in contact with a solid wall of cold water that I realize I've fallen into the fountain.

"Riley!" a muffled voice calls out.

There is a splash as someone dives in after me.

I try to stand up, but the fountain is *way* deeper inside than it looked from the outside. I can't seem to find the floor. In fact, there is no beginning or end to this water as far as I can see, and there is a violent undertow. I swallow a mouthful of water, and it's so salty I gag, which only makes me swallow another mouthful. *Ugh.* My chest burns.

My Converses catch on the thick wavy strands of what appears to be a red seaweed forest, and my head spins. I fell into a water feature at a *shopping mall*. Why does it feel like I fell into the sea?

A body in the distance is swimming toward me, and the

water starts to tremble, as if each molecule is fighting for freedom. Slowly, the sea begins to rise, like a puppeteer pulling on a water marionette. And just when Emmett reaches me, and my chest is sure to explode, the water completely lifts away, above my shoulders and above my head. My body lifts with it, until gravity finds me, and I drop back down onto the waterless bottom of the Trevi Fountain with a *thud*.

"Riley, are you all right?!" Emmett demands from a few feet away. He's drenched from head to toe, his eyes wide. He scrambles over, searching my face. "Are you okay?"

"Guys, climb out of there!" I hear Taeyo shout. "I don't know how much longer I can hold it."

We both glance over to see Taeyo standing outside the fountain, surrounded by my parents and Dahl—all looking decidedly pale. My Horangi witch friend has his two hands open and raised, and his arms are shaking with effort.

"Get out of there, sweetheart!" Appa shouts.

"Quickly!" Eomma echoes.

That's when we notice the trembling mass of water above our heads, threatening to drop back down on us. We clamber out faster than you could say *Emmett has eyes the color of honey.* (Wait, did I just say that out loud?!)

The water crashes back down into the fountain the second we get out, and Taeyo crumples in an exhausted heap. Luckily, we all seem to be okay, including little Taggy, who is still somehow tucked into the crook of my neck, unharmed.

"That was *weird*," Emmett says quietly, clutching Boris, his voice almost drowned out by the roar of applause from the saram bystanders. They must think this is all part of the show. "It was like we weren't in Vegas anymore . . . like we were transported somewhere entirely different."

Taeyo rubs his wrists as he and Dahl peer over the lip of the fountain at the water, which has now returned to its shallow calmness. "Almost like you were transported to an actual ocean," Taeyo guesses.

Dahl pops the collar on his jacket. "Maybe it's more of the Godrealm leaking into our realm already. . . ."

I lean over and pick some stringy red stuff off Emmett's shoulder, momentarily forgetting the awkwardness I've been feeling around him. "Ugh, Em. I think you've got seaweed in your hair. It's so slimy. Gross."

He takes the long strands from me, and our fingers touch. I jolt back, and the uncomfortable tension returns just as fast as it'd left.

"I was so scared for a second there," he says with a look of genuine fear on his face.

"Uh, yeah, sorry, I, uh . . . I'm fine."

I swivel on my heels to hide my blushing cheeks. This is my best friend. We summoned the mother of all creation together, for Mago's sake. Why am I acting so *stupid* around him?!

Eomma and Appa don't look so hot, and as they return to the bench to rest, Dahl takes the seaweed from Emmett's hand. "Uh, guys? Not to raise the bells of alarm, but that wasn't the ocean in the Godrealm." He gulps. "It was the *Spiritrealm*."

As we stare blankly at him, he holds up the long red threads. "These are raw fibers from the Tree of Fate, which only grows in the Spiritrealm. Woven together, they create the Red Strings of Fate, which are used to tie souls together and bind their destinies."

I shudder, remembering the time Hattie and I ran into a Dalgyal Gwisin at the Gifted Carnival who tried to tie her soul with innocent children so she could take them down to hells with her.

Taeyo fiddles with his bow tie. "So does this mean the fabric between us and the Spiritrealm is ripping already, too? We should probably let the mayor know—"

"But hang on a hot second," Emmett interrupts. "It's *seaweed*."

Dahl nods. "They call it the Tree of Fate, but it's actually a whole forest of seaweed. You have to admit *Seaweed of Fate* doesn't have quite the same ring to it."

Emmett takes the long red threads from Dahl and studies it carefully. "As if today couldn't get *any* more bizarre . . ."

"Don't miss the wedding of the century!" a cheery voice announces from nearby, stealing our attention. There's what seems to be a human-size plushie in the shape of a wedding cake, handing out flyers to tourists.

"Charles and Maru will be tying the knot at the Venus Garden Chapel, and you are all invited! Don't be late or you'll miss all the delicious sweet treats."

A saram tourist takes a flyer and comments to her friend, "Oh, look, Elvis is officiating the wedding. That's cool."

Her friend's eyes light up as she scans the sheet of paper. "Gosh, it's not every day you see people get married in full horse costumes, is it? How cute is that itty-bitty-size groom."

"Just adorable," the friend agrees. "And they have wings! Just like the Pegasus in the fountain. The special effects are top-class."

Something about all of this is ringing a weird bell in the recesses of my mind, and I quickly grab a flyer from the walking wedding cake before they disappear. My parents and friends huddle around me to look over my shoulder.

The black-and-white flyer looks like it was pulled together in two minutes tops, using text boxes and clip art in Word, and then photocopied in an even greater hurry (as evidenced by the large fingerprints covering the flyer). The heading says *You are cordially invited to the wedding of Charles and Maru, united at long last!* Inside a large clip-art speech bubble that's attached to the mouth of an Elvis impersonator. Underneath is another clip-art shape—a huge heart, this time—inside of which is a photo of two winged horses. One is the most stunning white mare I've ever seen—sleek and chiseled to equine perfection. But the horse on her back, standing between her wings, is a horse that's a fraction of her size. In fact, the black stallion seems to be no bigger than a Chihuahua, and there's something about his proud toothy grin that looks oddly pompous and familiar. . . .

"Holy shirtballs, that's the cheollima guard from the temple laundromat!" Emmett breathes.

The penny drops. "The one that made us answer those riddles so we could get to the gifted library!"

"His name is Charles?" Emmett comments, eyebrow quirked. "Guess we never asked his name."

"Charles the cheollima," I echo. "It's got a good ring to it."

Dahl takes the flyer from me and studies it carefully. "Hey, kid. Surely it's not a coincidence that we saw cheollimas earlier in the sky, and now there's a wedding for two of them. Right?"

Taeyo points to a smudge on the paper. "And is it just me, or does that look like a . . . scale?"

"A *dragon* scale?" Dahl adds.

Emmett raises Boris up to the flyer and compares his scales against the one in the flyer. "Hard to say for sure, but it's definitely the right shape," he confirms.

Upon closer inspection, I realize the dark oval shape I mistook for thumbprints *could* be a scale. *Possibly.*

"Maybe it's a clue," Taeyo suggests.

"But why in the three realms would Yongwang the Dragon King be photocopying wedding flyers?" I ask. "It makes *no* sense."

Taeyo thinks. "Unless it was intentional. Yongwang knew we'd be here, and he knew we'd see the flyers. So he left us a cookie crumb to follow. Maybe there's a reason we need to see him at the wedding instead of here."

Emmett nods. "I think we should go to the wedding."

Dahl's face lights up, and he hugs the A4 to his chest. "A cheollima wedding officiated by Elvis in Vegas! I can't believe I didn't already have that on my bucket list!"

Emmett wrenches the flyer from him to look at the little hand-drawn map in the bottom right corner. "At least we don't have to go far. Looks like the Venus Garden Chapel is inside Caesars Palace."

"When does it start?" Taeyo asks. "I'm glad I'm wearing a bow tie!"

"You're always wearing a bow tie," Dahl comments approvingly.

Emmett starts walking toward my parents. "It's already started. Come on, let's go."

As we fetch my still-dazed parents to take them to the "wedding of the century," I hope to dear Mago that our small equine friend is as helpful as he was last time.

"Too bad we don't have any of my salted-caramel cookies," Emmett muses. "It's kinda rude to turn up to a wedding without a gift."

I nod in agreement. "They were his fave. The whole reason he helped us last time."

"They're your fave, too," he points out.

A warm fuzziness spreads from my chest all the way down my toes, and suddenly, I feel the intense desire to cough.

"*Mumble mumble* I hope they have food *mumble mumble*," I manage to say.

4.
Who Doesn't Like a Garden Wedding?

 As the name suggests, the Venus Garden Chapel is located in the courtyard gardens of Caesars Palace. There are tall palms and rich green shrubbery surrounding the ceremony area, and two fanned-out sections of stone pews stationed to have a perfect view of the wedding altar. The altar itself is a Greek-style domed gazebo held up by marble pillars, each of which have been wrapped with climbing vines and pink flowers. With romantic lights illuminating the garden, and the sneaky marble statues of robed harpists peeking out from the bushes, it's the perfect setup for a classic garden wedding... that is, except for the guests.

There is nothing classic about the wedding party in the slightest. There's about forty people here, but it looks *way* more than that, probably because half of them are four-legged and winged and *gigantic*. When Emmett and I were at the temple searching for the last fallen star, Charles had told us that he didn't fit in in the Godrealm because he was a runt. I can see now how true that is. The full-size cheollimas are a head taller and a half a shoulder wider than any horses I've seen in my lifetime, and they vary in color from metallic two-tones, to glow-in-the-dark, to star and crescent-stamped holographic spots, and even zebra stripes that look like molten rainbows. With a dull guiltache in my stomach, I realize they all must have found the tear in the realm gates for them to have made it down here for this wedding.

At least we don't have to worry about the saram attendees, though. Most of the humans are carrying the same flyers we saw, and they've got their phones out, squealing about how Vegas is "putting on its A-game" with the sky blackout special effects and now these uncannily realistic costumes. If they only knew . . .

"Rye, look, there's Charles!" Emmett points to the miniature black stallion, who's flapping his wings in the air, while his strapping fiancée stands tall and striking alongside him. They seem to be having a jovial conversation with another cheollima couple, both of whom have holographic ferns furling and unfurling like GIFs on their backs.

"Come on," I say to Emmett, already walking toward Charles. "Let's get to the happy couple before anyone else does."

Luckily, we approach just as the holographic-fern couple move on to the canapé station, which is overloaded with a variety of pastries, cookies, pies, desserts, and candied carrots. Literally every single item on the table is a sugar bomb.

"Charles!" I exclaim, waving excitedly. "Long time no see! Fancy seeing you here, right? Huge congrats on the big day!"

The mini cheollima studies me and Emmett, before landing on his fiancée's back and rubbing his cute little face against her mane. "These two humans must be your guests, my sweetie sugar dumpling."

"No, dear. Not mine," she confirms in a rich, rumbly voice.

Emmett leans into my ear. "I just realized we were Cosette and Adeline Chung the last time we met him. No wonder he has no idea who we are."

My heart drops. Of *course*. Cosette had glamoured us to look like her and her sister so we wouldn't get caught at the temple.

I open my mouth, adamant to explain how we know him, but Elvis's dulcet tone sings out from the gazebo.

"Ladies and gentlemen, two-legged, four-legged, winged and no-winged alike, please take your seats for the most *equiiisite* wedding of the year!"

Before I get a chance to open my mouth, Charles plants a big wet one on his fiancée's mouth before flapping his wings toward Elvis. "It's time, my winged sugarplum fairycakes! Sway those shapely buttocks, won't you? I'll be waiting at the end of the aisle for you!"

It seems like a weird time to be sitting at a wedding when, oh, you know, the sky is falling. But Emmett assures me we'll get a chance to talk to Charles after the ceremony. So begrudgingly, I let him lead me to a seat next to Dahl, Taeyo, and my parents. My parents are awfully quiet, but they smile back when I flash them one, so I think they're recovering, albeit slowly.

As requested, the rest of the wedding party finds their seats (although half of the cheollimas have had to resort to hovering above the marble pews because they take up too much space), and finally, the ceremony begins.

"Dearly beloved, we are gathered here tonight to join this man and—"

Charles coughs.

Elvis looks down at his preprepared script. "My apologies. I mean we are gathered here tonight to join this *cheollima* and this woma—"

Charles coughs again.

"We are gathered here tonight to join this cheollima and this other cheollima in horsey matrimony," Elvis finally manages, third time lucky.

"That officiant man's hair is hashtag goals," Dahl breathes from my left, pointing at Elvis. "Maybe it's time I switched up my hairstyle, too. New realm, new hair. Makes sense, doesn't it, kid?"

"It's essentially the same as yours," I point out. "Although yours is real. His is defo a wig."

"You're right. I'm already hair goals." He smooths the side of his moon-colored hair. "Bada bing, bada boom!"

"Love can be bold and passionate and make you feel all shook up," Elvis recites, doing a little jiggly hip thrust to accentuate the point. "That's the type of love we go to Heartbreak Hotel for, and even dress up as winged horses for. But love me tender, baby, because this crazy little thing called love is quiet and unassuming. True love doesn't shout—it whispers. True love doesn't fight—it nurtures."

The crowd is hanging on to Elvis's every word, and he

continues after a grunt that sounds more like *uh huh huh*. "True love, ladies and gentlemen—"

Charles coughs.

"—*and* cheollima folks, is to give. When you love, give with all that you have, and all that you are. Remember these words. Because the King of Rock 'n' Roll has spoken!"

Taeyo and Dahl sniffle next to me, not making any semblance of effort to hide how moved they are by this speech.

"That man really is a king," Dahl breathes.

Taeyo nods, wiping his eye. " '*True love doesn't shout—it whispers.*' "

" '*True love doesn't fight—it nurtures,*' " Dahl continues. "It's just so powerful."

Dahl squeezes Taeyo's hand. "Let's get matching T-shirts."

While the bromance between my brother and his Horangi friend rages strong, Emmett sits unusually still on my right. Elvis finally moves on from waxing lyrical about the meaning of love and gets to the part where the couple exchange their vows and rings. Although, in Charles and Maru's case, they're exchanging neck tubes painted to look like sugar-glazed donuts.

"By virtue of the authority vested in me as the King of Rock 'n' Roll, I now pronounce you husband and wife." He turns to Charles and grins widely. "You may kiss the bride!"

The crowd goes wild as Charles and Maru seal their fate with a kiss. The cheollimas neigh and snort, and the humans rise up on their feet to cheer. For a second, I'm sure I see that fox-red fur coat again—it's the same woman from the Trevi Fountain, with the heavy makeup—but I blink and she's gone.

Then the heavens open up, releasing bucketfuls of rain, interspersed with flashes of lightning and roiling thunder. I worry for Areum, who has still not returned from her flyby of all the training locations around the city.

"The wild weather's back," Emmett comments, frowning up at the darkened sky.

As if connected, my phone pings with a message from Hattie.

Rye, how are things going up there? Any news?

I quickly text back:

Yongwang wasn't at the fountain ☹

She responds:

Aww really?? I was SURE he'd be there . . . >.<

But we followed a clue to a cheollima wedding, I text back. *And yep, that's not a typo!!! Will text you as soon as we find anything xxx*

I wish I could say I'm surprised, but then again, I'm currently teaching the imugis a dance routine, so what is life even? ╰(*°▽°*)╯ *Anyway, keep me updated. I have a gut feeling you're close so don't stop looking k?*

I take a snap of the rained-out wedding fiasco where drenched cheollimas and humans are now dancing to some unusual electro music that sounds more like horses whinnying than anything resembling a melody. I send the photo to Hattie. *Don't worry, Hat. We won't give up x*

"Hey, kid, is it just me, or do our parents look a little . . . off?" Dahl points to Eomma and Appa, who are huddled near the canapés table.

"They're doing that weird staring-off-into-space thing

again," I murmur as I glance worriedly between our parents and at Charles, who is now doing the moonwalk on his wife's back.

"You go talk to the groom, kid," Dahl answers, reading my mind. "Taeyo and I will keep an eye on the parents. I'll let you know if it worsens."

I bite my lip but nod. Finding out what Charles knows is the best way I can help my parents right now. "Come on, Em," I say, feeling increasingly impatient. "We've waited long enough. Let's go talk to our friend."

It takes three attempts—the third involving Charles landing on my head and doing a triple spin on his front right hoof—before we finally manage to grab his attention.

"Oh, you want to *talk*?" he shouts above the pumping whinny-beats. "Right *now*? But this is my favorite song, sugar dumpling! DJ Maximus made this mix just for us!"

"I'm so sorry," I say, meaning it. "I really don't want to ruin your big day, but it's kinda urgent. And it won't take a minute."

Emmett reaches his hand up, and with that extra new height on him, he easily guides our cheollima friend away from the dance floor. Charles continues to fly-dance in place, *unce, unce, unc*ing in his high-pitched voice.

"First of all, let us introduce ourselves," Emmett begins. "The last time we met, we were glamoured as two Gumiho sisters, Cosette and Adeline Chung. Sorry for the deception, but this is us. The real us."

"Our real names are Riley Oh and Emmett Harrison," I add.

Charles stops doing the running man and narrows his eyes at us. "Hang on a hot toddy. What is this nonsense?" He stares us down for a full five seconds without a word, and I feel the full impact of each loaded second. Sweat beads on my upper lip.

"You really enjoyed my salted-caramel cookies, remember?" Emmett improvises. "Sorry we couldn't bring you any today. I totally would've if I'd had the time to bake."

I mumble something incomprehensible just to feel like I'm adding to the conversation.

Charles thinks for an extra few seconds. He moves his jaw as if remembering the action of chewing into Emmett's cookies. He closes his eyes, lost in a moment of bliss. Then the cheollima's tiny face breaks out into a full-toothed equine smile.

"Well, well, well, what a pleasant surprise, my delicious macarons! Those were the best salted-caramel cookies I'd ever had the pleasure of tasting. In fact, I enjoyed them so much I asked the chef to re-create them for the guests today. I'm afraid they're nothing compared to yours, Emmett. You will have to give me the recipe. I'm not sure if you know, but I have *quite* the sweet tooth! It's a cheollima thing."

Emmett and I exhale together. *Phew.*

"Anyway, what brings you sneaky sweet devils all the way out here?"

"Well, actually, it's a bit of a long story," I start, "but there's a tear in the fabric between the Mortalrealm and Godrealm, and—"

"Oh, I know, dear! How else do you think this wedding was possible? If it wasn't for Mago's Fire being stolen from Mount

Baekdu, I'd never have had the melons to confess my love to my childhood first crush!"

"Wait, what's Mago's Fire?" I ask, confused.

Charles whinnies. "Have you been hiding under a rock, my sweet persimmons? You don't know the famous purple fire that sits on the most famous mountain in the Godrealm?"

The image of Luxor Hotel's pyramid doubling up as a mountain flashes in my memory. Something barbed twists in the pit of my stomach.

As if reading my mind, Emmett asks, "Is Mago's Fire connected to the sky somehow?"

Charles shakes his head. "Gosh, my puffy éclairs, you were much brighter when you looked like the Chung sisters, it must be said! But since you are the creator of the most delicious cookies ever baked, I will be gracious."

He clears his throat and puts on a David Attenborough voice, as if narrating a wildlife documentary. "Mago's Fire is the first fire *ever* created. It's the most powerful energy source in the entire universe, and it's the origin of all light."

"And that's why the lights are off in the sky," Emmett summarizes, frowning. "Because someone basically stole the main lightbulb?"

"More like stole all electricity," Charles clarifies. "Without Mago's Fire, the world is a body without a heart. And without any light being pumped around the body, the sun and moon and stars can't shine. They're as good as dead."

My own heart starts beating faster. "What will happen if the sky doesn't get its light back?"

"Well, that's *exactly* why I was so eager to get my dumpling Maru down here so fast!" Charles exclaims. "If Mago's Fire isn't returned to its rightful place on Mount Baekdu soon, there will be dire consequences to all three realms." He lowers his voice. "Because without light, there can be no life. Without Mago's Fire, everything—every*one*—will eventually perish."

Emmett and I gape at him.

"And when the world is ending," Charles concludes, his voice lifting back into its cheerful lull, "you gotta grab what's left of life by the melons, and get busy living!"

"But I don't understand," I say, trying to keep up. "Why would anyone in their right mind steal Mago's Fire?"

Emmett tenses beside me. "It's a total suicide move."

Charles shrugs. "Who cares, my little sweet buttercups!" He looks lovingly toward Maru, who he beckons over. "What's important is that tomorrow's not guaranteed. So we must enjoy the gift of today. It's why we call it the *present!*" He snuggles into Maru's neck and does a little bottom jiggle, making his tail sway from side to side. "Now, let's go party!"

Emmett clutches Boris closer to him, making the scooter's scaly ears twitch nervously. And I remember why we came to this wedding in the first place.

"Wait, before you do," I call out, "you haven't heard anything about the Dragon King recently, have you?"

Charles looks blank, but Maru's ears perk up. "Oh, funny you should mention that. One of my bridesmaids was just saying that she'd seen Yongwang around the Strip. She was speculating whether he'd been hiding down here this entire time."

"Hiding?" I ask.

She nods. "About six hundred years ago, he was the talk of the golden realm. Word got out that the charming hunk of a Dragon King was immigrating from the Spiritrealm up into our realm. If you didn't want to be *with* him, you wanted to *be* him, if you get my drift. Very much in demand. But he never came."

"Your bridesmaid—where did she see him?" I demand.

"Hmm, something about a hotel and water." Maru's eyes brighten. "Oh yes, some kind of hotel with canals and fountains."

"Did you hear that, Rye?" Emmett breathes. "*Fountains.* Hattie was right."

Momentarily forgetting about the awkwardness between us, I grip my best friend's arm. It's surprisingly firm and solid, and I immediately let it go. "Dahl will know. It's probably on his bucket list. There can't be too many hotels that have canals in them. We can find it."

Hope rages through me, even though in the back of my mind, it does strike me as weird that Yongwang hasn't been seen in the Godrealm for hundreds of years. When we were down in the Spiritrealm, the ineo siblings had told us that the Dragon King had left his ambassadorial position in the underwater borough six hundred years ago. If he hasn't been in the Godrealm that whole time, where *has* he been?

"Uhhh, *kid.* You need to come over here. Pronto!" Dahl's voice calls out from the other side of the garden.

I look over to see my parents lined up in single file, marching like toy soldiers. At first, I wonder if they're doing some old-people dance move—this *is* a wedding, after all. But one look at the blank expressions on their faces tells me that dancing is *not* what they're doing right now. They march unhurried but with purpose out of the garden and toward the street.

Dahl and Taeyo rush over, their faces as pale as garae-tteok.

"We need to follow them," Dahl says, hugging his leather jacket closer to his body. "We need to know where they're going."

5.
Museums Are So Hot
Right Now

I TRY OVER AND OVER AGAIN to get my parents' attention. I try pulling their arms, holding them still, and I even try tickling them (being tickled is Appa's kryptonite). But whatever it is that's trapped them in this weird trance, it's powerful. Nothing we do seems to snap them out of their daze.

Eventually, we resign ourselves to following them as they lead us northward up the Strip, hoping that wherever they're headed, it's close by. We've walked a few blocks when we spot a group of witches I recognize from the training modules. They're also marching in that stunned, toy-soldier-like way up the main drag, in one long, snaking line.

"Annyeong haseyo," I call out as I walk alongside them and wave my hands in front of their faces.

Nothing.

"Where are you going?" Dahl asks, tapping one of the adults on the shoulder.

Still no response.

Instead, Eomma and Appa silently merge like a zip with the rest of the witches, and continue to trudge up the road on autopilot.

"Hey, kids, is this some kind of public theater performance?" a saram bystander asks us, their eyes curious.

"Um...Well...It's..." I mutter, not sure how to answer.

Luckily, my brother's motto is *Act it until you exact it*. "It's actually a silent pilgrimage," Dahl responds, popping his collar and smiling easily, as if he's not talking out of his backside. "It's a form of higher meditation, linked to our spiritual beliefs. Really powerful stuff."

The bystander nods seriously. "Oh yes, yes, of course. How profound."

Luckily, that encounter dispels the other saram in the vicinity, at least for the time being.

We walk for about ten minutes maybe, and we've just passed a Walgreens and a Sephora, when the adults abruptly step into a moving walkway covered by green-and-cream awnings.

"Wherever they're headed, we must be here," Emmett guesses.

We follow the adults up the incline, when Taeyo and Dahl shout together in unison.

"LOOK!"

To our left is a huge cream-colored marble building complex that looks identifiably European. A sign up front says it's a "hotel-resort-casino" (of course it is) called the Venetian, and right in front of it, where Taeyo and Dahl are pointing, is a fountain. Under the lights of the street lamp, I can see it doesn't have the full sculpture scene like the Trevi, but it is a fully functional marble feature with water flowing down from its upper plates.

"Could that be the fountain we're supposed to find?" Taeyo asks.

"Kid!" Dahl says excitedly, waving his phone at me. "Remember I told you about the hotel that's made to look like Venice in Italy?"

"I think so . . ." I murmur. The truth is, I don't. He's always going on about his bucket list, so you can't blame me for tuning out on occasion.

"Remember how I told you that in the old part of Venice they use gondolas to get around instead of cars because they have waterways instead of roads?"

Emmett exhales sharply, and Boris's ears flutter back and forth. "*Canals.*"

Maru's voice echoes in my ear. *Some kind of hotel with canals and fountains,* she'd said.

"That's got to be it!" I exclaim. "That has to be the fountain from Hattie's dream."

"What are we waiting for?" Taeyo asks.

"And the adults?" Emmett asks as we make it to the top of the moving walkway and into what appears to be the lobby of . . . *Madame Tussauds wax museum?*

"Kid, you and Emmett stick with the parents," Dahl suggests, pulling Taeyo down a parallel awning-covered moving walkway that leads down toward the Venetian. "We need to understand what's affecting our grown-ups. Taeyo and I'll go check out the fountain and text you if we find a single scale."

Before I can respond, my twin and Taeyo have disappeared down the path.

"You don't have to stay with me if you don't want," I find myself saying to Emmett, which as soon as I say it I realize makes no logical sense whatsoever.

He frowns with his whole face. "Why the shirtballs would I leave you, Rye? I'm not letting you out of my sight."

My face heats, and I quickly turn away from him, just to see the last few adults make their way into the wax museum.

"Well, come on, then," I mutter, rushing in after them. "Let's figure out where the adults are going."

I've never been to a Madame Tussauds before, but I've heard all about the chain of museums full of wax figures that are made in the exact likeness of celebrities. I remember a few years back, Jennie convinced us that she'd been hanging out with Ariana Grande, showing pics of them together as proof. I won't lie—I totally fell for it. It was only after Hattie started probing why Ariana was always wearing the same bedazzled black-lace crop top in every photo that the truth came out. Turns out she'd been taking selfies at Madame Tussauds in Hollywood.

Emmett and I follow the adults into the Vegas branch of the wax museum, and the interior is more or less how I'd imagined it. Plush red carpet at the entrance, dramatically placed lighting creating shadows in all the right places, and gold lettering and accents on the walls to give the place a slight circusy feel. There are a few tourists waiting for admission, but the reception counter is currently empty, except for a small sign that says *Be back in 5.*

"Look!" Emmett says, pointing toward my parents, who are now walking past the elevators and snaking around the corner.

I look apologetically at the tourists, who, unlike us, are patiently waiting in line. "We, uh, already have tickets," I lie as Emmett and I chase after the grown-ups. "We're with those guys."

We follow close on the heels of the witches, who weave intricately through the various exhibits, and a string of hiccups erupts from my throat. I shove my hands in my jeans. As if sensing my nerves, Taggy buries farther into my sweater.

"What's wrong?" Emmett asks from beside me.

"Nothing."

"You're hiccuping," he points out.

"So?"

He raises his eyebrows. "You forget I remember everything."

I sigh. When the feelings are churning inside me and they're too much to handle, bubbles of it tend to escape as hiccups. It's a super-annoying tell.

"Spill," he says.

Perhaps it's because I need a momentary distraction from what's waiting for us at the end of this snaking convoy, but I admit my fears to him.

"It's just, I feel like a fake and a liar, you know? We're supposed to be leading this army against the goddesses, but Dahl and I haven't even unlocked our powers, so we're no help to anyone. And I'm trying to put on a brave face because I don't want to disappoint anyone or come across ungrateful for the responsibility....”

We walk past an eerily real-looking Lady Gaga with her hair tied up into a huge bow on top of her head. “But I don’t have the answers. I’m just leading us all on this wild-goose chase, and what are we even doing? For all we know, we’re just on some stupid scavenger hunt organized by the goddesses, and we’re just walking straight into their trap. Our people deserve a *real* leader—an actual *hero*. Someone wise and strong and certain who doesn’t have a track record of putting her loved ones in danger and—”

Scenes of my parents being attacked by a possessed Hattie spring to mind, as does snippets of Emmett being expunged off the face of the universe, his limbs burning into oblivion, inch by inch. I shudder, wishing the memories would disappear, but at the same time hoping that they remain burned into my mind. I never want to forget what my actions can lead to.

“The prophecy is wrong, Em,” I say. “I’m not cut out for all of this. I have no idea what I’m doing. I’m a *fraud*.”

“Imposter syndrome” is his response as we walk past a wax figure of Bae Suzy.

“Huh?”

“It’s called imposter syndrome—I’ve read about it in *Psychology Today*. It’s when you think you don’t deserve to be where you are, or own the things you’ve achieved, even though it’s clear to everyone else you have. I’m not a licensed therapist or anything, *obviously*, but I’m telling you, Rye—you’re suffering from a serious case of it.”

“Since when do you read about psychology?”

He ignores me. "You think that because of the mistakes you made and the bad things that have happened, that you shouldn't be at the helm of our army. But you're only looking at one part of the picture. The rest of us see you for who you are—the courageous, selfless girl who is willing to go to any lengths for the people she loves. We don't look to you because you're the last fallen star, or even because the Haetae has you in another one of his wacko prophecies. We look to you because you've proven yourself as someone worthy of being a leader. *Our* leader."

My eyes sting. I wish I could believe what he's saying, but it all just sounds like pretty-sounding words meant for someone else. "But, Em, I can't explain it—I feel this dread inside. This deep, tugging feeling that I can't shake, that no matter how hard I try, terrible things are going to happen. To all of us."

My parents lead the convoy past an exhibition starring Miley Cyrus on a wrecking ball and IU in the role of Jang Man-wol from the K-drama *Hotel del Luna*. I hate to admit it at a time like this, but I'm not *not* enjoying seeing these wax figures right now.

"Dude, that's called anxiety, and that's totally normal, too. In fact, the article also said that people suffering from imposter syndrome are at a higher risk of anxiety. They put a huge amount of pressure on themselves to meet stupid, unattainable standards that no one else is expecting them to meet. So, honestly, knowing you, it'd be kinda weird if you *weren't* spiraling into an anxious puddle."

He pauses to nod appreciatively at the Simon Cowell wax figure who's standing next to Psy in mid–"Gangnam Style" gallop. "Plus, the article said anxiety is our brain's way of try-ing to protect us. It doesn't want you to get hurt, so sometimes it makes up scary stories to try to talk you out of doing stuff. Which I'll admit, seems kinda annoying. But also kinda nice, in that Asian Auntie way, if you know what I mean."

I'm half listening to Emmett and half coming to a hazy half-formed realization, when the adults lead us through the doors of a pop-up exhibition room featuring intricate scale models of whole cities and countries in various stages of development. There are accompanying signs that state some are BEFORE, while others are AFTER. There's even a huge wax figure of a fox with gleaming eyes and a sharp chin that I'm convinced keeps changing poses.

That's when it strikes me. Bae Suzy. IU. Psy...

"Hey, Em, since when does Madame Tussauds have so many Korean figures?"

He lifts Boris, pointing the scooter's tail toward one of the models—a humongous display of a majestic mountain with a violet fire at its summit. The sign in front says it's *The Original Yeo-ui-ju (also known as Mago's Fire) on Mount Baekdu, Godrealm.* "Uhh, since now, I guess."

"Mago's Fire is the yeo-ui-ju?" I murmur, reading the little plaque over and over again. "As in the pearl of wisdom?"

Growing up, we'd known the yeo-ui-ju—or the pearl of wisdom—to be a powerful and legendary relic. No human had ever had it in their possession to know its true power, but some believed it to grant immortality, while others believed it to carry the knowledge of the universe. Then, six months ago, down in the Spiritrealm, I'd learned that the yeo-ui-ju had been what the snake had retrieved for Mago in his attempt to become a dragon, only for Mago to ask him to return it to where he'd found it. Overcome by greed, he'd been unwilling to return the pearl to its rightful place, which is what had transformed him into a weird snake-yong hybrid monster (aka an imugi). After that, the pearl was never seen again.

"It tracks," Emmett says. "And it makes sense why no humans have had it in their possession before. It's been in the Godrealm the whole time."

The hairs on my arms rise up, and I glance nervously around the pop-up space. "Does that mean *we're* in the Godrealm right now? Why else would there be exhibits about Mago's Fire in here?" I gulp, the realization slowly dawning on me. "A wax museum in the Godrealm must've leaked over Madame Tussauds in Vegas...."

Emmett points to the adults, who are now continuing on to a smaller door on the opposite end of the pop-up space that looks sort of like those emergency-exit doors in the movie theaters. "They're leaving. We can't lose them."

He jumps on Boris and scooters after them, and I follow, leaving a generous amount of space between me and the wax fox figure. Something about it is creeping me out.

Emmett disappears through the threshold after my parents, quickly followed by a *"What the—"*

"What?" I demand, running after him. "What's in th—"

My jaw drops. On the other side of the threshold is a cavernous dug-out space as big as an airplane hangar—no, *bigger*. It's as if football field upon football field has been stitched onto the back of one another, creating a long, unending pit. And standing within it are hundreds of people. They look just like the wax figures we passed to get here, their eyes open, staring into nothingness, but they stand shoulder to shoulder, row upon row, in perfect equidistant lines.

My parents and the other witches climb down a long ladder into the pit, and I run toward them, pulling at their arms. "Eomma, Appa, *stop*! What are you doing? You can't go down there!"

But it's as if they can't hear me. They continue down into the pit, and one by one, they line up in formation to strengthen the creepy collection of wax figures.

Emmett and I climb down after them, but it seems they've reached their final destination. Having found their spots, they solidify in place with their eyes open and unblinking, as if they've become human-size action figures.

"What *is* this place?" Emmett says from a few rows down, his voice hoarse.

I tentatively reach out a hand and trace it down my eomma's face. It's cold and weirdly smooth under my touch. "It's like they're gone," I whisper. "Like they're not really here anymore."

Then I place the hand on my appa's chest, only for relief to shudder through me. "They still have heartbeats, Em. They're okay, I think. Just on standby. Waiting." I pause, snuggling into the hard waxy shoulder of my appa. "But for *what*?"

There is a shuffle of feet as Emmett makes his way down the pit.

"Sora? Austin?" he shouts from a little farther away. "Mr. and Mrs. Kim?"

I reluctantly turn away from my parents and toward Emmett, only to come face-to-face with Professor Ryu from Saturday School. And my auntie Okja.

"Auntie O?" I croak. "You're here, too?"

I start running down the aisles of wax figures, seeing one familiar face after another. Jennie's parents. Noah Noh's Taegwondo grandmaster dad. All the Horangi adults who have been training up witches with elemental magic. All the Gom healers stationed across the city.

Emmett's voice echoes down the cavernous space. "Rye, this is bad. *Really* bad. It looks like all the adult witches in Las Vegas are here, period."

I make a face. "But how come *we* haven't been turned into wax statues?"

I jump as my phone pings in my pocket. The sound echoes ominously down the pit.

Guys, all our grown-ups have disappeared! Jennie messages in the friend group chat. *They all just started walking off in a weird trance.*

Noah responds immediately. *SAME HERE! Me, Areum, and Cosette were stopping a fight, and the next minute, they all just turned on their heels and marched off. What is going on?*

Despite the chaos in my head, I let out a sigh of relief, knowing that Areum is okay. I haven't seen her since I sent her off on a flyby of the training locations around the city.

Is everyone safe? I demand. *No one's hurt?*

Jennie messages back. *Yeah, David and I are fine.*

Noah immediately after that. *Yep, we're okay. You guys?*

I snap a photo of the wax-figure pit and send it to the chat.

We're dealing with THIS . . . 💀💀 We're pretty sure this is where all the gifted adults are disappearing off to . . . .

Jennie responds to the picture.

OMG. Tell us where you are and we'll be there ASAP ☺

Before I can answer her question, my mind turns to Dahl and Taeyo, who I haven't heard from since we entered the wax museum.

Wait, Dahl? Taeyo? I thumb furiously. *Let us know you're okay.*

Silence.

Emmett taps his fingers on Boris's handlebars impatiently. Still silence.

I tap my foot on the dusty floor of the wax-adult pit.

Persistent silence.

KaTalk doesn't even have blinking ellipses, so I can't tell if they're just typing a long message.

Guys??? I try again. I'm pretty sure a vein is about to pop on my forehead.

Finally, a series of broken messages appear. It's from Dahl.

Hel

P

Canals

Egggg

BONGALKSJFKLH

!!!!!

Without another word, I run back to give Eomma and Appa a kiss on their unnatural waxy cheeks. "Saranghaeyo. Just . . . Just stay here. We're going to snap you out of this prison. I swear." I quickly turn away, not sure how I'm going to live up to that promise.

Not daring to look back at my frozen parents again, I climb up the ladder and follow Emmett and Boris out the way we came in. We sprint all the way down to the lobby of Madame Tussauds and burst out the doors onto the green-and-cream-covered moving walkway. And it's only when we're running toward the main entrance of the Venetian that it hits me.

The wax figure of the fox was missing from the exhibition room.

6.
Blue Eggs and Ham(strings)

 DAHL'S MESSAGE HAD DEFINITELY included the word *canals*, so I'm pretty sure they must be inside the Venetian. But Emmett and I stop by the fountain outside the building anyway, just in case. There doesn't seem to be any sign of a fight or struggle, though. Not a drop of water seems to have splashed out of the fountain. Satisfied we haven't missed any clues, we run inside.

Much like the rest of the city, the inside of this building is a surprise for the senses. It actually reminds me a little of the Miracle Mile Shops earlier, what with the domed ceiling made to look like the real sky (one that still has a sun and moon!). Except the inside of the Venetian is extra trippy because it's been designed to look like the quaint, canal-filled old town of Venice. Little waterways separate the European-looking buildings with balconies and little windows. There are cute little bridges and overpasses, dotted by antique-looking streetlamps. Tourists with shopping bags are riding gondolas and getting out at patio restaurants overlooking the water.

It's not hard to find Taeyo and Dahl once we're inside. Dahl's weird string of messages had suggested he was somewhat distracted when sending them, and as we follow the sounds of squeals, barks, and splashing water, it becomes apparent why.

"Holy shirtballs," Emmett breathes, pointing at a flock of large, peacock-like birds with long, ribboned tails circling a gondola in front of Steve Madden. "Are those the phoenixes your dad mentioned earlier?"

My eyes widen. The bird on the logo of Bonghwang Express had a long, wavy plumage of tails that seemed to be every color of the rainbow. These birds circling over Dahl seem to have reddish-brown ribbons with white tips that swim long and wavy behind them. But other than the color difference, they do indeed look like the bonghwangs.

"Get *away* from us!" Dahl screams from a gondola floating in the middle of the canal, his usually impeccable hair a floppy mess. "Just because you're stunningly beautiful doesn't mean you're any less annoying!"

Taeyo is standing on the brick bridge overpass, using his water-manipulation skills to throw jets of water into the air to stop the phoenixes' attacks. A small crowd of saram tourists are watching and filming the whole scene on their phones, excitedly chatting between themselves.

Emmett unfolds Boris and jumps on the scooter. "I'll head over first to help."

I run to catch up behind him, just in time to see one of the bonghwangs dive down and peck at Dahl's head as if it's fishing for a delicacy of human brains. Didn't Appa say the phoenixes were benevolent creatures?

"Get *away* from us!" Dahl shouts again, throwing himself protectively over what looks like a huge blue egg sitting in the gondola. It's not quite as big as a misshapen exercise ball, but almost. There's a cut above my soul twin's eye, and blood is trickling down his face.

I hurry over to meet Emmett, who is now standing next to Taeyo, rubbing his wrists together.

"I'm so glad you guys are here!" Taeyo exclaims, wiping sweat off his brow. "We need to stop these birds from getting their claws on that dragon egg."

"Dragon egg?" I breathe, staring at the blue-scaled thing my twin is protecting with his life.

"We found it in the fountain," Taeyo explains. "It's scaly, so we figured it was somehow connected to Yongwang. But then these bonghwangs appeared out of nowhere and won't stop trying to steal it from us."

Another bird swoops down and unsuccessfully attempts to snatch the egg from the gondola, but does unfortunately manage to scratch Dahl's arm with a talon.

"Watch out!" I scream as I lean over the handrail, feeling helpless.

"Take this!" Dahl throws the key of all keys over the rail at me. "They seem to be kinda scared of it."

I catch the Key and grip it so hard, my knuckles go white. Then, as more bonghwangs fly toward Dahl, I wave it in the air furiously, not quite sure what to do with it.

A jet of water flies over Dahl's head to block another attack, and suddenly, one of the metal guardrails separating land from water screeches as it bends and breaks off, seemingly throwing itself into the air.

I turn to see Emmett, with his forehead furrowed in concentration, his hands raised in front of him. He makes a motion like he's lifting an invisible weight, and then releases one hand, swinging it like a Ping-Pong paddle. The metal bar in the air swings with the action, chasing an unsuspecting bonghwang away.

"Wait, you can wield metal?" I say to Emmett, dumbfounded. "I thought you said that your saram side was preventing the chip from working."

A muscle leaps on Emmett's jaw with his exertion. "Turns out I just needed to practice more."

There's a clap of thunder outside the building, and for a split second, everyone stops and holds their breath. There's another clap, and it's so loud it's as if the storm is raging *inside*.

"Riley, *watch out!*"

I look up, just in time to see a bonghwang diving at me. Luckily, Emmett's metal railing flies across the air and swats it away before it digs its beak into my brain. Ugh.

"Why is it coming after *me?*" I cry, ducking down and covering my head with my hands. "I don't even have the yong egg!"

"On your left!" Taeyo warns while projecting a protective water dome over Dahl at the same time. "The big one. It keeps going for you, Riley!"

Gripping even tighter to the key of all keys, I stand back up. Everyone else is fighting, so I need to game up, too. I mean, how hard could it be? If they're already wary of it, I just need to point this thing into the air and keep wiggling it around . . . right?

From the corner of my eye, I see the largest bonghwang again—the one with the gleaming yellow eyes and fluffiest ribboned tails—do a figure eight in the sky above Dahl before locking its eyes on me. I swivel around to face it.

"Give it your best shot!" I call out, my voice shaking like the traitor it is. "I'll have you know, I'm not scared to use this!" I shake the fat knitting needle topped with Dahl's and my teardrop stones into the air, trying to come across as threatening as I can.

I swear the bonghwang smirks at me and then flies right toward me.

I gulp. I guess I asked for it, so there's no backing out now. I change my grip so both my hands are firmly on the Key, and I wait for the phoenix to charge. But at the last minute, the bird changes course. Instead of coming toward me, it diverts its path and heads toward Emmett, who is too lost in the task of breaking off another metal pole from the guardrail to see what's coming his way.

I don't even get a chance to warn him. Instead, my instincts take over. The blood rushes from my head down to my limbs, and I find myself moving at a speed I didn't know I could move. My hamstring pulls, but still, I push through my pain and rush to my best friend's side.

As the bonghwang tightens its body and corkscrews itself toward Emmett, I stop thinking. I snap my eyes shut, and I spear the Key through the flesh of the bird's side.

The creature lets out a trail of shrieks, except it's so high-pitched and loud it sounds more like a howling young puppy than a bird. It falls from the air and drops with a dull *thud*. Its body writhes in pain, and blood is gushing from the wound in its stomach.

I drop the key of all keys, and it clangs near my feet. I drop to my knees. I think I'm going to puke.

"*Oh my Mago. Oh my Mago. Oh my Mago.*"

I know I should be helping my friends right now, but I can't do anything but stare at this poor beautiful bird that I wounded. It's going to die. This creature is no longer going to live because of *me*.

Get ahold of yourself! I tell myself. *This isn't the first time you've killed. You're the gold-destroyer. You're the one that ended the Cave Bear Goddess, for crying out loud. This is what you're destined to do!*

But for some reason, this feels different. This time there is literal blood on my hands, and this is a divine bird, not so different from Areum. . . . And to make things worse, Appa had said bonghwangs were benevolent. Maybe they were being controlled by someone, like when Bada attacked Dahl in the River of Reincarnation. And if that's true, I just took an innocent being's life.

I think I hear people calling my name. I think there's a new flurry of action around me. But everything starts to go hazy, as if there's a vignette around the spasming bird bleeding out on the stone floor of the Venetian. The only words I can hear are the words *murderer, murderer, murderer* ringing in my ears. My chest feels tight. *Too* tight. I realize I can't breathe anymore.

What's happening to me? Is it just me, or are the bird's tails growing? Am I hallucinating?

I am on the verge of passing out and joining this bird in the afterlife when something tickles me on my neck. Taggy is rubbing their head against my skin in a calm, soothing manner, as if to say, *Breathe. Just breathe, Riley. You can do this. Just breathe.*

At some point, I realize a real voice is talking into my ear. "Just breathe, Riley Oh. Breathe. I am here and I will protect you. Just breathe."

"Areum?" I whisper. "Is that you?"

"Indeed," she says smoothly, a warbly chattering sound warming my ears. "It is I. I am back. Everything is going to be okay."

"What just happened to me?" I ask, still feeling like I could be sick at any minute.

"I believe you had a panic attack, Riley Oh. Perfectly understandable, given the circumstances."

It takes a while, but slowly, the pain in my chest subsides. And when the spots in my vision disappear, it seems all the other bonghwangs have been chased away. In fact, all the tourists are gone, too.

Dahl, Taeyo, and Emmett are huddled around the scaly blue yong egg, which has been taken out of the gondola and put on the ground. They all look a little shell-shocked and weary, but apart from a few scratches here and there, they seem to be safe.

"You feeling a little better, kid?" Dahl asks, coming over. "You did good."

I shake my head. "No need to lie so blatantly." I stare at the bleeding bonghwang still lying on the ground at my feet.

"No really," Taeyo says reassuringly, adjusting his orange bow tie, which has gone off-kilter. "This big one was out for blood. You stopped it. And when you did, all the other ones just disappeared."

The bird stops spasming.

"Is it dead?" I whisper to no one in particular.

"I think so," Dahl responds.

"How odd—its tails look bigger and bushier on the ground, don't you think?" Taeyo points out, wiping some blood off his cheek.

I hang my head.

"You were just defending yourself," Emmett says quietly. "No, you were protecting *me*. In your place, I would've done the same thing."

All my friends nod, and I suddenly desperately want to change the subject. I don't want them to see that I'm struggling with this. This is *war*. There's probably a lot more of this fighting and killing I'm supposed to do from here on out, and just because I was raised a healer doesn't mean I can't take on this new job. They can't see me weak like this.

I wave my hand around the complex. "Where have all the saram bystanders gone?"

"I told them we were having a production team meeting, and that they needed to vacate the premises," Dahl explains. "They were surprisingly happy to comply."

Taeyo smooths down his striped dress shirt. "They didn't want the magic to be ruined, I think."

I nod toward the dragon egg in Dahl's arms. "Is that thing supposed to be shuddering like that?"

"It's been doing it for a while now," Dahl responds. "I think it's about to hatch."

I take out my phone. "I think we should call Hattie. She'll know what to do."

I'm so grateful in that moment that despite *my* weaknesses, I have a natural strong leader like Hattie. She is always brave. And she always knows what to do.

"Rye!" Hattie cries as her face pops up next to the mayor's. They're in the H-Mart food forest again. "You okay? What's happened? Did you find Yongwang? Tell me everything. Every tiny detail."

I don't even know how to explain everything that's transpired since we last spoke to Hattie, but luckily, Dahl is blessed with the gift of gab. He gets our sister and the mayor up to date, and with dramatic flair, at that.

"This must be the start of the war," the mayor says solemnly. "It has begun." He cups his hands behind his back and exhales deeply. "However, now that you have located Yongwang, we can work together to stop this war from ruining our realms. Please do not lose hope."

Dahl shakes his head. "Sorry to disappoint, Mayor, but we haven't actually found Yongwang yet. Only this egg."

"Yongwang did always like his elaborate outfits," the mayor says, with a quirk in his brow.

I run my hand over the blue scales of the yong egg in Dahl's arms. It's trembling uncontrollably now, as if it's got the chills.

"Wait, you're not suggesting that this egg could actually *be* Yongwang?"

Emmett scowls. "The Dragon King is an...*egg*?"

Hattie looks uncertain, but the mayor smiles knowingly. "It does look like an egg, doesn't it. But I recall Yongwang using this disguise on occasion in the Spiritrealm. Once when he was ailing from a terrible flu, and once when there was a minor uprising in the underwater borough that he was loathe to deal with. It's a protective act I believe, shrinking and curling up into a ball. It helps him preserve his energies."

"Like burying yourself in your bed and pulling the blankets over your head," I muse. "I wouldn't mind doing that...." I say that second bit under my breath.

"But how do we wake him?" Taeyo asks, studying the egg from all angles. "If I could figure out the mechanics of this disguise, I could see if there's a way I can pry it open. But that might involve having to—"

"I think I have an idea." Hattie, who has been surprisingly silent considering she's the one who had the dream about the Dragon King, finally speaks up. "Dahl, can you please draw a mun between our realms?"

I chew my lip. "Hat, that's what created the tear between our realms in the first place. Are you sure you want to—"

"Trust me, Rye. I have a gut feeling about this. I think I know how we can wake him."

Dahl draws a portal using the mun-pen Sharpie. Then he picks up the blood-covered key of all keys, still lying on the floor, to turn the mun into a portal.

A bright red light explodes behind the door, and Hattie swings it open from her side.

"I'm sending Namjoon through. Just put the egg in front of him, okay?"

All my friends leap back from the door.

"Uh, you're gonna send an *imugi* through the door?" Emmett asks, his voice cracking. "Are you sure it's a good idea to send a hellbeast up to the Mortalrealm?"

"I think it's the *best* idea," Hattie responds. "Namjoon is part yong. The Dragon King *is* a yong. They're cut from the same cloth. And something tells me that Namjoon will know how to get to Yongwang. Just trust me. Let him do his thing."

We hold our breaths as Namjoon sniffs the threshold between the two realms and then crosses over to the land of the living. He pauses, as if to see if he's still in one piece. And when he feels certain nothing is off, he walks confidently toward the yong egg, ignoring everyone else.

Emmett, Taeyo, Dahl, and I exhale in relief. Dahl and I know firsthand the joys of being imminent imugi lunch. And Emmett and Taeyo have heard all about it. The TL;DR being: *NOT FUN.*

As Namjoon sniffs the scales on the egg, I point my phone at him so Hattie and the mayor can see what's happening. He then licks it, which triggers a bit of PTSD from the time he licked me to create a cup of saliva-brewed coffee. *Ugh.* But then the imugi does the last thing I expect it to. It sits on top of the egg like a hen. He's warming it and letting it know that it's safe.

"See?" Hattie says through the screen on my phone. "He's a natural." She sounds like a proud mom.

At first, nothing happens. And I wonder if Hattie's gut was wrong this time.

But then Namjoon picks himself off the egg and gives it one final lick. And that's when the scaly blue thing starts to unfurl. It looks like a scaly blue armadillo. But then it keeps growing. And growing. And growing. It continues to stretch and morph, until before our very eyes appears a . . . *woman*.

She's statuesque and built like a warrior, with toned Michelle Obama arms. She's wearing black leather pants and a spaghetti-strap tank top that's steeped with blood under her left rib. Her skin has a blue tinge to it, and as she shakes out her shoulders, the outline of scales shimmers on her skin like a holograph. The movement makes her clutch her stomach, and her eyes darken in pain.

I gasp. No wonder she was curled up in a ball. She's injured. And really bad, by the looks of things.

"Wait, *what?*" Hattie asks from my phone, sounding very confused. "The Dragon King is a woman?!"

Yongwang opens her palm, revealing a fidget spinner. One of those small sensory toys you hold and spin around and around in your hand.

"Finally," the woman says hoarsely in a strong southern drawl. "You have located me." She winces.

Hearing the woman's pained voice, Namjoon whimpers and bends his legs as if bowing, before running back through the mun to the Spiritrealm. Even Boris's tail goes limp in Emmett's arms. And Hattie exhales sharply.

"*No. Freaking. Way,*" my sister breathes, obviously coming to a conclusion that no one else but Namjoon and Boris have.

"What is it, Hat?" I demand. "Share!"

Hattie's face pales like a rice sheet. "You're not going to believe me. But, um, it appears that Yongwang here . . . is the Water Dragon Goddess."

7.
Even Princess Jasmine
Needed Her Space

I GLANCE BETWEEN HATTIE on my phone's screen and the injured warrior woman holding the fidget spinner in her hand. I let out a snort-laugh.

"Is this some kind of joke?" I demand. "What do you mean, Yongwang is the Water Dragon Goddess?" I shake my head so hard, bits of hair fall out of my ponytail.

"What have you done with the Dragon King?" the mayor demands from my phone. He sounds genuinely upset. "Reveal yourself! Who in Mago's name are you?"

The warrior woman waves to my phone and attempts a weak smile. "Well, hello there, my old friend. Fancy seeing you again after all these years. Things going well down under?"

The mayor raises his hand and flicks his fingers outward in the sky of the snack forest, as if zooming into the image of the woman's face. "Is . . . Is that really *you*, Yongwang?"

She nods, which makes her cough, which makes her double over, which makes her cough again.

"Wait, so she *is* the Dragon King?" Dahl asks, sounding as confused as I feel. "Can someone please explain what in the heaven and hells is going on right now?"

The woman steadies herself. "I am, indeed Yongwang—"

"We found the Dragon King, Riley Oh!" Areum screeches happily from my shoulder.

"So Yongwang *is* a woman," Emmett clarifies.

"—but it is also true that I am the Water Dragon Goddess."

The word *goddess* rings like an alarm bell in my head. And like a well-trained muscle, I find myself leaping in front of my friends, sticking my arms out protectively.

"Don't you dare lay a *hand* on my friends, you hear me?" I shout. "I won't let you hurt them. Not on my watch!"

The woman doesn't respond. Instead, she nudges the fidget spinner toward me, her palm still open.

"What of it?" I demand, not stupid enough to take it from her.

The woman groans and clutches her stomach again. Fresh blood seeps out of her wound, and I feel a moment of compassion for her. Ugh. Why did my parents do such a good job instilling healer values into me?

Careful not to hurt Taggy, I shrug off my sweater and throw it at Yongwang. "Until we figure out what you're scheming, push this against your wound. You have to stop the flow of blood."

Hattie's voice rings out from my phone, which is still gripped in my hand. "Rye, I know this goes against everything we know, but I think we need to listen to her. I don't think she's here to end us. I think she's here to . . . to *help* us."

I keep my guard up—this won't be the first time the goddesses have pulled a sneaky on us.

"You have two minutes," I say cautiously.

She nods and points to a patio chair that's sitting outside Steve Madden. "Do you mind if I take a seat? I'm not . . . I'm not feeling so well."

I nod. "But no funny business."

Areum morphs into her full seven-foot stature and flies toward her, narrowing her avian eyes suspiciously at the Dragon King/Water Dragon Goddess.

"Well?" Emmett says impatiently, his eyes narrowed. "Out with it, Goddess."

The woman looks around as if to check we're alone. She looks . . . worried.

"Have you all seen *Aladdin*?" she finally says.

Dahl nods enthusiastically. "Oh, have I ever! I discovered it when I moved up here. It's a whole new world!"

"Are you serious?" I direct at the king/goddess. "We're at war, and you want to know about our movie tastes?" I nod over at Areum, who starts approaching the woman with a menacing *caw-caw*.

The goddess raises a hand in surrender. "I was just wanting to illustrate my point. Princess Jasmine wanted time away from the palace, and so did I. I wanted to escape the stifling restrictions and unreasonable expectations of the golden realm."

I raise my hand to stop Areum. "Continue."

"Being a major goddess in the Godrealm comes with lots of benefits. But it also comes with many shortfalls. You can't go anywhere without being recognized. There's always a minor god or divine citizen hiding around the corner, trying to pull you down, or use you to climb up the ranks...the rat race is just *relentless*. Not to mention what it's like living with all your sisters in one house. Do you know how big celestial egos can get? Can you imagine sharing a bathroom with that lot?"

She shudders. "Which is why I disguised myself as the Dragon King and spent some time in the Spiritrealm. To get away from it all. My time as the ambassador to the underwater borough was life-changing for me. All thanks to the gracious mayor who gave me the distinguished post."

The mayor exhales. "You really were the best candidate for the job," he admits. "I just don't understand how you got away with the disguise for so long."

The woman shrugs. "Being sisters with the Nine-Tailed Fox means you pick up a few tricks of illusion."

"How did you even get to the Spiritrealm?" Dahl asks. "We thought you and your sisters were trapped in the Godrealm. Isn't that why you tried to kill my sister in the first place?"

"That was the Cave Bear Goddess, *not* me," the goddess is quick to clarify. "And also, the entire three-realm system is designed with the land-dweller in mind. Even the boundaries between the realms are blurred when it comes to the sea. It means those of us who call the water home often get forgotten. Which I used to my advantage."

She grimaces as she repositions herself on the chair. "For example, no one knows that there's a path connecting the three realms by water, because no one has bothered to look. At first, my sisters didn't even notice I'd gone. It really was as easy as that." Her eyes get all dreamy and nostalgic. "Good times, indeed."

Down in the Spiritrealm, Bada the ineo had explained that land-dwellers' ignorance was also the reason why so many didn't know about the existence of the third underwater borough. We are so obsessed with our own lives on land that we don't even realize the majority of the world is actually below water. Mago forbid, we might not be the center of the universe.

"But eventually, my sisters started wondering where I was. They threatened to tell Mother I'd broken her rules and escaped. Jealous, petty, and closed-minded, my sisters." She scowls. "So I had no choice but to leave my post and return to the Godrealm."

Dahl nods. "Right, which makes sense why the Dragon King—well, why *you*, haven't been seen down in the underwater borough for six hundred years."

"And why the Dragon King never immigrated to the Godrealm," Emmett adds, recalling what Maru the cheollima had told us about the anxiously anticipated arrival of the Dragon King that never eventuated.

"Don't forget to press on the wound," I remind her, noticing the fresh flow of blood and the sweat beading on her face. "It's bleeding again."

The goddess pushes my balled-up sweater into her wound and shudders. Her skin has turned a sickly shade of blue. The scales are no longer holographic, but are now dark and defined on the exposed skin of her arms and shoulders, almost as if she's drying out in front of our eyes. I'll admit—she's not looking so hot.

"That's all good and well," Dahl says, "but that doesn't explain why you're here now. With us."

"Looking seriously crap, no offense," Emmett says.

"And why have you been visiting me in my dreams?" Hattie demands. "What does this all *mean*?"

The goddess sighs deeply and opens her palm again. "It's all to do with *this*."

"Because of a *fidget spinner*?" I feel my voice squeak in frustration.

Instead of answering, she plays with the sensory toy, spinning it around and around on her fingers. I am about to *really* lose my cool with her, when, suddenly, above the spinning whirr of color, a small bonfire appears. It's tiny—the same size as the toy itself. But the flame is resplendently purple.

Everyone gasps and shields their eyes.

"Is that . . . ? Is that what I *think* it is?" I demand, squinting through my fingers.

It burns so bright, it physically hurts. But I can't look away. Dahl grunts, and I know what he's feeling because it's happening to me, too. It's that same gut punch we felt when the bulgae was circling Mount Baekdu, right before the sky broke. That feeling of finality. Of impending darkness. Of the *end*.

The goddess stops spinning the toy and snaps it still in her palm, the violent flames disappearing with its stillness. She pants, almost as if it took all her energy to contain the fire in her hand without passing out.

"Did you know that Mago's Fire was created at the beginning of time itself?" she asks. "The Mother was creating the world, but she was tired because the world is vast. And right then, as exhaustion overwhelmed her, she shed a tear. As the tear rolled down her cheek and off her chin, it exploded.

"It was such an explosion—some call it the big bang—that the teardrop immediately caught aflame. And there it was. The birth of the most powerful energy in all the realms that could *never* be extinguished. A fire that exploded the world into being."

"*You're* the one who stole it," I say quietly, finally joining the dots. "And your wound? Who did that to you?"

"My sisters, who attempted to kill me for doing what I believed was right." Her eyes bore directly into me. "For trying to bring it to *you*."

"*Me?*"

I stagger back. The phone flips with the movement, and Hattie's stern voice comes from the screen. "We can't see, Rye! Put it upright!"

I obey, but now my hands are shaking. Why in the three realms would I want to have Mago's Fire?

"But why steal the thing that is the source of all light?" my sister demands, reading my mind. "Won't the world end if it's not returned to the mountain?"

The goddess's chest heaves, and I realize she's crying.

"Because as much as I love my sisters, they are misguided. I even tried turning a blind eye, leaving the Godrealm for another leave of absence. But . . . But . . ."

"But what?" I ask softly.

"But I couldn't sit back and watch. They were going to take the Fire for themselves—to use its extraordinary power to destroy *everything* that our mother created. I tried, but they won't be satiated by mere war. They want to topple the entire three-realm system and start afresh. They want to create a MegaRealm."

"A *MegaRealm?*" Dahl asks, bewildered.

The goddess nods solemnly, her voice hoarse with emotion. "They want to rule supreme over all beings, divine, mortal, and spirit. Because they believe *they* are destined to be the universe's rightful leaders." She sobs openly now. "I wish it weren't true, but my sisters...my dear beloved sisters...they *must* be stopped."

My heart wrenches like a dish towel for this warrior woman. It's so clear by the way she speaks about her sisters that, despite their wrongdoings, she still cares for them. They attacked her to the point of almost death, and yet, she loves them. If Hattie or Dahl did the same to me, how would it feel? I can't even imagine.

"I understand this is a lot to take in," the goddess says, her scales now starting to flake off her dark ocean-blue skin. "But I assure you, everything I have uttered is the truth."

"But why me?" I demand. "Why have you brought the fidget spinner—I mean Mago's Fire—to *me*?"

The goddess tries to stand from her chair but doesn't make it up. She's too weak now. Instead, as Areum narrows her eyes and fluffs her feathers protectively, the goddess opens her palm and offers me the sensory toy for what I'm sure is the third or fourth time since we met.

"Because, gold-destroyer, the Mother's teardrop contains within it the biggest destructive power known in all existence.

If you are going to win a war against my sisters, you will need to be prepared."

"Kid!" Dahl cries from behind me. "This is it! This is what we've been looking for. Don't you see?"

I swivel to see my soul twin waving his arms around like those blow-up stick-figure balloons outside car dealerships.

"See what?"

"The Haetae!" Dahl says, talking so fast his words slur together. "He said we'd unlock our true potential. *This* has got to be it! We needed to find the Water Dragon Goddess to find it." He gasps for air. "Mago's Fire is our superpower!"

As realization dawns on me, relief sparks through me like a firecracker. "Dahl, if you're right, we've finally unlocked our true—" Something moves in the edge of my vision, and I stop dead in my tracks.

Because the thing is *huge*.

It has beady yellow eyes, a razor-sharp chin, and it's covered in reddish-brown fur . . . and there are white tips on each of its *nine bushy tails*.

"ARGH!" Emmett cries. "It's another goddess!"

Taeyo rubs his wrists together, preparing a wall of water to attack at a moment's notice. Areum flies to me and stands between me and the Nine-Tailed Fox Goddess, her humongous wings outstretched protectively. But I just stand there like a stone statue, gawking. Two goddesses in one day is two goddesses too many!

"*Oh no*," the Water Dragon Goddess moans, her eyes now half-closed. "I'm already too late."

"ENOUGH!" the fox goddess cries, her gleaming eyes sharp and accusing. "I will no longer lie here and take this slander my traitorous sister has been spreading about us!" There is red liquid on her furry stomach, shrinking and disappearing before our eyes.

"Lie *where?*" Hattie asks from my phone. "Do you mean to say the Nine-Tailed Fox Goddess has been there with you this *entire* time?"

"And you've all been none the wiser, you stupid mortals!" the goddess sneers. "Thanks to the tear in the gates you conveniently made for yours truly, I've been able to do some sneaky reconnaissance here in your realm. I was at the Trevi Fountain. The cheollima wedding. I was even glamoured as a bonghwang. And you didn't suspect a thing!"

A shiver runs down my spine. I look down at the floor where the bonghwang I thought I'd killed earlier was lying.

But it's gone.

And so is the key of all keys.

"Oh my Mago," I breathe, dread filling my gut. "The woman with the fur coat and the heavy makeup at the Trevi. You pushed me in, didn't you?" I shake my head in disbelief, but also in disappointment at myself. How did I miss it? "I knew I saw you again at the wedding. I *knew* it."

Emmett groans. "And the missing wax figure at Madame Tussauds. She's been following us this whole time! But why just follow? Why not attack?"

"Because she needed us," I say slowly, it all falling into place. "She *needed* us to find her missing sister so she could steal Mago's Fire from her. I should have known!" I hit my head with my palm, frustrated.

"And you think you have what it takes to outwit *us*," the fox goddess says bitingly. "HA! And despite what my back-stabbing sister might claim, I will have you know that we are *not* misguided! We are *enlightened!*" She points the key of all keys—*our* key of all keys—at us smugly. "When Mother brought us into this world, she gave us free will. And then she took it away. We are doing nothing more than taking back what belongs to us, and making the world a better place. It's only natural. Expected. Virtuous, even. And if you don't want to join us, then that is your choice. Feel free to enjoy your doom!"

And with that, she leaps over to the Water Dragon Goddess, who is now slumped over the chair, only half-conscious. She moves so fast, she's all but a blur of auburn-and-white tails. I thought I'd killed that bonghwang—or should I say, the Nine-Tailed Fox Goddess *glamoured* as a bonghwang—but it's clear it was all an act. An illusion. Before any of us can register what is happening, she swipes Mago's Fire out of the Water Dragon Goddess's open palm.

"The thingamajig!" Emmett shouts. "She's getting away with it!"

The Nine-Tailed Fox Goddess's eyes shine as she looks back over her shoulder. "Choose wisely, children. Your fate is in your hands."

Then her nine tails start spinning like the blades on a helicopter, around and around and around. Her body starts to shimmer, reminding me of the way Areum's body glimmers when Cosette glamours us to be invisible.

I realize too late what is about to happen.

"No!" Dahl cries, coming to the same conclusion. "She's disappearing!"

And sure enough, soon all we see are the two yellow spots of her eyes, like two headlights of a car just before it crashes into you.

I blink, and then her eyes are gone. Along with Mago's Fire—aka the *one* way Dahl and I unlock our true potential and win the war.

Yep. True story.

8.
Is a Two-Star Hotel Really Just a Motel?

"I DON'T GET IT," DAHL CRIES, burying his head in his hands. "I get why she wanted the fidget spinner. It's got Mago's Fire inside—"

"To birth the *MegaRealm*." Taeyo shudders, adjusting his bow tie.

"Right. But why did she take our key of all keys, is what I wanna know," Dahl shakes his leg nervously and doesn't even care when the left side of his collar folds over, which is saying something.

I glance down at my phone, where Hattie is still standing in the food forest next to the mayor—both of them looking shell-shocked. "But without the Key, that means . . ." I murmur, tears welling in my eyes.

"That you won't be able to come see me anymore," Hattie finishes for me. Her eyes are wide, and she clutches the mayor's arm, while Namjoon whimpers at her side.

It's hurting me to watch Hattie trying to hold it together, so I shove my phone into Areum's feathers. "Please, take this."

"We'll find a way," I hear the mayor's voice from my phone, muffled by Areum's plumage. "We'll get to the bottom of your coma, Hattie, and you'll get to see your family again. Don't worry. Where there's a will, there's a way. It wouldn't be such a well-used saying otherwise, hmm?"

"Maybe they're going to use it to summon the Haetae," Dahl guesses, unable to stop grieving our lost relic. "Or maybe they know how to make it do that light-shooting thing it did at the Spring of Eternal Life. Or to create a telepathic link like we did that one time."

I shake my head, lost for words. All I can think about is the fact that we finally discovered how to awaken our true potential. The Fire that was going to help us win the war.... And we lost it.

Dahl paces back and forth a few times before storming up to the Water Dragon Goddess. "Do you and you sisters know something about the key of all keys that Riley and I don't? Do you know what they're going to do with it?"

The goddess is slumped over in the chair, and she doesn't respond.

Dahl pokes her gently in the shoulder with a finger. "Uh, Goddess—you all good?"

Nothing.

His voice is uncertain as he shakes a loose scale off his finger. "Guys, I think we're losing her."

Taking in her frail form, my Gom upbringing springs back into action like an ottugi toy. I run over to her. "We need to help her," I think out loud. "But how? We can't take her to a saram hospital, and all the Gom healers are all wax figures in Madame Tussauds." I chew on my lip. "Maybe a saram hospital is still better than nothing."

"No," the goddess manages, lifting her head ever so slightly.

"But you need help," I argue.

"It's too late for me, fallen star." She moans. "But I need you to do something for me."

I lean in.

"Hattie," she whispers. "Please take me to Hattie."

"I . . . I can't!" I say, tears filling my eyes. "I want to see her, too, but your sister took our key of all keys. We can't open the portal anymore."

The goddess grabs my arm. "No, please, take me to Hattie," she repeats again, so quietly I have to put my ear next to her mouth to hear. "Quickly. Before it's too late."

I suddenly realize what she's asking of me. She isn't asking me to take her to the Spiritrealm. She's asking me to take her to Hattie's body. Here. In the Mortalrealm.

"Rye," Hattie's muffled voice says from inside Areum's wing. "Do as she says. Take her to me."

I place my hand over the goddess's cold, clammy hand.

"Areum," I call out to my bird-woman over my shoulder. "I need your help."

We leave the others behind, and Areum flies me and the Water Dragon Goddess to the two-star motel that my parents, Dahl, Areum, and I have been staying at. One upside of the sky falling and the whole city thinking it's some kind of citywide magic show is that Areum doesn't have to worry about being seen by saram eyes. She flaps her wings furiously, unrestrained and free.

"I can feel her," the goddess whispers as Areum descends into the parking lot of Hotel Galaxy. "She's close."

Areum and I carefully lead the goddess to our room overlooking the tiny pool. The goddess is flitting in and out of consciousness, and she is *heavy*. Half the scales on her exposed skin have flaked off now, and she's changed from a dark ocean blue to a sickly swampy green. It's obvious to anyone that she is running out of time.

I swing the door open to room 27. Hattie is lying in the bed near the window, just where we left her, with the blankets tucked up under her arms. She looked pretty bad even before I went down to the Spiritrealm, but six months stuck in a coma has made my sister's body deteriorate even further. She's a bag of bones with sunken cheeks, and it makes me well up just looking at her.

"She's here," I say to the goddess, pushing a chair next to the bed and helping the goddess into it. "I've brought you to her."

I grab my phone from Areum, ready to dial Hattie.

The goddess inches to the edge of the chair and leans over the bed to take Hattie's hand. "Oh, dear mortal child, your body has suffered even more since I last saw you."

My finger pauses above my phone, mid-dial.

"Wait, what do you mean since you *last* saw her?" I frown. "Hattie didn't seem to recognize you before."

"She may not remember me, but I do her."

"How?"

The goddess strokes Hattie's hand, as if my sister is someone she knows fondly—someone she genuinely cares about. "From her time in the Godrealm."

Areum squawks in surprise, and I take a step back, almost stepping on Areum's talons. "She never spoke about meeting you in the Godrealm."

"How could she have? She was deteriorating rapidly when I found her trapped in my sister's dungeon." She coughs violently, her entire body shaking with the force.

My fists curl. The Cave Bear Goddess kept Hattie in a *dungeon*? And to think I've been plagued with guilt at taking the goddess's life.

"I thought she wouldn't survive the day," the goddess continues weakly. "But this mortal child, she is strong. She is dogged, and she is determined. And she fought with all her might to stay alive."

I throw my phone onto the bed. Hattie doesn't need to relive the terrible things that happened to her in the Godrealm.

"And it moved me. Her persistence to cling on, to *live*, it awoke something inside me that I had long forgotten. So I helped her."

"You did?" I whisper.

"I fed her with my divine power—just tiny drops, because I knew too much could kill her. Just enough to give her the strength to keep fighting. To find her way back home." She wipes the tears from her eyes. "For my sister's sins, it was the least I could do."

I put a hand on the goddess's flaky shoulder, and loose

scales stick to my palm. "You infused her with the divine power of the yong?"

I think back to last summer when Hattie was having her sleeping spells, and how she'd always know it was going to rain. Or how she'd conjured a storm in the sea of the Spiritrealm. It makes perfect sense now. It was because the spirit of the yong was inside my sister, and controlling the weather is what yongs do. It also explains her uncanny affinity with the yong hybrid hellbeasts!

The goddess nods and then winces. "I was merely trying to help. I didn't realize that my efforts would only make things worse."

I frown. "I don't follow."

"Once she returned to the Mortalrealm, she no longer had the constant drip of my divine power, but her body had become accustomed to it. She *needed* it." Trembling, she puts her forehead on Hattie's hand. "Without it, she became trapped in her own body."

"*You're* the reason she's stuck in a coma. . . ."

She nods.

"Then can you get her out of it," I demand.

The goddess releases Hattie's hand and uses all her strength to stand up. "It will gladly be the last thing I do."

Before I can ask for details, the goddess begins to sing. It's a sad song with ancient words I've never heard before. But the melancholy strikes me in my chest like a heavy anchor. It's raw and unflinching yet a soothing balm. It's like being pulled down into the darkest depths of the ocean while simultaneously taking the first breath of fresh air. It's longing and loss and ache and want...and *love*.

As tears stream down my cheeks, Areum tenderly wraps her warm wings around me, and I realize *this* is the lullaby Hattie had been hearing in her dreams. The Water Dragon Goddess was the one who'd cradled Hattie like a baby, nursing her back to health. They weren't dreams at all—they were *memories*.

Before our very eyes, shimmery ribbons of light come out of the goddess's mouth, as if the melody itself has become alive. They swim like seaweed around my sister's body, enveloping her in its embrace. And soon, her entire body is bathing in a glittery sheath of water.

"I leave you what's left of my divine soul," the goddess whispers to Hattie as the ribbons continue to sing their melody. "It is not much, but I leave you what's left of *me*. Thank you for the gift of motherhood. It was all but a glimpse, but it was what I yearned for and was never destined to have." The goddess kisses Hattie's forehead. "Good bye, dear child."

The intensity of the light swathing Hattie grows until it explodes. And it's so blinding I have to cover my eyes.

When the light dims, I move my hand away, only to see that the goddess has started to turn translucent, like a goddess-shaped body of water.

I rush to Hattie's side, standing opposite the goddess, as the last of the shimmery ribbons seep deep into my sister's skin. It fills her like a balloon, her gaunt cheeks blossoming to life and giving her pallid skin a warm glow. She looks *radiant*.

She stirs.

"Hattie?" I cry.

I look up with grateful tears blurring my vision, but the goddess is nothing but a hazy outline now.

"Thank you," I murmur. "Thank you for saving my sister. *Again.*"

The goddess nods once.

And then the last of her physical form disappears, leaving only her voice lingering like a mist in the air.

"You must retrieve the Mother's Fire and the key of all keys from my sisters. It's the only way to save the world."

"I know," I whisper back hoarsely. "But *how?*"

"A three-legged-crow feather will show you the way. But proceed with caution, bringer of the new era."

I grip the sheets on Hattie's bed. "Why?"

"Because," the goddess's voice says, no louder than a whisper in the wind now. *"The curtain of death never lingers far from you and your kin. You must be careful. You must be vigilant. And above all, you must be courageous. The future of the world is in your hands."*

9.
Meetings Should Always
Happen on Ferris Wheels

HATTIE SITS UP ON THE BED and stretches her arms over her head, as if she just woke up from a nap rather than six months of a coma that took her to the afterlife and back.

"Hat! Oh my Mago, you're *awake*! I can't believe you're here. Like *actually* here!"

I throw myself onto my sister and hug her with everything I have. She's solid and warm and real, and when I pull back to stare at her face, I pinch her cheeks because they're so full and rosy that I have to confirm I'm not hallucinating.

"Ouch!"

She leans over and squeezes my cheeks in response.

"Ouch!" I echo.

"Exactly."

"I was just trying to make sure you were really here," I cry, tears spilling down my cheeks. "Areum, can you believe it? Hattie is *back*!"

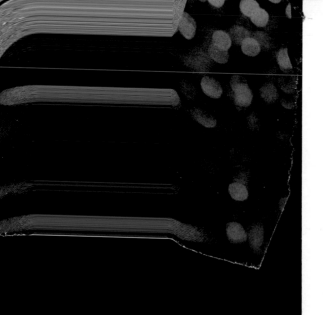

Areum squawks and pecks at Hattie's hair affectionately. "It is rather pleasant to have you back in the Mortalrealm with us, Hattie Oh."

Hattie rises to her feet, and I study her up and down, making sure all her limbs are there and in one piece.

"Stretch everything out. Just check everything works," I suggest. "Do your fingers and toes move?"

She jiggles her arms and legs like a jellyfish, and she grins. "Freaking hells, I feel good. No, I'm more than good—I feel *great*. It's so good to be alive again."

Her glee is infectious, and I do a little jellyfish jiggle myself, just to celebrate the moment in solidarity.

"The Water Dragon Goddess's essence must have pumped you up, because you look amazing," I say. "Like, even better than you looked in the Spiritrealm. I can't believe she... she..."

Hattie suddenly stops grinning and looks pensive. "I know what happened. I can't believe the goddess died...for *me*. And that she was the one who kept me alive all that time in the Godrealm." Her voice wobbles. "And I never even got to thank her."

"I'm sure she knew how you felt," I murmur, swallowing down the lump of emotion in my throat.

She nods bravely.

I put my hand on her shoulder. "Do you feel...*different* at all? Like, do you think having what was left of the Water Dragon Goddess's spirit has given you any of her divine powers?" The thought that Dahl and I might no longer be the only divine beings around to save the world is energizing. "Because, honestly, it would be uh-*may*-zing if you had superpowers. Especially since I have, like, nothing."

"I don't know," she says, staring at her open palms. "I don't *think* so. I feel strong, but I don't feel like I have any specific skills. It kinda just feels like I had a really good sleep and I'm amped for the day ahead."

For some reason, it dawns on me then that if Hattie is here with me now, she is no longer in the Spiritrealm.

"What about everyone down under?" I ask. "What about the imugis? They must be so worried their keeper has suddenly disappeared."

At the mention of her hellbeasts, she grins. "To be honest, I feel more connected to them than I did before. Maybe it's the yong spirit in me. In any case, something tells me this is not the last I'll be seeing of them. I can feel it in here." She points to her stomach.

My own stomach flutters, remembering what the goddess said to me before disappearing into thin air.

"Hat, before you woke up, the goddess told me that a three-legged-crow feather would show us the way to saving the world. What do you think it means?"

My sister puts her hands on her hips in that Boss Hattie way, and her eyes focus like lasers. "I think that means we need to regroup. The adults might not be here, but we are. We need a plan."

There is such conviction in her voice, I'm overcome with relief. She's a *real* leader, not a fraud like me. And now that my brave, headstrong sister is finally here, she and Dahl can take the reins, leaving me to sit in the backseat, where I belong.

There is the *ping* of a phone notification, and Hattie searches for her phone.

"Darn it! Guess my phone got left behind in the Spiritrealm," she says. She leans over and picks my phone up off the bed.

"Who's Phoebe?" she asks, putting in my passcode and opening the message.

I groan. "She's the leader of the RilOh Fan Club. They won't stop bugging me. Just ignore them."

Hattie immediately starts typing back. "If they're on our side, Rye, we need their help." She opens our friend group chat next. "In fact, they can join us for our strategic-planning meeting. Many heads are better than one. I'll let everyone know."

A moment later, responses start flying back from our friends.

Let's meet at the High Roller, Dahl suggests.

You mean that huge Ferris wheel? Jennie asks.

Yep! Dahl confirms. *It's 550 feet tall. The biggest observation wheel in North America. Isn't that amazing? Besides, it's a proven fact that you think better when you're moving.*

Taeyo, his BFF, jumps in to support. *They also say taking a step back and looking at the bigger picture helps when tackling problems. You can't get a bigger picture of the city than from the top of the wheel.*

Fine, fine, fineeee, Hattie texts back. *Everyone meet at the High Roller stat. We've got a plan to hatch!*

Hattie sends our meeting location to Phoebe and the RilOh stans, before pocketing my phone. "You okay if I keep this on me, right, Rye?"

Before I can answer, she walks toward the door, her eyes slightly dreamy. "Areum, let's get moving. I haven't seen Noah in *forever.*"

It turns out the High Roller is not your average Ferris wheel. Each carriage is fully air-conditioned and can fit up to thirty-five people. I'd imagined with so many of us there, it'd be a tight fit. Instead, as Areum counts heads as we each pile into the glass box, it feels like we're in a fancy floating boardroom at the top of the world. Or at least, on top of Las Vegas, which unlike the empty dark sky, is still alive with its bright neon lights.

"Hattie, you're back!" Dahl and Emmett cry, pulling her into a hug with a tail-wagging Boris wedged in between them.

Taeyo glances up from busily typing on his laptop and gives Hattie a wide grin. "Welcome back, Hattie."

"Took your sweet time," Jennie says with a teasing smirk, and Cosette flashes one of her pearly perfect smiles. David's rosy cheeks just get redder from the joy of being reunited with an old friend.

"And looking as radiant as ever," Noah Noh (aka Hattie's future husband) says, sporting the world's hugest lopsided grin.

Hattie blushes. "You're not looking too bad, either." She hesitates for only a moment before pulling Noah into a hug, too, and we all avert our eyes to give them some privacy.

Phoebe and her two friends, all wearing their RILOH STAN tops, giggle in the corner, definitely *not* giving them any privacy.

"It is common knowledge, young witches, that it is rude to stare," Areum lectures, opening her full-size right wing to block their view.

Unfortunately, this has the unwelcome effect of the fan club members turning their attention to me instead. I try not to meet their eyes as they point and excitedly whisper between themselves.

Luckily, Hattie finally calls the meeting to order with a loud *fwwht!* as she whistles with her fingers. "All right, now that we're all present, let's talk business. Like I mentioned on the group chat, the Water Dragon Goddess told Riley that a three-legged-crow feather will, quote unquote, 'show us the way.' If anyone as any initial thoughts at this point, please speak."

Jennie pipes up. "Back when our Samjogo clan still had the Three-Legged Crow Goddess as our patron, our elder used to say that one feather from the goddess's plumage was powerful enough to give you the Sight—basically, the ability to see anything, anywhere, whenever you wanted, without having to use your eyes. I think that's what the Water Dragon Goddess was talking about. That this feather will show us exactly where the goddesses are keeping the Key and Mago's Fire so we can go find them."

I chew my lip. "But that will involve us going to the Godrealm, won't it? Where else would we be able to find a rogue feather the Three-Legged Crow Goddess has molted?"

"You said Madame Tussauds had merged with a wax museum in the Godrealm, didn't you?" Dahl asks. "Maybe we could use that as a way in."

"Already beat you to it," Emmett answers as his dragon scooter waggles his ears to corroborate. "Boris and I dropped by on the way over, but the entire pop-up space and pit of wax adults is gone."

Phoebe and her friends gasp.

Cosette tucks her long, silky hair behind her ears. "If the doorways are sometimes there and sometimes not, it must mean the Godrealm hasn't completely solidified on top of our realm yet."

"Which is actually a *good* thing," Emmett reminds us.

"Definitely," echoes David and Noah.

"But while I was in the museum, I *did* find this." Emmett holds up a flyer advertising a *Realm-wide Town Hall Meeting.* "It's some kind of invitation for all Godrealm citizens to come to a big announcement the goddesses are making." He reads the flyer. "Oh, actually, the meeting's already been. But looks like the announcement was about addressing societal inequity."

Hattie raises her eyes. "Societal inequity is a thing up there, too?"

I turn to Areum, who's the only one in this room who used to live in the Godrealm. "Was it really that bad?" I ask.

She squawks. "Indeed, Riley Oh. In the Godrealm, the major goddesses—the old patrons of the gifted clans—are like royalty. They enjoy unscrupulous wealth and fame, while the minor gods complain incessantly about their inferior place in society."

"Minor gods?" Dahl asks.

"Yes, Dahl Oh. Lesser deities who don't have ruling power

like the goddesses but who still hold official titles—as outdated or forgotten as they may be."

"Like who?" Noah asks, nudging his trendy glasses up his nose.

"I was always fond of Onggi, the ancient god of earthenware pots."

"Never heard of him," Jennie comments.

"My point exactly," Areum answers.

"What about divine creatures like you?" I ask my inmyeonjo.

"And cheollimas and bulgaes and bonghwangs?" Emmett adds.

Areum *caw-caw*s, and it sounds a little sad. "We are but the working class of the golden realm. We have no titles, only the names of our species."

Jennie takes the flyer from Emmett and studies it. "Have divine creatures also been complaining about the societal issues up there?"

Areum bristles her feathers. "When one is busy working, one does not have the luxury to complain."

Everyone takes turns reading the flyer, in case we can glean anything new from it. And when it's David's turn, he speaks up in his small voice. "Maybe the town hall meeting was held so the goddesses could announce the new MegaRealm."

"That's got to be it, kid!" Dahl cries. "What better way to appease your disgruntled citizens than to announce a restructuring! Just look at Mayor Yeomra."

Jennie scoffs. "Except the reality of a world where mortals, gods, and souls live together would be total anarchy."

"Think of the overpopulation," Cosette says.

"The fight for resources," David adds.

Noah nods. "And let's face it—mortals would be at the bottom of the pecking order. It'd be absolute chaos."

As if picturing what would become of mortals in this proposed MegaRealm, everyone goes quiet.

We're all staring out into the empty night sky when Phoebe pipes up from the corner. "This might be a stupid question, but Areum mentioned before that there were various species of divine creatures. Are there other three-legged crows in the Godrealm that *aren't* the goddess?"

Hattie slaps her thigh. "New kid, I *like* you! I like you a *lot*." She turns to my bird-woman. "Please tell us there are, Areum. Please tell us there is a way we can get our hands on a three-legged-crow feather without having to steal it from a goddess."

Areum makes a weird coughy sound I've never heard before. She angles her face sideways all twitchy, and if I didn't know her better, I'd say she was . . . *embarrassed.*

"Areum?" I prod.

She eventually squawks and nods in that jolty avian way. "In fact, I do, Riley Oh. I do know a three-legged crow. Somewhat."

The whole floating boardroom breaks into a cheer.

"How do we find them?" Dahl asks, popping his collar excitedly.

Areum picks at a feather in her side, acting jittery. "I believe he is employed by Persimmon—the equivalent of Apple in the golden realm. We should be able to locate him there, Dahl Oh."

"That's presuming we can get into the Godrealm," Emmett says, frowning.

David scratches his cheek. "But surely if Godrealm creatures can use the doorways opening up to come to the Mortalrealm, then mortals could do the same to go to the Godrealm?" he suggests quietly. "We just need to find a doorway, no?"

"IT'S DONE!"

We all turn to Taeyo, who has not said a word since he greeted Hattie on the way into the glass cabin. He has been furiously working away on his laptop, and he's finally looking up, his eyes all red and shiny and triumphant.

"I did it! I used one of the Water Dragon Goddess's scales and some fallen fur from the Nine-Tailed Fox Goddess back at the Venetian to create a divine DNA profile."

"A divine DNA profile?" Cosette repeats curiously.

Taeyo continues excitedly. "Then I used the profile to locate all similar divinity signatures across the city." He swivels his laptop to show us a map of Las Vegas where some locations are dotted by a flashing light. "The areas where the beacons are shining the biggest and brightest is where the divine energy profiles are the strongest."

"*Whoa.*" Cosette's eyes light up like the beacon on the screen. "Which means you've created a literal map of all the doorways into the golden realm!"

For a second time, we all clap and cheer, this time at our Horangi friend's genius. His BFF, Dahl, even bows down to pretend to kiss his feet. "Bada bing, bada boom! And *that's* how it's done, folks!"

"It's not foolproof through," Taeyo says humbly. "Like

Cosette said before, the merging of the realms hasn't solidified yet. We might get there only for the doorway to close again. And we don't know where we'll come out the other side. It might be *miles* away from Persimmon's offices."

Boss as always, Hattie makes a decisive move. "Then we split up. There are enough of us. Whoever gets there first takes the lead and keeps us in the loop, and the rest of us will follow right behind."

No one argues with that.

Hattie takes the laptop from Taeyo and studies it carefully. "In that case, it looks like the largest divine energy signatures are currently over the Eiffel Tower replica, the Las Vegas Mob Museum, and M&M's World."

"I shotgun M&M's World!" Dahl announces. "It's on my bucket list."

I groan. "*Everything* is on your bucket list," I remind him.

He runs his palm down his pearly hair, unfazed and grinning wide. "Actually, nope, I've changed my mind, kid. I shotgun the Mob Museum. It's higher up on the list."

"Done," Hattie declares. "Dahl, Emmett, and Taeyo, you guys can take the Mob Museum." She points to Noah, Jennie, Cosette, and David. "You four check out the Eiffel Tower replica. Which leaves Riley, Areum, and me to go to M&M's World." She turns to Areum. "For the group that makes it through, how do we find our way to Persimmon?"

Before Areum can answer, Phoebe raises her hand as if we're in class and Hattie is the teacher. "What about us? Where do we go?"

Hattie doesn't miss a beat. "You three stay back here and

keep us updated on what's happening Mortalrealm-side. We need eyes on the ground. Do you accept your assignment, noobs?"

"Yes!" Phoebe and her friends shriek, jumping up and down. "We won't let you down."

As the High Roller finally finishes its revolution and brings us back to land, I can't help but notice again how stark and empty the sky looks against the neon backdrop of the city.

The sight should make me sad for the state of our realm. But right now, buried among the fluorescent lights of Las Vegas, I'm filled with hope.

If this one city on Earth can shine this bright when the sky is falling, then maybe we have more going for us than we think. Perhaps the goddesses have underestimated us mere mortals. We might just be harder to extinguish than they ever could've expected.

10.
Who Knew There Were So Many M&M Flavors!

 The M&M's World is a four-story building on the Strip, next to a building shaped like a Coca-Cola bottle. There's a gigantic yellow packet of M&M's on the front facade, making it look like the delicious little chocolates are spilling down into the entrance. The packet of chocolates is flanked by the red, yellow, and green M&M characters, looking mighty proud about the candy world built in their image.

Areum drops us at the entrance, and before I've even climbed off, Hattie is already walking through the doors. "There are four floors to cover, so let's start at the bottom and go up. Chop, chop."

The first floor is mostly just a gift store and character collections. The most interesting thing that happens there is a group of saram teens who, upon taking in Areum's full seven-foot stature, give her a spontaneous round of applause.

"Hands down the most impressive cosplay I've *ever* seen," one of them breathes.

"The feathers are just so *real*," another says, reaching out to touch Areum's wing.

Areum basks in her rare interaction with the saram population in her true form, before we decide to tackle level two. The sign next to the elevators says it's home to the M&M Candy Wall, the M&M Dispenser, Apparel, and Accessories. When the elevator doors open on the floor, our jaws open right along with them. As the sign suggested, the walls surrounding the displays of M&M's towers and gift boxes are covered in candy. More specifically, there are tall clear tubes lined up side by side, spanning the entire wall, looking like pipes on a church organ. Except each one is filled to the brim with a specific flavor or mix of M&M's.

"It's like we're on a candy spaceship!" I squeal, momentarily forgetting about the life-or-death situation we're in and only seeing the sheer beauty that is the rainbow candy wall. I always thought there were just two M&M's flavors: chocolate and peanut. It appears I was gleefully wrong.

"Ah, the candies even cover part of the ceiling," Areum points out, sounding rather excited herself.

I look up and see the same transparent pipes of candies traveling over a good portion of the ceiling.

"This place is heavenly," I breathe.

"Omigods, this one looks amazeballs!" Hattie exclaims as she pulls down the lever on the cylinder of red, orange, and burgundy M&M's and they start spilling onto her hands and all over the floor.

"Chili nut," Areum reads, peering over Hattie's shoulder. "I have never heard of this flavor combination. It sounds rather interesting."

"We should probably pay for them first," I point out, looking around the floor for the staff. But the only person behind the cash register is busy giving taste samples to a group of tourists.

"Looks like we're allowed to try a few," Hattie says, popping one of the Chili Nuts in her mouth.

"Right," I murmur as Hattie tries a teal-colored one from a different tube. "I guess it couldn't hurt to try one. . . ."

I study the selection closest to me, and I tentatively pull the lever for the yellow, tan, and brown mix of English toffee peanut when Areum starts moving all jagged-like in the corner of my eye, as if she has ants in her pants.

"You okay, Areum?" I ask.

She looks like she's doing a modified inmyeonjo version of the chicken dance. She shakes out her left feather in a weird angle, trying to swat at her back, which, unfortunately, seems to be the one place on her body she can't reach. The meticulously placed pyramid display of M&M's slot machines (this is Vegas, after all) tumbles to the ground as her body hits everything in her vicinity.

"The insect," Areum cries, swatting even harder at that awkward place on her back. "It is on me. Please tell it to remove itself from me, Riley Oh!"

"What insect?"

Hattie points to my neck. "I think she's talking about Taggy."

I look down to see that my wakerpillar has, indeed, disappeared from their favorite place in the crook of my neck.

"It is on my back. Please, Riley Oh. Please help me! It is tickling me to torture!"

Before I can remove my little Spiritrealm export from my inmyeonjo's back, Areum gives her wing an extra-large swing. It hits the wall with a spectacular *thud*. The impact takes her by surprise, and she jumps, almost leaping straight into Hattie's arms. Taggy gets propelled off Areum's body in the commotion, and I somehow manage to catch them safely in my cupped hands. *Phew!*

"Argh!" Hattie cries as the seven-foot bird-woman crashes into her.

"Argh!" Areum echoes back as she wraps her wings around Hattie at the last minute to prevent a full-on collision.

Something falls out of Hattie's hand and cracks on the ground. "Oh no, your phone!" She picks it up, only to find that the screen is cracked and completely black. She tries swiping up on the screen and pushes the buttons on the side again and again. She groans. "It's *dead*. How are we going to contact our friends now!"

As Areum shakes herself back together, something falls out of her feathers and clanks on the ground, too.

I bend over and pick up a round gold compact.

"I am sorry, Riley Oh! I was meant to keep that safe for you."

"Heyyy, it's my star compass! I forgot you had that." Taeyo had given it to me when I first met him, just before I'd been tasked with facing the wrath of Areum for the Horangi clan initiation. Then, when our house had been hexed by the Gom witches, I'd asked Areum to hold on to it while I went down to the Spiritrealm to find our clan a new patron.

I push the small button on the side of the cold metal, and the compass flips open, revealing the tiny black detailing around the edges and the slender golden arrow hovering inside.

Hattie looks over my shoulder. "Is it supposed to be shaking like that?"

The golden arrow is, indeed, trembling. "Weird. It's never done that before." In fact, the arrow never used to work at all.

Taggy, who's acting a little jittery from all the commotion, crawls down my forearm and climbs onto the face of the compass as if they, too, are curious about the contraption.

"Oh, look, Riley Oh," Areum says. "The arrow has stilled."

I peer at it closer. "Is it pointing north? That's what compasses do, right?"

"But we walked up the main drag this way," Hattie points out, gazing over her shoulder to the Strip outside the window of the building, "which means north is over there."

I focus on the slender gold arrow, following the destination of its tiny little prick. Looking up, my eyes land on a cylinder made of shimmering gold M&M's shaped like little stars and moons on the opposite wall.

"Surely it's not pointing at *those*?" I walk curiously over to the sparkling candies. "Also, since when do they make M&M's in different shapes?"

Areum squawks. "Perhaps your compass is pointing to the doorway to the Godrealm, Riley Oh."

Hattie pulls down on the lever and hands me a few candies as well as throws a few to Areum. "I wonder what flavor this one is."

Before I can say anything, Hattie pops a few in her mouth.

She swallows and then blinks a few times. Then her jaw gapes open.

"WHOA."

"What?" I demand. "What's happening? Are you feeling okay? Are they gross?"

"Just eat it. *Now!*" Hattie orders. "You too, Areum."

Areum and I look at each other and down at the glittery stars and moons in my hand and in hers (well, in her wing).

"Are you *sure* they aren't—"

Before I can finish the question, Hattie takes the candies from my open palm and shoves them down my mouth. I almost choke on one (thanks a lot, sis), but then the taste of cumulus clouds with a touch of rainbows fill my mouth. I bite down on them and realize with surprise they're chewy. Like gummies, not chocolate. I close my eyes to savor the intense new flavor. I don't exactly know how I know what clouds and rainbows taste like, but I just do. And it tastes *divine*.

"Riley Oh," Areum breathes from next to me. "Open your eyes. It appears we have found the tear in the gates."

I flutter my lids open and realize why Hattie's jaw had dropped before. What was until a second ago a candy wonderland of M&M's is now the lobby of what appears to be a clinical and sterile Very Important Company. There is a receptionist, but she's working two phones at the same time, all while typing furiously on her computer. Next to her is a restricted-entry gate manned by a guard that leads to the elevators, where people with cards attached to lanyards are scanning their access passes to get through. They're wearing suits or labcoats, looking extremely Busy and Important. But strikingly, every single one is sporting a tall top hat, as if a magician might need one to pull a bunny out of at any minute.

"Where the heavens *are* we?" Hattie asks.

Areum points her wing at the big sign behind the receptionist desk, which reads *Tokki Pharmaceuticals: The Proud Home of My Gummy.* "It appears the gateway in the M&M's World has sent us to Tokki Pharmaceuticals."

"*Tokki?*" I repeat. "As in the Moon Rabbit Goddess?"

"One and the same, Riley Oh," Areum answers, opening her large wings and trying to usher us out the main glass doors. "Unfortunately, this means we are not within vicinity of Persimmon. We will need to hurry. Their offices are on the other side of the gilded city."

Hattie halts abruptly before the doors, making the people behind us grumble in annoyance as they weave around us. "*Whoa.* Hold the bus. Why does the Moon Rabbit Goddess run a pharmaceutical company?" She points at the sign behind reception. "Also, why does it say *The Proud Home of My Gummy?*"

My Gummy is Hattie's favorite gummy candies we get from the H-Mart. They come in lots of different flavors, but Hattie's number one is grape. My fave is peach.

Bowing her head apologetically to the company staff, who are giving us nasty looks, Areum redirects us to a quieter corner of the company's lobby instead. "Back in the Age of the

Godrealm," Areum starts, "there was a rabbit, a fox, and a monkey—"

"This isn't going to be like one of Appa's dad jokes, is it?" Hattie interrupts. "They always start with three people or three animals walking into a bar."

Areum squawks. "Do you want to hear the story or not, Hattie Oh?"

Hattie makes a zipping motion over her lips. "Of course, yes, you have the floor."

"As I was saying, a rabbit, a fox, and a monkey were living in a village, when Mago Halmi came to them disguised as a beggar. The beggar asked the animals each to bring her something to eat. Being the kind and generous animals they were, they immediately set out to honor the poor man's request."

A few security guards on the other side of the lobby spot us, and Areum pushes us farther into the corner near the emergency exit before continuing. We're the only ones here that aren't wearing top hats, which seem to be part of the uniform. It's obvious we don't belong.

"The fox was the first to return to the beggar with a fat, meaty fish caught from the local river. The monkey then arrived, carrying a delicious handful of ripened fruit picked from the trees. The rabbit, however, being small and timid, was only able to bring back a mouthful of grass from the meadow. When she saw what the other animals had brought, the rabbit was ashamed. Despite it being the juiciest grasses from the greenest part of the meadow, she felt that her offering was not sufficient. That she had let the beggar down."

"But it was the best she could offer," Hattie points out.

I nod. "From the greenest part of the meadow."

Areum continues. "But then the rabbit had an idea. She collected the grass she brought from the meadow and lit it on fire. Then she threw herself into the flames."

Hattie and I grab on to each other and gasp violently.

"Why in the three realms would she do *that?*" I demand, horrified.

"Because," Areum answers, "it was an act of self-sacrifice. She wanted the beggar to have a proper meal, and that was the best way she knew how to give it to him."

"Ugh, that's a bit OTT, though, isn't it?" Hattie argues, looking a little green. "She could've just used the same fire to cook the fish and roast the fruit, and that would've been her value-add. She didn't have to, you know, literally jump into the fire herself."

I nod with Hattie's argument, but somewhere deep down, I kind of get it. The rabbit didn't feel like anything she had to offer was worthy of the man. So she had to go next level. She had to do the unthinkable.

"Perhaps," Areum says. "But that was the rabbit's decision. And it moved Mago Halmi. It affected her such that she decided to offer the rabbit a piece of her divinity. She placed the rabbit on the moon to be its guardian and asked her what would make her happy. The rabbit said that she'd always dreamed of making sweet rice cakes, so Mago gifted her a mortar and pestle with which the rabbit could pound her sweet rice. And thus was born the Moon Rabbit Goddess. The original Tokki."

My eyes linger on the logo underneath the signage, of the iconic Moon Rabbit Goddess portrayed with her humongous mortar and pestle, as she always is.

"The Tokki Goddess moved to the Godrealm shortly afterward. Must have been rather lonely up on the moon by herself. But they say even today, if you look up at the moon, you can see the old shadow of the rabbit and her mortar and pestle, pounding away."

"Wow," I breathe. "I can't believe we've never heard that story before."

"Right?" Hattie says. "It makes a lot of sense why David Kim's parents run a restaurant."

I nod. "And why the Tokki clan is—well, *were*—so good at making potions and tonics. It's their legacy."

"It's also why the goddess started this company," Areum concludes. "She found that residents of the Godrealm were deficient in some vital nutrients and minerals, but they were also terrible at taking their vitamins. So she had this brilliant idea of hiding the vitamins inside gummies, which everyone loves. Vitamin deficiency is all but a myth now in the Godrealm."

The security guards have left their posts and started walking toward us, pointing in our direction. Their fancy hats sit miraculously still on their heads as they stride our way, and if their bunched brows are anything to go by, they don't seem to like the look of us.

"Um, Areum," I start, "maybe it's time we start making our way to Persimmon. . . ."

Getting whiff of the trouble coming our way, Areum

squawks. The guards are blocking the path between us and the main exit, which means we're stuck between the quickly advancing officers and the shadowed corner of the lobby.

Areum opens her wings full-span to block the view of the guards and nods her beak toward the emergency exit. "Quick."

We push through the doors into a dim stairwell illuminated by one errant bulb, as Areum slams the door shut behind her. She rests her entire body weight against it, and we look around. The steps go up as well as down, but on the other end is a door to the outside.

"Out through there," Areum counsels as the guards start pounding at the door. "As soon as we get outside, jump on my back and I will fly us to Persimmon."

Hattie rushes for the handle, but it's either locked or hasn't been used in a while, because she struggles to pry it open. Taggy tickles my neck, and instead of helping, I find myself taking out my compass and flipping open the top.

"What are you doing, Rye?" Hattie demands. "Come help me open this door!"

"Gimme a second," I say breathlessly as I study the tiny sliver of an arrow inside the compact. Maybe, just maybe, my compass will show us the way again.

As Areum grunts with the effort of keeping the door to the lobby closed, the golden arrow trembles like before. Then, as it did last time, it decides on a direction and locks it in.

I point up toward the stairwell. "It wants us to go upstairs!"

"Shouldn't we go down?" Hattie asks, giving up on the jammed door. "We can't exactly jump out of a second-story window, can we?"

I shake my head, holding up the compass for Hattie to see. "The compass says up."

She harrumphs before pushing me up the stairs. "Oh, look at us jumping straight into the fire," she says dryly. "The Moon Rabbit Goddess would be *so* proud."

"Run," Areum calls out from behind us. "I am right behind you."

And run is what we do, up the stairs and out onto the second floor of Tokki Pharmaceuticals, as the guards follow hot on our heels.

Areum steers us down the long clinical hallway, all while looking over her shoulder. We turn a sharp corner and come to a set of doors labeled with the word LABORATORY.

"You two, hide in there," she warbles hurriedly. "I will lose our tail and meet you later. Please be safe, Riley Oh and Hattie Oh."

She squawks loudly and flies toward the grunting guards, leading them down the opposite fork in the hallway.

"You too," I whisper to Areum's back.

Hattie grips my hand, and together, we sneak into the laboratory of the Moon Rabbit Goddess's pharmaceutical company.

11.

Ever Wondered Where
My Gummy Is Made?

AT FIRST, THE LABORATORY inside Tokki Pharmaceuticals reminds me of David Kim's infusionarium in the basement of his house. Both have technical-looking equipment stationed on the long workstations covering the floor, and there are glass receptacles of all sizes filling every inch of the walls. There are even countless number of Cuckoo rice cookers at each station (of course).

But that's where the similarities end. For one, the lab is *way* bigger. And secondly, this place is so white and sterile, it feels like the entire room was dunked in a humongous vat of bleach. Even the scientists' lab coats are blindingly white. The only thing filling the space with color are their magician hats, the posters on the wall advertising *The MegaRealm: The Answer to All Our (Lack of) Prayers*, and the concoctions the staff are working on.

Their glass beakers and receptacles are full of bright violets and fuchsias, neon greens and lightning blues. Transparent pipes cover the walls, not in neat rows like back at M&M's World, but more like zipping maps taking whatever these colorful substances are to a different part of the factory. There's even a glimmering gold substance that's being transported out through some clear pipes on the back end of the lab, reminding me of the star- and moon-shaped M&M's that Hattie forced into my mouth.

We sneak behind a screen that's been set up to separate the lab area from what looks like a snack table, and watch for a moment as they add powders and gases and incantations to their concoctions. Then they peer into the little eyepieces attached to their contraptions, as if checking the cellular makeup of their elixirs. They're all so engrossed in their work that none of them seem to notice that two kids have snuck onto the floor.

"Quite a snack table," Hattie whispers, nodding at the spread behind us. It seems to be a vegetarian buffet with lots of different green salads, a few varieties of rice cakes, and carrots of all colors and sizes. Who knew there were blue and orange spotted carrots? Bright green ones that are as wide as they are long? Even little mini transparent ones that seem to be filled with a pink Jell-O–like substance, and a little bowl of what looks like mayonnaise for dipping. I steal a particularly juicy looking mugwort leaf and pass it to Taggy to nibble on.

Hattie exhales sharply, pointing a finger at the scientist working near us. "Rye, over there, the one working on the purple liquid."

The scientist is taking a break from his work and pulls the

top hat off from his head. Two long, droopy ears shake themselves out from their cramped confines and shoot up toward the ceiling. He musses his black hair, which settles into place around the tall pair of pointed ears.

"They're *bunnies?*" I whisper incredulously, staring back down at the selection of carrots and salads.

There is a ruffle of feathers as the screen shifts slightly, and a shrunken Areum flies to land on my shoulder. "They are related to rabbits on Earth, in the way that a lizard is distantly related to a dragon. But they are not bunnies, no," Areum responds.

I snug my head against Areum's, glad she managed to lose the security guards and is back safe with us.

"But they're obviously not just average humans," Hattie points out under her breath.

"They're not humans at all," Areum clarifies. "They're moon rabbits. Relations of the Moon Rabbit Goddess."

I think of what Areum explained earlier, about how divine creatures are the working class of the Godrealm. That they were too busy working to complain about how unfair things were for them.

"They're all related?" Hattie asks, trying hard to keep her voice down. "But everyone in the lobby were wearing those hats, too. There must be a gazillion of them!"

Areum nods. "Not dissimilar to breeding habits of rabbits in the Mortalrealm, the moon rabbit community believes in large families."

"What are they doing exactly?" I ask, watching the scientists create new mixture after new mixture.

Before Areum can answer, there is an excited yelp from the other side of the lab.

"Eureka! I think I've got a working formula!"

The various hats on the moon rabbits' heads all fling off simultaneously across the lab. Long, impossibly soft-looking bunny ears unshackle themselves from their tight holds and all shoot up into the air, as if a mob of meerkats have popped up to see a predator on the horizon. I have to cover my mouth to stop the uncontrollable "Aww!" from escaping my throat. Why is it that rabbits—even their Godrealm's counterparts— are so darn cute?! Many of them stop what they're doing and run toward the triumphant scientist. Their runs seem to have a slight hop to them.

"Did you do it?" one asks eagerly. "Do you think Big Aunt will approve?"

"I don't know," the Eureka scientist says. "I hope so. I guess we won't find out until we test it on the kids."

"Do it!" another urges. "Send it off. I can't wait to see what Big Aunt says!"

"Can you imagine the yummy meal she'll treat us to if you're successful?!" another exclaims.

Eureka moon rabbit claps her hands and rubs them together. "Here goes nothing!"

She pours the green liquid with the consistency of slime from her Nutribullet into a goldfish-bowl-shaped glass receptacle on the wall. Then, taking a big breath, she pushes a big red button underneath the bowl. The liquid shoots up a set of glass pipes that climb up the wall and snakes off into the ceiling.

"What do you think they're making?" Hattie whispers. "And if they're relatives, do you think Big Aunt could be the Moon Rabbit Goddess?"

I look down at my compass, which has now decided to bend and point toward the ceiling where the green contents of the pipe disappeared. "I don't know, but something tells me we need to follow the green slime," I whisper back.

Areum nods in that birdlike way. "Then follow the slime we will, Riley Oh."

I'm in the process of closing the compass lid when my finger accidentally presses on the rough patch on the back. Immediately, small blades shoot out of the edges, making the compass look like a golden star. I'd forgotten it could do that.

"Argh!" I cry as one of the blades pierces my skin. I drop the compass, and it clatters onto the shiny hard floor of the lab. The sound startles Hattie and Areum, who both take a step back, only to knock into the snack table. Eclectic carrots, rice cakes, and green leaves fly into the air. The mayonnaise is thrown out of its open bowl and lands unceremoniously on top of the dropped compass like a great dollop of bird poop.

"Who's there?!"

There's a pitter-patter of (hopping) feet as the scientists rush over to see what the commotion is about.

"Please leave some of the Jell-O carrots!" another cries, mistaking us for snack thieves. "I was saving those for later!"

The screen is ripped aside, and there are at least thirty sets of twitching bunny ears and round beady eyes, focused solely on us. Areum squawks protectively and morphs into full size, wrapping her large wings around us.

"Um, hi!" Hattie manages weakly, and raises her hand with a V sign. "We come in peace."

"Who are you?" the Eureka moon rabbit asks suspiciously.

"And why are you messing up our snacks?" another asks, staring at the food on the floor, sounding genuinely forlorn. Inside his lab coat, he's wearing a T-shirt that says SNACKS ARE LIFE. He sniffles.

I swallow. "We, uh, um . . ."

I try to think what Dahl would do if he were here. I've seen that boy in action—he can talk himself out of almost any situation. And that's when I find myself recalling what the Eureka scientist said before about the green liquid. *We won't find out until we test it on the kids,* she'd said.

"We . . . We're here for the test," I blurt out. I nod toward Areum. "And this is our chaperone."

Eureka moon rabbit's one ear bends in a frustratingly cute manner. "What test?"

"The test for the green . . . the green . . ." I mumble, trying to put on my confident voice. (What confident voice?!) "We're the kids for the test."

The scientist's ear perks back up, and there's a moment of pause. "The kids for the test?" Her entire face lights up with a smile. "Oh, the *kids*! For the *test*! Oh, wow, *wow*, it's such an honor to meet you! I have to say, we really are thankful for all that you're doing for the cause."

"The cause?" I slowly repeat, hoping she'll elaborate.

Instead, she reaches over to shake my hand, and then Hattie's. "Yes! If it weren't for volunteers like yourselves, we wouldn't be able to confirm the efficacy of our work. We really owe it to you. Such honorable behavior for mere mortals, no offense. Your sacrifice is received with utmost gratitude."

Hattie yelps and squeezes my arm. "Sacrifice?"

I think of how the Moon Rabbit Goddess jumped into the fire in an act of self-sacrifice, and goose bumps coat my skin. What in the three realms—or the MegaRealm, should I say—are these tests? And why are they being done on *kids*?

One of the other moon rabbits picks up a handful of blue and orange spotted carrots, wipes them on his lab coat, and offers them to us. "Do you want a snack before we take you to the testing center? It's the least we can do. After all that you're doing for us."

"They're peanut-butter-and-blueberry-jelly flavor," another explains. "My favorite, personally speaking."

Hattie takes the carrot tentatively, scared to offend, and I take the opportunity to grab a napkin from the floor. I bend down and, wiping as much of the mayo off with my top as I can, I pick up my compass and disable the blades.

"Look, it's been a treat," Hattie says, inching us away from the moon rabbits. "But we better get going now to the, uh, testing center."

"Please, let me escort you," Eureka says.

"No, really, there's no need," Hattie argues. "We can make—"

"I *insist*," Eureka responds.

Hattie opens her mouth to argue again, but I nudge her in the side.

"This testing center," I start. "That doesn't happen to be where that pipe of your green stuff leads to, is it?"

Hattie looks down at the closed compass in my hand, and she nods, following my drift.

Eureka smiles a big, proud toothy grin. "Indeed. My formula has been sent straight to the gummification machine, which is located at the heart of the testing room."

"Thank you," I say. "In that case, we would be very grateful for your help."

Eureka leads us to the elevators and up to the seventh floor, chatting excitedly the entire way. She talks more about how enlightened we are for believing in the cause despite being humans, and how she's guaranteed to get a promotion after all of this, which means she'll finally get to move into her dream burrow with the meadow views and the extra en suite. She's so open and chatty that I decide to probe a little.

"So this gummification machine you spoke of earlier," I prompt. "What exactly does it do?"

Eureka's eyes brighten. "Oh, it's amazing. Big Aunt's invention. Our solutions get sent to the machine, and they come out the other size as gummies. Everyone loves gummies!"

Hattie nods in agreement. "I mean, it's true. My Gummy *is* my favorite candy."

"And *obviously* we know exactly what the gummies are for," I continue carefully. "But in your own words, how would you describe the purpose of these gummies? And by all means, share as much detail as you'd like." Man, Dahl would be proud of me.

"It's all got to do with the limitations of Big Aunt's sister, the Three-Legged Crow Goddess," she responds easily.

Areum's feathers perk up at the mention of the crow.

"The Three-Legged Crow Goddess is famous for her Sight, but she also has the ability to bend the mortal brain in incredible ways."

I think of Jennie Byun and the Samjogo clan, and how they were able to see visions and premonitions. It makes sense those gifts came from the goddess who can control mortal minds.

"But she cannot influence children," Eureka explains. "Mortal children like yourselves are yet to be sullied by adulthood, which makes you utterly immune to the Three-Legged Crow Goddess. Your minds are too wild, too free, and too pure to be manipulated by her force."

"I've never been happier to still be a kid," Hattie whispers into my ear.

"Which is why Big Aunt tasked us with formulating a gummy that could do what the Three-Legged Crow Goddess couldn't," Eureka says. "We may not be able to use mind control, but we are connoisseurs of good taste. We make the sweetest, chewiest, yummiest gummy candy, and I have to this day never met a child who could resist."

Hattie gulps, and I would, too, if I gobbled up gummies at the rate my sister does.

"Do you mean to say," I murmur, trying not to have a full-on freak-out in the middle of this hallway, "that you're trying to make a gummy that can control the minds of mortal children?"

Eureka grins widely. "Yes, of course. But you already knew that, you enlightened human children! All for the cause! For the peaceful future of the MegaRealm!"

"Rye," Hattie says to me under her breath as Eureka continues to lead us down a burrow-like maze of hallways, "you remember that lesson in history when Mr. Bell from saram school told us about the terra-cotta warriors in China?" Her voice sounds agitated, as if she's just figured something out. Something bad.

I shake my head. "Not really. Why?"

She starts whispering real fast, and I almost hear a slight lisp coming through. "Mr. Bell said that when the first emperor of China died, they created thousands and thousands of terra-cotta soldiers to be made and buried in a funeral pit as big as multiple airport hangers."

"Okay . . . ?"

"They made the soldiers so that the emperor wouldn't be alone in his grave." She pauses, and when she continues, her voice breaks. "So that the emperor would have his *army* by his side."

I hear a whimper, and it's only when Hattie squeezes my hand that I realize it came from me. And just like that, the clues piece themselves together. The poisoned spring water in the Spiritrealm had taken over the minds of Saint Heo Jun and Bada the ineo. I remember the way their eyes clouded over until there was nothing but black. The way they were no longer in control over their own bodies, merely following the orders of a higher power.

"The goddesses are preparing their army," I whisper out loud, the dread expanding and pushing against my rib cage. "The Three-Legged Crow Goddess has brainwashed all the adults to enlist in their personal army at the wax museum, and now they're trying to use Tokki Pharmaceuticals to control all us kids, too."

"But why are they yet to deploy the adult army?" Areum asks, a tremor in her warbly voice.

Hattie nods grimly. "What are they waiting for?"

I take a deep breath. "I don't know, but—"

"We're here!"

Eureka the moon rabbit stops us at an entranceway that has the words TESTING CENTER: TRESPASSERS WILL BE DENIED SNACKS FOR TWO FULL DAYS on the front.

"I'm afraid my journey with you ends here," Eureka says, opening one of the two heavyset doors. "But I just wanted to reiterate again how much of an honor it has been to meet you in the flesh, and how grateful we are as a realm for your sacrifice."

With that, she pushes us into the room, and the door slams shut behind us.

"We are doomed," Hattie whispers in the dark. "They are going to tempt us with the most delicious gummies ever made that no one in their right mind could refuse. Especially me." She gulps. "And then they're going to take over our minds. Take away our free will. It's sick. It's completely evil. It's—"

"It's how they're going to win the war," I conclude, fear filling my chest.

Areum fumbles against the wall, looking for the light switch.

A crackle of light expands from the ceiling, illuminating the dark room. It's as big as the sanctuary at the gifted temple. Except at the heart of the room is not the cauldron housing the sand from the beginning of time. There is, instead, a gigantic machine with pipes for hair. The pipes are coming out of the ceiling, and one of them is carrying a familiar bright green solution. Peering at the opposite side of the machine, I see tiny green brain-shaped gummies are being churned out, pooling out into a large silver bowl.

But that's not the most bizarre part.

That would be the cages lining the walls. Cages too big for cats or dogs, but too small for, say, horses or elephants or even adults.

They're cages that are a perfect size for *kids.*

Areum squawks loudly as if in pain, and Hattie shrieks, "No. They. Didn't!"

I follow their gazes to see a group of occupied cages to our right. Inside I recognize four unconscious bodies with four familiar faces, lying on the cold floors of their human cages: Cosette Chung, David Kim, Jennie Byun, and Hattie's future husband, Noah (Oh-)Noh.

"How did they get here?" I demand in a shaky voice, the Water Dragon Goddess's omen ringing like a siren in my head. *The curtain of death never lingers far from you and your kin. You must be careful. You must be vigilant.* "Are they . . . ? Are they alive?"

But I don't get the chance to know the answer. Because as soon as the question leaves my lips, a sweet-scented gas is released from the vents above, whirring like a fan, tasting of my favorite peachy flavor of My Gummy.

The next thing I know, I feel light-headed, and my head hits the floor.

12.
Always Choose Free-Range Friends Over Caged

I DON'T KNOW HOW LONG I've been out. But the next thing I know, people are calling my name.

"Open your eyes, Riley Oh!"

"Rye, get up!"

I groan and try to sit up, only for my head to hit something hard and solid.

"My head," I moan, clutching it. "Why is the world spinning?"

"Because we got drugged by the biggest drug company in the world," Hattie says from somewhere to my left.

I rub my eyes and poke my head toward the sound of my sister's voice, only for my head to hit something hard again. My fingers grip around the metal bars in front of me. I trail my fingers above and behind me, only to find solid metal on all sides. I'm trapped. In a cage.

"They locked us in?" I yelp, pulling at the bars without luck.

"I detest cages, Riley Oh!" a shrunken Areum shrieks from the cage to my right.

"You guys doing okay?" a familiar soft voice calls out from the opposite end of the room.

I rub my eyes and squint. "David, is that you?"

I see him nod, but it's Jennie's voice that responds. "We're all here. Me, David, Cosette, and Noah."

It comes rushing back to me now, being led to the gummification room by Eureka the moon rabbit scientist, and seeing our friends' unconscious bodies in their cages.

"We found the gateway to the Godrealm at the Eiffel Tower replica," Jennie explains, "but sucks for us, it took us directly to the Mountain Tiger Goddess's college campus."

"Turns out she runs the most prestigious university in the Godrealm," Cosette adds.

"Then her mountain tiger underlings captured us and brought us here," Noah says.

"Who looked like us but had furry ears and full-on tiger tails," David explains.

Jennie leans her face against the bars of her cell. "I think we were out when you guys were brought in, but we've been up for a few hours now. The moon rabbits only just left."

"We've been unconscious for *hours*?" Hattie asks from the cage to my left.

"Did . . . Did they *hurt* you?" I dare to ask, my throat closing.

Noah groans. "If you call sugar overloading a valid form of torture, then yes."

As if to corroborate his claim, Cosette clutches her stomach. "Honestly, I can't do any more gummies. I just want a big, fat, salty gimchi bacon burger right now. Extra grease."

I take a nervous glance over at the gummification machine.

A horrible feeling builds in the pit of my stomach. "Did they feed you the brain gummies?"

David points to the green gummies still shooting out of the machine. "Those ones? Nope, they said those weren't perfected yet."

I let out an exhale.

"But they fed us a *whole* lot of other ones."

Areum squawks in concern.

"Which ones?" Hattie asks.

"There were the ones that made our skin go neon orange," Jennie says.

"Honestly, we looked like traffic cones," Cosette confirms. "Like fake tanner gone wrong."

"And there were the ones that made us laugh and cry at the same time," Noah says. "I almost peed my pants it was so intense."

David cringes. "Not as bad as the one that made us fart and burp nonstop."

Jennie shudders. "That was the worst. You're right. And they had to go and make those ones apple flavor. My favorite. Ruined forever."

Noah nudges his trendy glasses up his nose. "The worst for me was the one that made us talk backward. My brain still hurts from getting my head around all those back-to-front sentences."

The Water Dragon Goddess's warning hums in my ears, and I grip harder on to the metal bars of my cage. "We need to get out of here before they feed us the brain gummies. Once they perfect that, we're done for."

Hattie studies the room as if looking for something, while rubbing her wrists. "Anyone see any soil? Been a while since I used my elemental magic."

"Don't bother," Cosette explains from her cage, flicking back her luscious locks. "We tried that, but our biochips don't work here. I think it's because the Horangi tech draws from the power of nature in the Mortalrealm. Here in the Godrealm, there's nothing for our biochips to draw from."

My heart sinks. "So you're all powerless here?"

Noah frowns. "If only we had the crowbar."

"The crowbar?" I ask.

"At least that's what I think the moon rabbits were calling it," Noah responds. "It looked like some kind of stick with a bird's claw on the end, but whatever it was, they used it to lock us in our cages."

"A *crowbal*," Areum corrects us. "It is a type of key fashioned from the unique shape of a three-legged crow's feet."

"Must be why it's called a crow*bal*," David says "Because *bal* is Korean for 'foot.'"

I bite my lip. How are we going to find one of *those*?

"Do you guys still have your phones?" I ask. "Mine died, but maybe we could ask Emmett, Taeyo, and Dahl to find—"

"Someone is coming," Areum squawks nervously from her cage. "We may already be too late."

"Pretend to be sleeping!" Hattie whisper-yells.

We all slump back down on the floor of our cages, with our eyes sealed shut, trying to stay as still as possible. My heart is beating so loud, I can feel it pounding in my head.

The door to the gummification room swings open, and I hold my breath.

A pause.

"Anyone in here?" a voice calls out tentatively.

A flutter of feathers.

"It's Sahm. I've come to help."

"*Sahm?*" Areum stands up abruptly and makes a shrill screeching sound.

The mystery person half flaps, half runs and appears in front of Areum's cage in an instant, carrying a large sack. "*There* you are! I've been looking everywhere for you."

The rest of us rush to get a good look at our visiting stranger, who seems to be part man, part bird. He is as tall as Areum when she's in her full stature, but he's slighter in the shoulders. He's covered in a thick plumage of shiny black feathers, and he has ... three legs?!

"Sahm of the Sisterhood," Areum says quietly, acting uncharacteristically jittery. "It has been a while. A long while." She makes a high-pitched whistling sound with her throat that I'm pretty sure I learned in a wildlife documentary was a bird mating call. (Yep, not awkward at all ...)

Sahm ruffles the neck of his feathers to be big and fluffy, making it look like he's stuffed an entire ball inside his shiny black chest. "Wow, it really is *you*. I haven't seen you in forever, but hot dang, you look *amazing*, Sister of the Sisterhood."

"I have a name now. Areum."

"*Areum*," he repeats, his eyes wide. "Meaning 'beautiful.' I can't think of a more perfect name." Sahm makes a soft rattling sound and then bows slightly, splaying his shiny black wings to be almost parallel to the ground. That's when I realize he only has one wing. The other looks like a little stump, as if it never fully grew out. He coos and looks up at Areum from his bowed stance with a sparkle in his eye. I get the distinct feeling some special bird language is happening between these two that I am not following, nor do I really *want* to be. . . .

"You never responded to any of my messages," Sahm says slowly.

Areum growls, but it doesn't sound angry. It sounds more vulnerable than anything. "I was confused," she finally says. "It has taken a long time for me to accept myself for who I am. My human, Riley Oh, has helped me see that I am more than the mistakes of my ancestors." She pauses. "That I am worthy of beauty. And perhaps even worthy of . . . of . . ."

"Of love," Sahm answers softly.

Areum giggles—yes, she actually *giggles*. And I find myself grinning so hard my cheeks hurt. I think Areum *likes* this bird-man. It takes me back to the first time I met my inmyeonjo, when she was frenzied and furious, wanting to destroy all the buildings on the Horangi campus because the mirrors reflected back what she didn't want to see. She thought she was ugly, and that she didn't deserve to be treated with compassion. I remember hurting for her, because she had lived her entire life believing such a terrible, ridiculous lie.

"How did you know to come here?" Areum asks, as if finally remembering the rest of us are in the room.

"Friends of yours came and found me at work," he responds.

That's when it clicks that Sahm of the Sisterhood is

the very three-legged crow Areum wanted us to find. Dahl, Emmett, and Taeyo must've made it to Persimmon to find him!

Sahm keeps his eyes glued on Areum, as if he's worried she'll disappear if he looks away. "When they couldn't get a hold of the rest of you, the smart one merged his divine energy profile software with his mortal DNA to reverse his technology."

Cosette exhales in her cage, obviously impressed. "Taeyo made a map of all the mortal energy signatures in the Godrealm!"

Sahm nods. "And it led me here to you. Not every day you get a bunch of mortal kids in one place in the gilded city, I suppose."

"Where are they now?" I ask him. "Our friends."

"They're still at Persimmon, recruiting fresh blood," Sahm explains. "The one with the pearly hair and the shiny leather jacket—he's quite the orator. He made a passionate plea at lunch, and suddenly, there were people lining up to join the anti-MegaRealm movement."

He studies the lock on Areum's cage, and I warm at the thought of Dahl working his charm on the Persimmon staff. Trust him to be building allies in the most unexpected of places.

Sahm rummages through his sack and finally takes out a few different prosthetic-like gadgets. One looks similar to his own foot, but with the claws bent in slightly different angles. Holding it up to the lock on the cage, he finally decides on one before attaching the contraption to the farthest left of his three feet.

"A crowbal," Hattie breathes.

"You're all lucky I work in security," he says, to which Areum *caw-caws*, the sound filled with pride.

I, too, am overwhelmed by gratitude toward this bird-man. But when he takes his sweet, sweet time unlocking us from our cages, I start to get a little impatient.

"Um, Sahm, not to be rude, but you couldn't hurry it up ever so slightly, could you?" I ask, trying to hide my frustration.

He shakes out his little stump-side wing. "Don't you worry, the big ears won't be coming back in here anytime soon. The building's deserted."

"It is?" Hattie asks. "Is it home time already?"

Sahm shakes his head. "They've all gone to the tournament."

"What tournament?" I ask.

Having opened the final cage, he takes out a court jester mask from his Santa sack. "The goddesses are putting on a realm-wide competition to find the new MegaRealm's first ever prime minister. It was announced at the town hall meeting, and it's all anyone's been talking about, really."

My stomach drops at the mention of the MegaRealm. The goddesses are so confident about winning the war that they're acting like it's already been formed.

"Wait, why would the goddesses give away power to someone else, and through a public tournament at that?" Jennie asks, frowning. "I thought *they* wanted to rule supreme."

Sahm shakes his head. "At the town hall meeting, the goddesses made it clear they had no desire to hold public office. They're happy to sit there and look regal and have their pretty faces on the coins. Oh, and throw amazing parties—they're really ace at that." He waggles the court jester mask as if that explains everything. "But they're happy to let other people do the hard work of actually *running* a realm."

My mind begins to reel. "But what about the army of witches at the wax museum? I thought they wanted to use our adults to win the war."

"You mean the Witch Peace Corp?" Sahm clarifies, scratching his side with one of his three talons. "They said the mortal witches had volunteered themselves to be defenders of the peace and public harmony in the new realm. There was zero talk of war or an army."

Our friends groan, and my heart drops. The goddesses have been using the town hall meeting to spread insidious lies, trying to lobby their divine citizens to get on board with their terrible takeover plans.

Sahm looks sheepish. "Sorry to be the bearer of bad news. All I know is that the winner of the masquerade-ball-themed tournament is going to be publicly elected prime minister, and that they'll be knighted with the Key to the Final Eclipse, which will be used to birth the new MegaRealm."

"The Key to the Final Eclipse?" Hattie repeats. "Rye, that can't be a coincidence."

My heart starts to race, as I recite the Haetae's prophecy in my head:

When the dark sun and moon are united once more,
Together they'll unlock the key of all keys.
That opens the door to the dawn of an era,
Of which they'll call the Age of the Final Eclipse.

I gasp, the pieces slowly coming together to form a

disturbing picture. "Guys, remember when the Water Dragon Goddess told us that Mago's Fire had the greatest destructive power in all existence?"

You must retrieve the Mother's Fire and the key of all keys back from my sisters, the Water Dragon Goddess had said in her dying breath.

"It must be connected with the Key somehow," Hattie says, quickly catching up to my line of thought.

"It explains why the Nine-Tailed Fox Goddess stole the Key," David suggests, making my insides squirm nervously.

"Maybe they need to use them both to kick-start this supposed MegaRealm," Noah surmises.

Areum squawks solemnly. "And to end the world as we know it."

Hattie grabs my arm. "You know what this means, don't you?" But she doesn't even give me a chance to process the question. "It means you need to enter the tournament."

"WHAT?" I gape at her.

"She's right," Jennie pipes up. "If you win, you'll literally be served Mago's Fire on a silver platter."

Cosette nods. "And without it, they can't bring about the end of the world."

Noah puts his arm around Hattie, and he grins proudly. "Hattie's on the money. *This* is how we're going to win the war. By winning the tournament!'

Before I spell out the gazillion and one reasons why this is the most terrible idea Hattie has ever had, David yelps and leaps into the air as if he's seen a gwisin.

"Guys, there's someone over there!" He points toward the opposite side of the room. "There, in the wall!"

My eyes shoot over to a large metal grate in the wall. It's some kind of large air vent.

"Where?" Noah calls out, heading toward it. "I don't see anything."

Sahm and Areum follow Noah to check it out, but Hattie's high-pitched squeal is enough to stop them in their tracks.

"No. Freaking. Way!"

I peer closer. And that's when I see it behind the grate.

Two piercing blue eyes.

Two very *familiar* piercing blue eyes.

"Namjoon!" Hattie cries, rushing toward the vent. "You're here!"

13.
Does This Mask
Look Good on Me?

WITH SAHM AND AREUM'S HELP, Hattie and I
manage to pull the grate open to let my sister's
right-hand hellbeast out of the wall vent.

"Namjoon!" Hattie cries again, pulling him
into a big hug. "I can't believe you're here."

The snake-yong hybrid creature with the piercing blue eyes
shakes out his knobbly legs, and his wet-looking white scales
glisten under the light of the gummification room.

"It's *so* nice to see you here, my good boy," Hattie murmurs into his neck, and his acid-laced tail wags in the air
behind him.

Here.

It suddenly dawns on me what it means that a hellbeast is
here and not in the underworld.

"Namjoon," I start, "how exactly did you make it up here?"

The imugi makes weird gurgly sounds, as if he's going to
cough up a huge globule of phlegm. I take a step back, remembering how his saliva was so intense it could brew coffee just

by being added to beans. How it stung like bees when he slathered it all over my face to taste my soul. I'd rather stay a lifetime away from imugi saliva if I can help it.

Hattie, on the other hand, leans in toward him. "What's that, you said? Oh, hmm, is that right? Oh, wow, yeah, that *is* bad news."

It takes both my sister and me a minute to realize what is happening.

"You can understand imugi?" I ask.

"I can understand imugi?" she asks herself at the same time.

We both stare at each other, and then Hattie fist-pumps the air. "I can understand imugi!"

Namjoon wags his tail weapon (which makes Areum and Sahm leap back in alarm) and Hattie pulls him in for another smooshy hug.

"It must be from the Water Dragon Goddess's spirit," I think out loud. "Because she's the highest-level yong. So it makes sense you'd have a special connection with anything that's yong-adjacent."

Hattie's excitement tempers when she remembers why the Water Dragon Goddess left the way she did. She releases her hellbeast and clears her throat. "Namjoon says the fabric between the realms has ripped even further, and there are now tears all over the Spiritrealm, too."

I look down at my trembling hands. I'd almost forgotten that Emmett and I had fallen into a fountain in Vegas and somehow almost drowned in the sea of the Spiritrealm. The leaks must have worsened since then.

Namjoon gurgles some more, and Hattie nods. "That's how

he managed to get up here—through one of the torn gateways," Hattie interprets. "The mayor was worried we wouldn't know what was happening, so he sent Namjoon up to let us know, and to help us in any way he can."

I send a wave of gratitude to the mayor. He's really made some progress since his days of being a head-in-the-sand sort of leader. He's actively helping us, giving me faith that despite what the goddesses are plotting, we have a strong alliance with the Spiritrealm.

"So, it's settled, then," Hattie concludes, abruptly returning to the conversation we were having before Namjoon turned up. "You, Rye, go enter the tournament and win. The rest of us will go join the boys at Persimmon and help recruit more allies."

"But won't the Persimmon staff be at the tournament, too?" Noah asks.

Sahm chuckles. "Judging by the waves your pearly-haired friend was making, I'd bet there's a sizeable contingent of my colleagues who decided to give it a miss. The bonghwangs from the software-development team seemed particularly moved."

I chew on the inside of my cheek. "Um, in that case, Hat, how about *you* enter the tournament and *I* go with the others to Persimmon?" I suggest. "You're the more natural leader. You're brave, you're strong, and you're not scared of anything. If anyone can win that tournament, it's *you*, not me."

Sahm clears his throat. "I should add that the tournament is only open to Godrealm citizens, which I may be assuming here, but might exclude the both of you?"

"Godrealm citizens are all those with divine blood," Areum clarifies.

"So it has to be you," Hattie jumps to add. "You're the last fallen star, Rye. Not me."

"But you now have Water Dragon Goddess's spirit in you," I quickly point out. "So you're also technically a Godrealm citizen."

"Touché," Hattie says.

She pauses, and I think I've convinced her. I'm not lying when I say that my sister was the one born for greatness, not me. The survival of the Mortalrealm (and the Spiritrealm now, too) would be safer in her hands.

"No," Hattie finally concludes. "*You're* the one the prophecy said would lead us into the new era, Rye, not me. It's time you believe in what everyone else has known from the start. You are the gold-destroyer, the last fallen star, and our leader. It's time to stop running away and step up."

She pauses and looks squarely in my eyes. "But don't do it because it's your destiny. Do it because you *choose* to."

"Everything she said," Jennie pipes up, and the rest of our friends murmur in agreement. Areum squawks in support, and even Namjoon gives a small wag of his acidic tail.

"Whoa. Tough love," Sahm says.

Right? I say to him with my eyes.

"Mad respect, though," he adds.

My eyes toward him narrow.

"It's *time*," Hattie says simply. "It's Mago's Fire that will awaken your true potential, and that's what you get if you win the competition. Don't you see? It's all how it's meant to be." She puts her hands on her hips. "Plus, I might only be older by one month but it's still one more than you, so what I say goes."

Geez. Hattie is starting to sound very Asian Auntie on me.

Buuut it *does* make me think about what Emmett said. That I'm suffering from imposter syndrome. That it's a real affliction where you feel you don't deserve to be where you are, even when it's clear to everyone you do. He read it in some fancy psychology magazine, so it must be true. And if it is true, and I really *am* suffering from it, then maybe I need to trust that my family and friends are the ones that've got it right. Maybe I *am* supposed to enter that tournament and win the fidget spinner so Dahl and I can awaken our true powers to save the world.

I clear my throat uncomfortably. "I mean, if you think it's the best course of actio—"

"It's the *only* course of action," Hattie confirms.

Cosette ties her shiny hair up in a bun, all ready to go, and she claps her hands together. "Great, so Sahm, tell us—what's the quickest way to Persimmon?"

Before he can respond, David clears his throat and speaks in that soft way of his. "Actually, I think I'll stay here."

We all stare at him.

"Like Mago you will!" Jennie quips. "We're test rats here. It's dangerous!"

He shakes his head, his eyes determined despite his eternally ruddy cheeks. "Perhaps, but I'll be more use here than at Persimmon. You know I'm not much of a talker, let alone a scout for allies." He points to the green brain-shaped gummies solidifying next to the gummification machine. "I was taking notes before when the moon rabbits were discussing the gummy formulas, and I think if I can use their lab, I might be able to reverse engineer them."

Noah's eyes widen. "You mean, to create a gummy that could *un*-brainwash people that have been mind-controlled?"

David nods excitedly. "Exactly!"

I think of how the moon rabbits' lab reminded me of David's infusionarium in the basement of his house. If anyone could get the job done, it'd be our resident Tokki witch.

"Besides," David adds, "Sahm said everyone's at the tournament. I'll have run of the roost here. I'll be safe."

"Well, I'm staying with you," Jennie says. "You know you work best when I'm nagging in your ear."

"And I'll stay as guard, just in case anyone comes back from the tournament early," Cosette adds.

Noah looks to Hattie and smiles shyly. "I'm coming with you. We've spent enough time apart."

My sister grins, lapping up Noah's affection like a thirsty dog after a run. "It's settled, then."

"I'll take you and Noah to Persimmon," Sahm says to Hattie. He holds up his stump wing. "I'll have to put on my prosthetic before I can fly, though."

"And I'll take Riley Oh to the tournament," Areum says to me. "Although, won't the goddesses recognize you? Surely, they will not allow the last fallen star to compete in the tournament willingly."

Sahm makes an excited warbling sound and picks up his mini Santa sack from the floor. "It's a masquerade-themed tournament, remember?"

He pulls out a mask that looks like a creepy medieval clown. "This is a Venetian-style mask. Very classic. It'd look great on you."

There are small bronze bells attached to the pointy ends of the clown's hat, and I shake my head. "Those bells remind me of the ones attached to the Spiritrealm's hell gavels." I shudder. "Sorry, PTSD. Do you have any other ones?"

He pulls out another—this time a lacy number with peacock feathers attached to the sides. "What about this one? Or this one?" He reveals another with a huge protruding beak, that kind of looks like those suits that doctors used to wear during the plague. Except made out of papier-mâché and painted a fluorescent pink.

This time, Cosette shakes her head. "Both of those are . . . a *lot*. Maybe something a little less . . . well, just *less*, so she doesn't stand out so much?"

"Fine, fine." He rummages in the sack and brings out a much smaller, simpler mask. It's white, and it covers three quarters of the face on an angle. It reminds me of the mask from *The Phantom of the Opera*. "What about this one?"

I nod and take it gratefully. "Guess that could work. Lucky you had so many of these in your bag."

He waves his solo wing across his face, as if to feign modesty. "Just a little hobby of mine."

"You made all these, Sahm?" Areum asks curiously. "These are not skills we were taught at the Sisterhood."

He grins, and there's a sparkle in his eyes that makes me want to look away and give them some space. "Papier-mâché. Crocheting. Aerial yoga. There are lots of things I can do now that we weren't taught at the Sisterhood, Areum."

Areum's plumage fluffs up like she's been electrocuted, and she coughs a few times.

"And the last finishing touch," Sahm announces as he pulls two feathers from his side and crisscrosses them artfully across the head of my mask. "Your friends who came to find me—they explained why you were looking for me."

I run my fingers along the two three-legged-crow feathers.

"They aren't nearly as powerful as those of the Three-Legged Crow Goddess," he explains. "They won't give you the Sight. But if you whisper the specific item you seek into each feather, it should help guide you in their general direction. It'll feel like the pull of a magnet when you're close."

I'm starting to think the Water Dragon Goddess's message to acquire a three-legged-crow feather was more about finding Sahm than the quills themselves. But still, I gratefully whisper *"Mago's Fire"* and *"key of all keys"* to each of the black feathers. Then I put the mask on. "Thank you so much, Sahm. We seriously owe you."

Cosette, our resident illusion expert, studies my face and shakes her head. "The mask helps, but it's still obvious it's you. We need something else."

"What if you were also disguised as a moon rabbit?" David suggests, picking up a bunch of poop-shaped gummies from a small glass bowl. "These were the ones that made us grow moon rabbit ears temporarily."

Cosette nods encouragingly. "Great idea. They didn't last long, though, so you probably want to take the whole lot."

I scoop up the six gummies left in the bowl and pocket them for later.

"Don't worry, they taste like cola," David offers, "so nothing like poop."

"How would you even know what poop tastes like, you doofus?" Jennie adds.

David chuckles good-naturedly, and before I know it, we're all moving, heading in our respective directions.

"Where is the tournament being held, Sahm of the Sisterhood?" Areum asks. "Where should I take my human?"

Sahm grins wide. He makes a funny wing-flapping motion that looks like he might be trying to hit a ball or something. "At Hungry Holes!"

We all look at him blankly, even Areum.

He groans. "You guys really need to get out more. It's the coolest glow-in-the-dark mini golf in the realm! Plus, they have the best avocado milkshakes I've ever tried."

Hattie makes a face. "*Avocado* milkshakes?"

"Have you tried them before?" Sahm asks.

Hattie shakes her head.

"Well, you can hardly judge, then, can you? The ones at Hungry Holes are Mago's gift to livingkind. Trust me."

I throw my head back and laugh. Because honestly, what else can you do when you find out that avocado milkshakes are a thing, and that the divine tournament to become the MegaRealm's prime minister is going to be held at *mini golf*?

Also, here is a fact lesser known about me. . . .

In some parts of the world (aka in my family), I am also known as Hole-in-One Riley.

14.
Why Don't Perfumes
Smell Like Food?

 MY ENTIRE LIFE, I ALWAYS WISHED I could be more like my sister. Despite only being one month older, Hattie was always stronger, louder, prouder, and just more *everything* than me. And I know, I know. By this point, that's old news.

What may be *new* news, though, is that there was one area in our lives in which I always excelled. One activity where I was *always* superior to Hattie.

Mini golf.

Yup. I know, it's not even *real* golf. It's just the putting part. But *still*. I've always been good at it. There's this place, Zany Zoo Mini Golf, where our parents used to take us as kids. There were only nine holes, but the place was decked out with humongous animals. You'd have to hit the ball up the narrow path of a giraffe's bent-over neck, or make it bounce off a Tasmanian devil to avoid falling into the small pond, and of course, the ninth hole—my personal fave—where you'd have to make the ball shoot straight into the hippo's mouth. A hole in one there scored you a free ice cream. A two-scoop, in fact. On a waffle cone! Not to hoot my own horn, but I had a *lot* of free ice cream at Zany Zoo Mini Golf. Just saying.

The funny thing is that, as I've said before—Hattie is stronger, she has better aim, and she's more competitive. But her downfall is that she's impatient and impulsive. And that's where I have the upper hand. While Hattie just hits the ball willy-nilly and hopes for the best, I think hard before I make my shots. I study the angles, I do the calculations, I think a few moves ahead like I'm playing baduk. And I always do several practice shots without the ball just to get a feel of the swing before committing. Sure, it makes for long games, and it drives Hattie bonkers, but what can I say? It works for me.

That's why, as Areum lands in a large, empty parking lot, having followed Sahm's directions, I feel a sense of excitement blooming inside me. If being good at mini golf is going to score me that fidget spinner, then perhaps I do have what it takes to win this tournament, after all. Maybe the prophecy is actually going to come true, my imposter syndrome be damned. I take out one of the poop-shaped gummies from my pocket and pop one into my mouth. Like David said, it's cola flavor, which honestly, is such a relief.

"Hey, before we go in," I say to my inmyeonjo, "can I ask you a question about Sahm?"

She nods. "Of course, Riley Oh."

"You keep calling him Sahm of the Sisterhood. What is that?"

"The Sisterhood of the Inmyeonjo is the convent in which

I grew up, Riley Oh. Sahm was born with one wing, and he was rejected by his flock of three-legged crows for it. They deemed him faulty. Broken." She screeches angrily. "He was abandoned by his kin, and the Sisterhood took him in."

"Wow," I say, feeling grateful for the Sisterhood's compassion. Then I add, "He really seems to like you."

Areum makes a high-pitched chattering noise and covers her face with her wing, as if she can't bear to look me in the eyes.

I laugh. "Don't tell me you're embarrassed!"

She squawks and swats at me affectionately with her other wing, before pointing her beak to the closed doors we're rapidly approaching. "We're here."

I adjust my Phantom of the Opera mask as my ears start to tingle. "Are you sure this is where Sahm said it is?"

I reach my hand up over my head, and my moon rabbit ears have materialized. They shiver a little as I run my hand up and down them. They're impossibly soft. I let them spring back up so they point to the dark, moonless sky, and focus on the lit-up sign above the doors.

"Wait a second. It says it's a cosmic bowling alley." My heart clatters on the pavement. "I thought it was supposed to be mini golf, not tenpin bowling!" It also dawns on me that we're in a *parking lot*, which must mean on the flight over from Tokki Pharmaceuticals, we somehow transitioned back into the Mortalrealm.

Areum narrows her avian eyes at the sign. "Look, Riley Oh. The sign is changing."

When I look back up at the building, it has turned into a

Stairbucks. Not the Mortalrealm version with the green tea frappuccinos I love and would kill for right now, but the one spelled with the letter *i*. As in the Spiritrealm version that houses the stairways between heaven and the hells.

"It's just as the imugi said, Riley Oh," Areum murmurs. "It appears the fabric between the realms is getting thinner by the minute. The netherrealm is closer than ever."

As we both stare at the entrance, the facade changes again. This time it reveals a set of puffy doors that look like they're made of clouds. On them float the big bold words *HUNGRY HOLES—The Godrealm's First and Finest Indoor Mini Golf*. Underneath are smaller floating letters, which claim that the establishment was *EST: The Beginning of Time*.

Beneath that is a floating glass noticeboard where someone has used a fluro glass pen to write *Mondays, Humpdays, and Stardays are now glow-in-the-dark! Bring a friend and an avo shake is on the house!*

"Quick," I say, pulling on the door and hurrying inside. "Before it changes again!"

The first thing that happens when the cloud doors shut behind us is drool. A lot of drool. All coming from my mouth.

"Do you smell that?" I ask Areum, trying not to get saliva on my Converses. Honestly, it's flowing like a tap. There's meaty galbi (heavy on the garlic) and sizzling samgyeopssal wafting in from my left, with notes of melting sugar and caramelized sweet potatoes flying in from the right. Except everything is heightened. I haven't even tasted anything, but it smells like the foods have been condensed down into its most potent form. Like how grapes are sweet, but raisins are *way* sweeter. Suddenly, I'm very curious about that avo shake. Maybe I *should* give it a go.

"Do not be confused, Riley Oh," Areum explains. "What you are smelling is not food. It is perfume."

I stare at her.

"Wearing food scents is very popular in the Godrealm," she says matter-of-factly. "Floral and musk went out of fashion a few centuries ago. Dulce Ga-banana is the realm's leading perfumery, and they have made a divine fortune from their two best-selling scents: L'eau de Bulgogi and L'eau de Dalgona. Even I have a small bottle of the latter."

I nod, trying to make sense of what Areum is saying, and finally register the space around us. Truthfully, I was expecting something a bit, well, *more*, since we are in the land of the gods. But it really does just look like a cool indoor glow-in-the-dark mini golf. It's slightly bigger than the one we used to go to as kids, so it's probably an eighteen-hole course. There's an arrow pointing to the bumper-car riding zone, and another that leads to the arcade games. Next to the sign is a counter where you get your club and ball, and there's even a little photo station where you can get selfies in front of a six-foot-tall avo shake cardboard cutout sporting a cheesy smile. A speech bubble is coming out of the shake's mouth that says AVO GREAT TIME!

There are only three things that make me feel various levels of unease.

The first is how high the ceilings are. For a space that isn't that big, the headspace in here is unnecessarily spacious. Like, so tall that I can't actually see where the roof is.

Two, there are Wanted posters sporting Dahl's and my faces all over the walls, claiming we're charged with the death of the Cave Bear Goddess, the suspected disappearance of the Water Dragon Goddess, and the theft of Mago's Fire from Mount Baekdu. They look fresh and crisp, as if they've only just been put up, and the reward for our capture is in Prayer Dollars (whatever that is) with a *lot* of zeroes. My jaw clenches with the injustice of it all. How *dare* they try to blame it all on us?! All I can say is, this disguise was a *very* good idea.

The third thing that is making me uneasy is my viewpoint. It feels like I'm looking through a fish-eye lens. The things directly in front of me—like a group of scantily clad moon rabbits sporting lacy, gold-filigree masquerade masks—look super big and focused. While things in my sizeable periphery look distorted and stretched. Such as the two-story-high fried-potato tornado stick (hole 5, par 3), or the long black sausages on my right, curled to look like slithering snakes (hole 465, par 3). It's almost like . . .

"Wait a second," I say out loud. "Hole *four hundred and sixty five*? How big *is* this course?"

"Sahm said it is the most popular course in the realm," Areum says.

"But it *looks* tiny," I point out.

Areum nods, as if remembering I'm new to this realm. "They have merely folded space to look small, Riley Oh. It is common practice in the Godrealm."

"You can't *fold* space. It's not paper."

"It is just like paper, in fact. As long as you do it with skill and precision, large spaces can be condensed into smaller ones for ease of access, and for ease of vision. How else could they host a tournament for an entire realm inside one indoor mini golf venue?"

She makes it sound so obvious, which I guess it kind of is, when you're divine and have lots of powers at your disposal. But all I can think about is how greedy the Godrealm is for keeping this magic to themselves. Imagine how useful it would be to just fold over the highways in LA, and *boom!* Traffic jams would be a thing of the past. Or if you could fold the globe over and you could go from LA to Seoul with one footstep instead of by plane. Imagine the wonders that would do to our carbon footprints.

"Try tilting your head and pinching out at the edges of your vision," Areum suggests. "You should be able to zoom out to see the folded-over portions."

I tilt my head to the left and gather my index finger and thumb before making them slide away from each other. Suddenly, the course opens up, and it scrolls so fast, everything is a blur. When I use my fingers to pinch the air in an attempt at pushing pause, my vision stops at hole 156. It's a par 3, where you have to navigate the ball through a scattering of gimbap pieces to get to the hole. Ooh, tough, but I could ace that one pretty confidently.

"Everything is food-themed here," I point out to Areum, zooming back out to my original fish-eye view.

"The Godrealm has an insatiable obsession with what can be consumed. They wear it. Eat it. Bless it. Inspire it."

"Guess they're not that different from us, huh?"

She nods, then fluffs up her wings. "I will go scope out

the area, Riley Oh. I will admit I am very nervous about you entering this tournament. I want to make sure I know where the exits are, and check if there are any threats. Please stay here until I return."

With my only companion gone, I decide to take the time to study my potential opponents. There are a lot of people here now, all dressed up in their masquerade getups, milling around and waiting for the formalities to start. It's hard to see with all the masks, but apart from some bonghwangs, cheollimas, and other head-to-toe divine creatures, many of the Godrealm's citizens look very human, with the exception of small details—moon bunny ears (like mine, which I can't stop touching), large wings, bushy tails, claws and talons, even some hooves. Some of them are drinking creamy pale green beverages, which I assume are the famous avo shakes. Others have already collected their glow-in-the-dark clubs and balls from the counter, and my fingers itch to get a hold of mine.

I eagerly get into the line for the counter and start thinking through my tried-and-tested strategies, which have never failed me before. To help me think, I take out my compass and fiddle with the hard, smooth metal, running my finger across the rough patch on the back, releasing and folding the blades absentmindedly.

"No way. You have a moral compass!"

I turn toward the voice behind me, a short, balding man who apart from his long orange-and-black-striped tail and furry ears looks like a human man—albeit one who is decked out in a colorful lucha libre mask and accompanying wrestling spandex. He smells extremely of garlic-and-soy-sauce-marinated beef. I'm going to go out on a limb and say he's wearing the famous L'eau de Bulgogi.

"Wow, moral compasses are so rare. You're so lucky to have one. It should definitely give you an upper hand in the competition."

Since he's in line for a club and ball, I assume he's also a competitor. And my parents always said sportsmanship was just as important as the game. So I try to be as polite as possible, even though my logic tells me that with a tail like that, he must be related to the Mountain Tiger Goddess's lineage, and that I should be on guard at all times.

"A moral compass is a person's ability to judge what's right and wrong, and to act according to their judgment, no?" I say politely. "Surely, it's not *that* rare."

He shakes his head and points down at my golden star compass. "No, no, I mean your Moral Compass!"

"You mean, this thing?" I bring the relic up to my eyes to study it more carefully. "My friend Taeyo, who's a Horang"—I stop myself before admitting that my friend is a mortal witch—"I mean, my friend gave it to me a while back. He thought it might help me find my way back home one day." It had been such a thoughtful gift, given during a time when I needed it the most. In some ways, the compass embodied my discovery that people are not always as they seem, and that there are always two (or more) sides to every story.

The Lucha Libre man nods approvingly. "Must be a good friend to give you such a valuable gift."

I look away and cough to clear my throat. "So, uh, random question. But what does a Moral Compass do, exactly?"

He laughs and slaps me on the shoulder, and it's so force-ful I almost do a full 360 twirl. I search my neck, worried for Taggy's safety, but luckily they're okay. They climb up higher on my neck, though, back toward the safe spot in my ear. Smart move.

When I don't laugh back, the man raises his eyebrows. Well, at least his mask lifts where his eyebrows would be if I could see them. "You don't know?" He sounds surprised. "It's a compass that shows you your true north."

When I continue to remain silent, he is decent enough to explain. "You know how people always say you should follow your gut? That's great, but there's so much noise in there, how do you actually know what it's telling you?" He pats his latex-covered belly, as if to illustrate. "Or when people say that they have a sixth sense. That's just another way of saying that they have a really loud gut voice. They can *know* things that oth-ers can't."

"Like having a really strong intuition?"

"Exactly. A Moral Compass calibrates to your internal true north, to give your gut a chance to speak. To help manifest your sixth sense in a way that's immediately visible."

"Wow." I think back to how the compass helped us find the lab at the pharmaceutical company and then to locate our friends in the gummification room. I'd assumed the com-pass had some form of magic attached to it, but if this man is to believed, it was just translating what my intuition already knew.

Unable to curb my curiosity, I flip the compass open right there in front of him.

This time, the slender gold pointer trembles before pointing in the direction of the ice-cream counter. There is a sign advertising their new seven-scoop waffle cone with avocado ice cream. Immediately, I think of my proud legacy of hole-in-one waffle cones at Zany Zoo Mini Golf.

"What's it saying?" the man asks eagerly. "Any tips for the game?"

I smile. "It's saying that for the first time in my life, I might just be confident about something, after all."

I'm next up at the counter, and the attendee helps pick out a club that's right for my height. I grab a bright yellow ball from the basket—the color of the sun—and I snap my compass shut.

You've got this, I coach myself. *You're just suffering from imposter syndrome. It's a real thing. Emmett said so. You can win the tournament, and you can use Mago's Fire to unlock your true potential. Then you and Dahl are going to save the world! Aja! Aja!*

"Loyal and distinguished citizens of the soon-to-be MegaRealm, the tournament is about to commence," a voice booms through the speaker system. "Contestants, please collect your clubs and balls from the counter and stand by for the formal proceedings to begin."

"Oh, wow, there they are!" the tiger-tailed wrestler man exclaims. He points into the air above the golf course, where something shimmers like a star. "It's really them!" He tilts his head and pinches at the air next to his temple, acting like whoever he's seeing is an A-list celebrity.

I copy the motion to zoom into the sparkle floating in the air, only to realize it's not a star at all. Zoomed in, it's a chariot in the shape of a pear-shaped bottle gourd, cut right down the middle, with gigantic glittery wings. There are four figures sitting inside the hollow of the gourd, and immediately, Sahm's feathers on my mask shiver, tugging at the chariot by an invisible cord.

It'll feel like the pull of a magnet when you're close, Sahm had said, and I get a rush of adrenaline. The fidget spinner and our Key must be in that gourd. I go to zoom in even closer, but the winged chariot keels to one side and glides across the expanse of the golf course. I chase the flying vehicle in my vision by pinching in and out, until eventually I get the full view of the passengers, each cloaked by a royal mantle.

A fox with gleaming eyes and a sharp chin, with nine perfectly bushy tails spread out like a fan behind her.

A sleek black crow with purple streaks running down her back, with three taloned feet underneath her plumage.

A rabbit with impossibly soft fur and ears pointing to the moon, carrying a pestle the size of a baseball bat in her hand.

And an orange-and-black-striped tiger, strong and majestic, with a muscular tail swishing menacingly behind her.

The tiger's red eyes are sharp and alarming, and as I try to calm my pounding heart, her gaze lowers until they're staring directly at *me*.

"The goddesses," I breathe as a shiver runs down my spine. "They're *here*."

15.
Infomercials Have Their Place...Or Do They?

LUCHA LIBRE DUDE BOWS DEEPLY to the four divine royals, until his forehead touches the ground. "The deliverers of the new MegaRealm," he whispers reverently. "The new Mothers of our *future*."

"Welcome to this marvelous day, great citizens of the soon-to-be MegaRealm!" a commanding female voice announces through the speaker system. "Welcome to history in the making!"

Lucha Libre man squeals. "Ahhh! It's the Mountain Tiger Goddess!"

I'm still holding my breath as I stare frozen at the orange-and-black-striped goddess holding the mic from the flying chariot. But if she's seen me, she hasn't registered who I am. I touch my mask and moon rabbit ears with gratitude. *Phew.*

"My sisters and I are truly honored to host this momentous occasion, and we are so happy to see that we have received such a plentiful turnout. As you all know, we have invited you all here today, to this grand tournament, to publicly choose the prime minister of the MegaRealm."

There is a roar of excited cheering and applause that spreads across the venue like a tidal wave.

The goddess clears her throat. "Now, before we get stuck into the tournament, my sisters and I have prepared a short video for your viewing pleasure. A lot of thought and care went into this, so we hope you enjoy."

She clicks her fingers, and immediately, a virtual screen appears in my vision. On it, a video begins to play.

It's all in black-and-white, with dramatic, sad violin music in the background. Divine citizens are at the supermarket, frowning at the empty aisles, their hungry children crying in the shopping carts. Cut to a scene of Godrealm residents trying to get money out of an ATM, only to find the bank no longer exists. Finally, a peaceful suburban neighborhood at night, until the houses suddenly disappear into thin air, leaving families exposed on the street with no roof over their heads.

"Are you tired of being beholden to the fickle loyalty of mortals?" asks the Nine-Tailed Fox goddess narrator from the screen, dressed like the woman with the caked-on makeup and fur coat at the Trevi Fountain. She puts on an exaggerated sad face. "Are you one of the hundreds and thousands of Godrealm citizens who have suffered from the plummeting faith of the Mortalrealm?"

The Lucha Libre man beside me exhales deeply, as if reliving some deep trauma.

"For much too long, we have held on to the old ways," the Nine-Tailed Fox Goddess continues in a melodramatic manner. "We have desperately clung to the days when mortal prayers were plentiful, and legends of the divine were passed down from generation to generation like precious treasures. *Those* were the days when our realm prospered, our economy bolstered by mortal devotion. *Those* were the golden days when our banks were full of Prayer Dollars and our supermarkets were stocked to the brim of altar offerings. *Those* were the glory days when homes didn't disappear over our sleeping children because mortals forgot we even existed!"

The crowd of divine citizens around me wails in grief.

"Well, loyal citizens of the Godrealm, our somber days are behind us!"

Suddenly, the screen comes alive in full Technicolor. The sad violin music is replaced with an epic movie-trailer soundtrack, and the scene explodes with rainbows and clouds and lots (and *lots*) of food. The Moon Rabbit Goddess replaces the Nine-Tailed Fox Goddess as the narrator on the screen, her plump form wearing a floral dress, her two long bunny ears braided with ribbon down to her belly button.

"We intend to start afresh!" she says in an overly chirpy voice. "In the new MegaRealm, we will no longer need to rely on the humans who have forgotten our legends, our myths, our stories. We will no longer suffer at the hands of humankind's fickle disloyalty, because we will sever the link that binds us. We will give birth to a new world where we will be in control of our *own* futures. A safe, stable, and prosperous realm where we will finally be *free*!"

As scenes of happy moon rabbit children run and laugh through tulip-filled meadows in the background with their nine-tailed fox friends, a new goddess now appears on the screen. Unlike the Nine-Tailed Fox Goddess's melodrama, or the Moon Rabbit Goddess's overcheeriness, the Mountain Tiger Goddess is sober and pensive.

"The mortals killed our sister the Cave Bear Goddess. Then they took our Water Dragon Goddess sister hostage. Now the mortals have stolen our precious Mago's Fire from Mount Baekdu and torn the fabric between the three realms, destroying everything the Mother created. It is *our* divine responsibility to put things right. We must rise above the insolence of mortalkind and restore the universe to the glory of Mago!"

The Mountain Tiger Goddess is joined by her three other sisters, and together they recite in unison to the camera, "Long live the MegaRealm!"

The video ends, and the divine audience roars with emotion, repeating the phrase *Long live the MegaRealm* over and over like a prayer.

"Which is why we've gathered you all here today," the Mountain Tiger Goddess announces in the flesh from the winged gourd chariot. "To search for our first prime minister to rule our new MegaRealm. We will do away with the class divides that have plagued our realm with inequality and strife. This time, we will do it right. Together, openly and transparently, we will choose our new prime minister, and together, we will build a new realm of peace and prosperity. For *all* of us."

Lucha Libre man's shoulders shudder, and he wipes his eyes.

"My gods, that was *beautiful.* Just absolutely *inspiring,* don't you think?"

The goddess gives the floor to the Three-Legged Crow Goddess, who launches into some other big speech. But I find myself standing there in my own world, gripping tight to my golf club and ball, trying to digest what I just saw and heard.

The goddesses have definitely put spin on their message to sway their audience, like any good infomercial would do. I mean, we *definitely* didn't take the Water Dragon Goddess hostage—she came to *us.* And it wasn't us that stole Mago's Fire from Mount Baekdu—it was their sister. But at the same time, I can't help but feel a spark of sympathy for them in a way I never expected to feel. I didn't realize the waning faith of mortals in the divine was directly affecting the Godrealm's well-being. And while it doesn't change all the terrible things they've done, and all the horrible things they're continuing to do, I can see now that the goddesses think what they're doing is *right.* They truly believe that the MegaRealm is what's best for their divine citizens.

And it makes me wonder. . . . Is what they're doing for their people any different than what I'm doing for mine? Am I so different from the goddesses?

"—so now that all the rules of the tournament have been squared away, I officially deem this tournament commenced!" I catch the Three-Legged Crow Goddess conclude.

"Wait, what?!"

Lost in my thoughts, I'd totally zoned out and missed the goddess's speech, which now appears to have been the rules of the game.

Panicked, I turn to Lucha Libre man. "Wh-what did she say again?" I stammer. "Can you repeat what she said? Please?"

The man looks at me pityingly. "I'm a pretty competitive guy, and I wouldn't normally do this. But you look like you'd hardly be a worthy competitor, so I'll give you the summary." He stands taller and grins. "Gosh, the goddess's speech has really brought out the community in me."

I nod gratefully. "Thank you, thank you!"

"So there's a total of three rounds. The first is a qualifier, and only those who get a hole in one on their first go get through. Mini golf is the realm-favorite sport, after all. Anyone who can't play a mean game doesn't deserve to become prime minister."

I grip my club even harder. A hole in one on the first try at an unfamiliar hole is tough, but not impossible.

"The next two rounds are Command and Commitment—both qualities the goddesses deem essential for the position."

"How are they going to test those at mini golf?" I ask, suddenly confused.

"Who said the next two rounds would be golf?"

My heart starts to pound in my chest as it dawns on me what this means. "But you don't understand. I'm *only* good at mini golf!"

He gives me another pitying look and points to the strip of green lights that have appeared to my left and right. They look like the lighting that flight attendants tell you to follow in the event of an emergency.

"Just follow the lights, kiddo, and do your best—it's all any of us can do." He turns to leave, but before he does, he points to my right ear. "And you might want to check that out. Looks infected or something."

My hand shoots up to touch my long moon bunny ear, and luckily, it's not infected. It's just in the process of disappearing.

Quickly, I grab another one of the poop-shaped gummies from my pocket and pop it into my mouth. Under my touch, the bunny ear solidifies again and stretches tall. Phew.

Areum is still not back from her flyby of the mini golf, and I decide to stay where I am in case she can't find me. But when the speaker's voice booms over the venue warning that the game will start in five minutes, I start to panic. Do I wait? Do I go? What do I do?

Eventually, I decide it'd be worse if I missed the game entirely. Then all of this would've been for nothing.

Grateful for something to focus on, I follow the green-lit path, until I find myself at hole 123, which is a par 3, and modeled off a cross-section of a boba tea that's fallen on its side. The hole is at the top tip of the straw, and little chewy balls of tapioca have "spilled" across the path that the ball will have to navigate.

At first glance, it doesn't seem like a difficult hole, and for a second, I feel preemptively triumphant. I'll just need to get the ball through the bobas and use the walls as bounce-offs to make a clear shot for the hole. Easy!

But then I remember this isn't a par 3. I need a hole in one. I look closer and get a bout of hiccups.

Thanks to the rogue "bobas" spilled on the green, there

is no clear straight path from the tee to the hole. There is *no* way I can make this hole-in-one shot. For the first time in my life, I have dark feelings toward boba tea.

What's worse is that as I circle the hole to look at the curvatures in the green, I realize that there is an incline halfway up the green, which then tapers back down to the hole. This means I'll need to get the power of the shot *just* right, or else I could overshoot the hole completely.

As the goddess's voice announces over the speaker that there are two minutes remaining until tee-off, I drop my head in my hands.

Who am I kidding?

I'm no Hole-in-One Riley.

I am *doomed*!

16.
Get Ready to Have Your Photo Taken!

 "ALL RIGHT, CONTENDERS, we are about to start the clock," the voice announces over the speaker system. "You will have ten minutes—and not a second over—within which to make your one and only shot. And remember, only those who get a hole in one will qualify for the next round. Good luck, everyone. May the best putters win!"

A big red number 3 flashes in the air in front of me, followed by a 2, then a 1. A loud foghorn sounds across the venue.

"Your time starts now!"

The numbers are replaced with a timer that counts down from ten minutes. A man wearing a dokkaebi mask (ugh) to my right starts hopping on his feet and making loud howling noises, as if he's trying to rile himself up. The woman to my left with two fox tails is placing her club down horizontally from the tee to calculate the best angle to hit the ball.

Areum still isn't here, and it suddenly hits me how much is riding on this one shot. If I don't make this hole in one, all our plans to save the Mortalrealm will be dashed. I will have failed. Not just myself, but *everyone*.

My chest tightens. I try to take a breath, but it's like my lungs are at capacity and can't take in any more air. I start to see spots in my vision. My club and ball are squirming in my hands. Oh no, am I having another panic attack?

My wakerpillar tickles my skin.

"Taggy?" I gasp, feeling woozy.

They rub their head against my earlobe in a calm, soothing manner. *Breathe, Riley,* they seem to be saying to me. *You can do this. And you've got time. Just take a deep breath.*

I focus on the soft pattering of Taggy's legs against my skin, and I put my club and ball down on the ground. Over my shoulder, I see one of those old-school photo booths where you sit inside and get a strip of photos taken. It looks unoccupied.

Hurrying inside, I swipe the curtain closed, grateful to have a moment to myself. I sit on the hard seat and stare blankly at the touch screen, trying to focus on my breathing. I manage one small inhale, and then another. And another. Eventually, I suck in a deep, sweet lungful of air, and the spots fade from my vision.

That's when I realize there's no camera in the photo booth. Instead, there is a big button on the touch screen that says, *Push this button to receive a random selection of photos from people who are currently thinking about you.*

Curious about this weird reverse photo booth, I push the

button. Almost instantaneously, a new message pops up on the screen.

Your request has been processed! Please collect your photos from the collection slot outside the machine.

I slide the curtain to exit the booth, and there in the slot on its side is a strip of photos. I hold it up to see it clearer, and there are four tiny images.

One is of Phoebe and the RilOh stans standing out on the Strip with a group of saram. A few cheollimas are flying in the air above their heads, and judging by the looks on the tourists' faces, it seems the ruse that a huge magic show is being filmed in the city is starting to wear off. They look worried. Scared, even.

The second one is of Hattie at some techy-looking offices with Namjoon at her side, giving some kind of speech to a crowd. Her cheeks are flushed, her hands are raised in mid-gesture, and there's a peek of Dahl's moon-colored hair in the corner. She must be recruiting allies at Persimmon.

The last two photos are of Emmett. They're close-ups of his face, both wearing that funny expression that makes me feel like someone's dropped a bowl of Skittles inside my stomach.

Does that mean Emmett is currently thinking about me? Twice over, even?

Clutching the strip of photos close to my chest, I feel a slight boost of confidence. Knowing that the RilOh stans, my sister, and my best friend are thinking of me, it makes me feel braver. That I'm not alone. And more importantly, that I'm doing this for *them*.

"Okay," I murmur to myself as I glance up at the timer. Five minutes left. "I'm Hole-in-One Riley. All those years at Zany Zoo were not in vain. Think of all those double scoops. I've got this."

Picking up my bright yellow ball, I put it down at the tee. I stand with my feet planted firmly on the ground, imagining myself as a tree with its roots shooting downward. Then I squat slightly and wrap my hands around the club, left first, then my right, linking my right pinky with my left index finger.

The club still feels like it's squirming under my touch, so I take another deep breath and gaze left toward the hole, picturing the path the ball will need to take to navigate the forest of scattered boba pearls and get to its destination. Testing the club's movement, I get a feel of its weight, its rhythm, and to release some of my tension.

Then, thinking of Emmett, Hattie, and my RilOh fan club, I swing the club back and let the momentum guide it toward the ball.

"Argh!" my golf club shrieks. "Don't you *dare* swing me anywhere *near* that lying scumbag of a ball!"

I drop the club and leap back. "Argh!" I shriek. "Why can you talk?!"

"Why can *you* talk?" it retorts. "How rude!"

I take a tentative step toward the club, just in time to see a pair of eyes and a mouth appear on the head of the putter. It has very long fake-looking eyelashes.

"Don't stare!" she scolds. "Staring is also very rude. You're really just a very rude person, aren't you?" She points her putter head at my ball. "Not unlike *someone else* I know."

Just when things couldn't get weirder, my bright yellow ball spins to look up at me, also sporting two eyes and a mouth. Less eyelashes, but very purple lipstick. "Can you please tell that frustratingly attractive club that if she's going to keep playing these silly games, I don't want to play ball with her, either."

I shriek again. "You can talk, too?!"

"On second thought, maybe she's right. You *are* rather rude."

"I— I— How— What—"

I'm still mumbling, trying to figure out a way to get the question—*any* question—out of my mouth, when the club starts to sniffle.

"You never called me!" she whines. "I waited and I waited and I waited. You promised to call. But you didn't. Why?"

The ball rolls toward the club. "I wanted to call, I promise. But the number you gave me was a disconnected line. I thought you'd played me for a fool!"

"Lies," the club hisses. "Why would I give you a fake number?"

"I don't know. Why *did* you give me a fake number?" the ball shoots back.

"I didn't! We totally hit it off. Why would I have any reason to give you any number but mine?"

"Then tell me this. Why was it a disconnected number? I made it very clear I had a ball of a time with you!"

I glance up at the timer. There's four minutes left, and I'm quickly getting the impression this conversation is going in circles.

"Um, hey, you two," I interrupt. "I'm really sorry to cut off the, uh, *reunion*. But I was wondering if you'd both do me a solid and let me make my shot before you continue your conversation? It's kind of really important for me to get this hole in one."

They both shoot death glares at me.

"There is no way I'm going anywhere near that lying son of a ball," the club seethes.

"You're not touching us until we're finished our convo, moon bunny," the ball echoes.

They go back to running conversation circles around each other, and I sigh in exasperation. The dokkaebi man to my right grunts loudly as he finally hits his ball, and I can immediately see that he's used *way* too much force. The ball bounces off the set of life-size chopsticks and rebounds straight into his shin.

"Owww!" he yelps before he disappears completely, his club and ball and all, into a cloud of red.

Nervously, I look over to my left, and the two-tailed fox woman is just about to take her shot. I hold my breath, and like a pro, she navigates the upward incline through the wavy seaweed forest and dunks it into the hole.

"YUS!" she cries as she disappears into a cloud of green.

I exhale sharply. So red is fail and green is pass?

My club and ball, on the other hand, are still at each other's throats, their voices even louder and more emotive than before. The timer now says there are three minutes left on the clock.

"I really am *doomed*," I whisper to Taggy, who is on the edge of my shoulder, watching with full interest. "There's no way they're going to finish talking before my time is up. What am I supposed to do now?"

Taggy rubs their front legs together.

And that's when I remember.

My *Moral Compass*. The guide to my inner true north. It helped me before, and it can help me again.

Quickly, I fish it out of my pocket and open the lid, waiting for the slender gold pointer to point to the answer.

Nothing. Not even a tremble.

I close it, activate the blades, and then flip it open, again. Maybe it needs to be in star form.

Still nothing. The gold pointer lays flat and unmoving on the face of the compact.

I groan. If anything, all I feel is a slight breeze coming from inside. But no helpful message amplifying my gut voice or manifesting my sixth sense. Maybe my intuition is faulty. Or was Lucha Libre having me on? Maybe there's no such thing as a Moral Compass.

The ever-so-slight breeze from the compass moves a strand of hair into my face, tickling my nose. I scratch away the tickle, but now it seems the air is getting stronger. My compass is blowing out wind.

Wait, *wind?*

Suddenly, I know what I have to do.

"Hey, you two!" I call out. "Sorry to be rude and interrupt again, but I was wondering if you'd be willing to hear me out. I think I might be able to help."

"Take your best shot, moon bunny," the ball grunts. "Not like we're going anywhere anytime soon."

The club grumbles but doesn't say no.

I clear my throat. "Well, I get the impression you obviously still care for each other, am I right? Or else you wouldn't be so upset."

They turn away from each other but both mumble what sound like *yeah, I guess so* under their breaths.

"And I also get the impression that there might have been a simple misunderstanding." I point to the ball. "Sorry, what was your name?"

"Gong. She/her are my pronouns."

"So, Gong, you claim the number you were given didn't work."

She nods.

I point toward the club. "And you—?"

"Chae. She/her are my pronouns."

"And you, Chae, claim you never got a call."

She nods.

"So could it be a reasonable and possible sequence of events, then, that Chae, in her excitement to have met Gong, accidentally wrote her phone number wrong when passing it over? And therefore, Gong might be, in fact, telling the truth when she says she tried to call Chae?"

They both pause, thinking that through.

"But even if that were true," Chae says, "how can I trust that she's telling the truth? How do I know that she isn't lying now, just like she could've lied about having tried to call me? I have trust issues, okay? This is very triggering for me."

Gong rolls forward, about to defend her position. But I go first.

"Well," I start, holding up my compass. The wind coming out of its open top is almost gusty now. "I guess you might never know for sure. But that's the thing about faith. It's kinda invisible, but doesn't mean it's not there."

Gong bounces erratically as if to say, *Talk like it makes sense, moon bunny!*

I jiggle my fingers above my open compass. "Even though you can't see the wind, we feel it. It helps cool us on a hot day. It spins turbines to power electricity. It helps push the sails on ships to get sailors home to their families." I think of Emmett, Hattie, and my RilOh stans, cheering me on without them even knowing it. "I think faith works a little like that."

When they both remain silent, I take that as encouragement. "So if you really like each other, maybe wipe the slate clean and start afresh. Because just because you can't prove anything doesn't mean it's not true. Perhaps it's worth taking a leap of faith. For each other, but for yourselves, too."

"Like the wind, eh?" Chae murmurs under her breath.

"Invisible but there," Gong echoes.

I glance up at the clock. Only twenty seconds left.

I blanch. "It's too late," I whisper to Taggy, feeling my throat close up. "I tried my best, but it's too late. There's only twenty seconds left. No, nineteen. Now eighteen."

"Pffft." Chae hops over and snuggles her rubber grip into my hands. "After that therapy session, I thought you'd have more follow-through, moon bunny."

"There's only fourteen seconds left," I whisper, my voice hardly audible as I grip on tighter to Chae's grip.

"You mean, there's *still* fourteen seconds left," Gong finishes, rolling over to the fairway and settling herself onto the tee.

Chae physically pulls me over to Gong.

Ten seconds on the clock.

"Now, surrender to me," Chae coos. "Just hold on to me, and trust me. Like you said, have faith."

"Let us be your wind," Gong chimes.

My eyes dart up to the clock.

Five seconds left.

Either way, I'm going to disappear. And I *want* to believe. I really *want* to have faith. So I close my eyes. And surrender.

My arm swings back involuntarily with Chae's guidance, and she hits Gong with a satisfying tap.

With my heart in my throat, I open my eyes, just in time to see Gong expertly weaving through the scattered boba pearls on the green and sinking gracefully into the hole.

In one.

Single.

Shot.

My heart bursts.

Hole-in-One Riley is still in business, baby!

And then everything goes green.

17.
There Is No Such Thing
as Too Much Butter

I AM STILL BASKING IN THE GLORY of my triumph when the green cloud dissipates and I find myself in a strange room. The club and ball have disappeared, and I wish I'd gotten a chance to say good-bye. I wouldn't have been able to make it without them, and with mere seconds on the clock, at that.

Curious voices murmur around me.

"Oooh, there's the contender!"

"She's a moon rabbit!"

"Do you think she has what it takes?"

It appears I have been plopped right into the center of an ice rink. See-through protection screens have been put up along the periphery, as if to protect the audience from whatever is going to happen in here . . . which, frankly, does not give me any kind of comfort about what this round might entail. Definitely not mini golf. Maybe hockey? Figure skating?

Through the transparent barriers, I see what must be at least a few hundred pairs of eyes locked on me, their bodies packed tightly into the stands, waiting for the event to begin. Some eager bystanders have plastered themselves right against the screens to get a closer look. I even see a certain white-winged mare and a small black-winged stallion bouncing on top of her. They're wearing lacy masks, but it's definitely the newlyweds. Funny place to come on a honeymoon. Although, it *is* nice to see two familiar faces.

Attempting to drown out the voices speculating about me and the game, I tentatively move my feet. I am mightily pleased to find that the floor is, in fact, not made of ice. Whatever it is, it's firm and not slippery, which is great, considering ice-skating and me aren't friends.

I take small steps, though, just in case, inching forward, to get a feel of what might be on offer. The Lucha Libre man had said the second round would be about Command, but how are they going to test that here, and what does that really mean, anyway?

A loudspeaker crackles into action, and a voice clears its throat. "Congratulations, moon rabbit from hole one hundred twenty-three! You were one of the two hundred and five successful candidates in the qualifiers that have made it to the Command round. Well done!"

There is a round of applause from the audience, and I suddenly feel *very* exposed.

"Without further ado, please let me introduce the rules of this round," the voice continues. "But first, you will need to choose from the three doors now appearing in front of you."

Three doors do, indeed, begin to materialize in front of me, all simple with glazed wooded panels. I look behind them, but they don't seem to lead anywhere. They're just three identical doorframes. The only difference between them is that the first has a picture of a flame on its surface. The second has an image of a raindrop. The third has a simple drawing of a mountain.

"What—what do they mean?" I find myself asking out loud to the voice.

"Fire. Water. Earth," the voice responds. "You must choose one. You have six seconds to open the door, or your chance will be forfeited. Six. Five. Four—"

Before I can start to panic, the crowd starts shouting their suggestions.

"*Fire!*"

"*Earth!*"

"*No, water!*"

The voice continues the countdown. "Three. Two—"

Argh. Without thinking, I run toward the closest door—the one with the flame on it—and yank it open.

"You have chosen fire!"

Dry ice begins rolling out of the open entrance. It's so thick that for a moment, all I see is white. I wade through it to clear my vision, and when the white plumes settle, the entire rink has been filled up to my ankles with fluffy white clouds. In surprise, I reach down and cup a handful into my palm and run it over my left forearm. It's cool and soothing and spreads like butter. Weird. Could they actually be *clouds*?

There's a loud bark from somewhere near me, and the

crowd cheers. When I look up from staring at the clouds near my feet, I realize why my door had a flame on it. In front of me on the rink, is a dog. And it's on fire.

"*It's a bulgae!*" the crowd yells excitedly.

I gulp, remembering the canine-shaped fireball, the size of a rhino, galloping across the broken night sky earlier. Areum had said they were the dogs of the Godrealm. This one is the size of a Great Dane, so maybe it's a puppy. What in the world are they expecting me to do with *him*?

As if hearing my question, the voice answers.

"The Command round is about seeing whether you have what it takes to be a true master of the many. Can you command respect, obedience, and loyalty from your populace? Will you be able to control the most uncontrollable of forces?"

My heart sinks as I begin to realize where this is going. Memories of Mong as an excitable puppy come flooding back, him tearing around the house and me failing abysmally to get him to sit. I can't imagine controlling a flammable divine puppy is going to be any easier. . . .

As if hearing my thoughts, the bulgae barks loudly and wags his fiery tail, sending tiny balls of fire into the audience. Luckily, the Perspex screens block the flames. (I can see now why they're there.) He lopes toward me like he wants to lick my face, except when he nears, the fire burns my skin.

"Argh!" I cry, shielding my face with my arms.

Sensing my fear, the bulgae stops. But not before the hair on my right arm singes off completely. Weirdly, the hairs on my left arm remain intact.

"The aim of this round is simple. You must make the bulgae light a bonfire using the materials provided."

"What materia—" I start to ask.

A huge heap of scrap appears in front of me, the clouds parting like billowing dust as they land with a *thud*. There are wooden planks, coils of rope, a mound of old car tires, and a bunch of sticks of varying lengths. It looks like part of a junkyard just got spilled out onto the ground.

"You must ensure every single item provided is lit on fire. We have doused the materials with fuel to give you a helping hand. And we have provided you some tools, if you wish to use them."

A collar, a long leash, and a leather whip appear at my feet.

"Those are the entirety of the rules," the voice concludes. "Good luck, contender. You have thirty minutes, which begins *now.*"

The same floating countdown clock materializes in the air above me, and the crowd goes wild. I hear Charles's and Maru's whinnying particularly loudly, as they shimmy to get an even better view of the game.

The bulgae approaches the mountain of junk curiously and sniffs it from a distance. He makes a face, obviously deciding he's not interested, and lopes off the other way. Instead, he turns his attention to the clouds on the ground. He barks happily, wags his tail, then rolls around in the white fluff.

Looking down at my unsinged left arm hairs, I take a leaf from his book. I get down and roll myself in the clouds, covering as much of my body as I can with the cool white plumes.

I'm sure that's what protected me from getting burnt. It can't hurt to be cautious.

The bulgae looks over at me and barks, as if he thinks I'm hilarious, and I study him, strategizing the task at hand. So I need to make the bulgae light a bonfire using all this junk. Surely if I can just get him close enough, the fire from his fur will light everything on fire. This should be a piece of cake.

I pick up the collar and leash, kicking the whip to the side. There is no realm in which I'd be okay using a whip on a living animal. *None.*

"Hey, fire doggy," I start instead, making a clicking sound with my tongue. "Do you mind if I put this collar and leash on you? Then we can go for a little walk. Would you like a walk?"

The bulgae looks over his shoulder at me and promptly turns away. He doesn't seem remotely interested.

I keep trying to talk to him nicely, telling him how much I love his fiery fur and how it's so cool his tail can wag out fireballs. But the bulgae isn't even listening. He plops himself down on the cloudy floor and scratches his flaming ear, oblivious to my existence.

I look up at the time. I've spent over five minutes cajoling the creature, and there's not a single lick of fire to be seen. I try to think of anything I know about bulgaes to help me, but all I can think about is Areum saying they're *extremely intelligent but notoriously difficult to train.*

I groan. Just my luck.

Hooking the collar onto the leash, I decide I'll try to lasso him. If I can get the collar on, perhaps I could pull him by sheer force toward the kindle.

As the crowd murmurs their opinions on my approach, I swing my lasso in the air in circles as I inch closer toward him.

He senses me approaching from a mile away and gives me a dirty look before bounding to the opposite side of the rink. Still, with the clock ticking, I give it a go. And a few more. And a few more after that. But each time, my sad attempt at being a cowgirl ends with a mortifying *thump* as the leash falls flat on the ground.

I am persistent; that much is clear. But as I tire and my aim worsens, all that results is a more-annoyed bulgae. When I try the lasso for the eighth time, he lowers his head and growls at me, his eyes narrowed. That's when I notice his teeth as sharp as knives. *Gulp.* The clock says I've wasted ten more minutes, and even the audience seem to be getting tired of my stubborn and unoriginal attempts.

I glance over at the whip on the ground, and for a split second, I consider what would happen if I picked it up. If I used such brutal force on this creature to save the world. Would it be worth it?

But as quickly as the thought comes, I shove it away. No way. No way in all the heaven and hells. I'll just have to find another way.

Finally, I decide I'll try running at him. I've already covered myself in cloud protection, so surely if I could catch him in my arms, I could just sprint for the kindle and use him like an oversize candle to light the thing on fire. Some dogs like being carried...don't they?

Before I can think myself out of it, I make a mad dash for the fire dog.

At first, his eyes widen, as if he doesn't know how to react. But then they narrow back down in challenge. He howls with his head arched up and charges toward *me*.

The crowd gasps as the tables turn and I become the one being chased in circles around the rink. Fortunately, the cloud cream really is effective, and despite us getting pretty close several times, my skin remains unblistered.

By the time the bulgae tires of chasing me, I only have thirteen minutes left on the clock, and I am spent.

I sigh and drop to the floor to cool off. What am I going to do now?!

As the clouds soothe my heated skin, I sit there and catch my breath and do the only other thing I can think of. I take out my Moral Compass.

This time when I open the compact, the inside lid has turned into a mirror. That's new. I look at it from all angles in case I'm missing some kind of clasp or release, but all I see is the reflection of the audience, where Charles and Maru are front and center. Despite my poor efforts, they seem to be cheering with full enthusiasm. They might as well have pom-poms.

I turn the compass again, and this time the mirror on the lid shows me the bulgae's reflection. His long tongue is hanging out the left side of his mouth, drooping down and dripping saliva onto the clouds.

There is a visceral pang in my chest as I realize how much I miss our dog, Mong. He does the exact same thing with his tongue out the left side of his mouth. Knowing we'd be in Vegas for a while with the training modules, we'd had no choice but to leave him at a long-stay doggy day care.

As I stare into the bulgae's eyes, I think of how I'd gone to great lengths to spell out Mong's needs to the doggy day care staff. For example, I'd explained that Samoyeds were super smart and got bored really easily, so it was important to give him lots of stimulation, or else he'd start looking for trouble. Lest we forget the day our house was covered in toilet paper from top to tail. . . .

The bulgae sighs and paws the clouds in front of him, looking bored out of his mind.

And that's when it hits me.

They're extremely intelligent but notoriously difficult to train, Areum had explained. *They only ever want to* play.

"You're just like our Mong, aren't you?" I say to the bulgae, getting back up on my feet. "Do you like games?"

His ears perk up at the word, and suddenly, I have an idea.

I close my compass, put it in my pocket, and run toward Charles and Maru.

"Hey, lovebirds," I say, through the gap in the see-through screen. "You can't see my face, but it's me, Riley Oh."

Charles looks suspiciously up at my moon rabbit ears. "Sure, sugarplum," he says with a chuckle. "And I'm Pegasus."

"No, really, I am!" I insist. "And I need your help."

"I don't know if that's allowed," Maru says in her deep, velvety voice.

"They didn't say anything about audience participation not being allowed. They just said I needed to make the bulgae light the stuff on fire."

Charles whinnies loudly. "If we were to help you, Supposedly Riley, what would we get out of it?"

I think about that one. "By the sounds of your enthusiastic cheering, I'd say you two would rather be *in* the game than watching it. If you join me, think of all the stories you could tell your friends afterward. About the time you helped a humble girl become prime minister."

They consider my offer.

"And, uh, I also have these." I hold out my palm, sporting two slightly sweaty but still edible poop-shaped gummies.

"Ooh, honey, look, gummies!" Maru exclaims.

By the sparkle in both the cheollima's eyes, I know I've hooked them. Sweet treats are a cheollima's kryptonite. I know it. They know it. We all know it.

"You should have led with that, my little petite chouchou!" Charles cries excitedly. "We're definitely listening now."

Maru rises on her hind legs to kick the Perspex screen down, but Charles stops her.

"But surely, you can do better than two, hmm?" he fishes, glancing down expectantly at my pocket.

I chew my lip. My ears will fade soon, and I'll need to have a top-up gummy. But at the same time, if I don't get their help, I won't be around to need a gummy.

I grunt and take out the last two remaining candies from my pocket. "These are all I've got."

Charles grins and picks the gummies out of my open palm. "What are we waiting for then—let's get the fire started!"

Maru completes the task of kicking the screen down, and my heart stops for a moment as I wait for the voice to announce a breach of the rules. But all I hear are the excited gasps from the audience. Their interest is well and truly piqued. The bulgae watches us like a hawk from his side of the rink, but I just look over and wave.

Eight minutes.

Ample time.

Trying to remember what I saw Hattie and her hellbeasts using at the Spiritrealm's Central Park, I get Charles and Maru straight to work. We put a long wooden plank over a smaller chunk of wood to create a seesaw. Then we use sticks of varying lengths and the rope to fashion a few makeshift hurdle jumps. We line the old rubber tires and tie them up to create a few tunnels. And we even use the leather whip to hang a tire from a wooden A-frame, then add a wooden ramp to complete our very own tire jump.

When we're done, we all step back to admire our work.

"Well, if that's not the snazziest canine obstacle course I've ever seen!" Charles whinnies proudly. "But how are we going to get the bulgae to cooperate, caramel puff? Surely you'll need some kind of incentive? Dog treats, perhaps? Too bad you've run out of those delightful gummies."

I grin widely. "I've got something even better."

As Charles's eyes widen, I heap a thick layer of cloud butter over his beautiful black fur. "This stuff will protect you," I assure him.

He neighs in an extra-high pitch, and flaps his itty-bitty wings to hide behind Maru. "Wifey dearest, do tell this deranged human that I am *not* live-bait material! You know I don't have the temperament for this type of performance!"

Maru chuckles and ushers her husband forward with an encouraging push of her wing. "I rather think this role suits you very well, Charlie dear. You definitely look the part."

As Charles grumbles loudly about how you can't trust anyone these days, I turn to the bulgae and whistle.

"Hey, buddy, sorry for making you wait. And also for chasing you before. And trying to trap you in a lasso. That was all pretty mean of me. Sorry!"

The bulgae lowers his head suspiciously, but his eyes lose a little of their bite.

"So I thought I could offer you a truce. By offering to play a game with you. That is, if you wanted to."

At the sound of the word *game*, the bulgae's ears flick up again, and his tail wags ever so slightly.

I clap my hands. "Well, the game is pretty simple. It's called Catch the Cheollima."

Charles squeals nervously, but Maru murmurs sweet words into his ear, which seems to calm him down.

I point to the hanging tire. "To catch Charles, you will need to first run up that ramp and jump through the tire. Then run up and down the seesaw. Do you think you could do that?"

The bulgae's tail wags more obviously now, sending a fire shower into the air.

"Then all you have to do to complete the course is jump over those two sets of hurdles and run through those tire tunnels. Got it?"

The bulgae's butt and nose both wiggle with anticipation.

"There's only one rule. No teeth, okay? This is a game, so we don't want real tears."

"Or blood!" Charles adds grumpily.

The bulgae looks to me with a gleeful glimmer in his eye and nods eagerly. He whimpers, desperate to get started.

There's only one minute left on the clock, but I'm not even flustered. That time was well spent, because I already know this is going to work.

"The things you do for love!" Charles cries as he reluctantly gets into position behind the tire.

"Ready, steady, go!" I announce.

The flaming dog easily lopes up the wooden ramp and runs through the tire toward Charles. The cheollima shrieks as the ramp and hoop immediately ignite on fire, and the crowd explodes with applause. The bulgae quickly runs up and down the seesaw before barking triumphantly, missing a furiously flapping Charles only by an inch.

"This better be worth it, cinnamon rolls!" Charles shouts as he flies over the hurdles and the bulgae chases him at full speed. The bulgae leaps over them both in one go—too high, in fact, missing the second hurdle entirely. He looks over his shoulder and, realizing the second hurdle hasn't ignited, runs back and scratches his butt against the last one, making that one explode into flame, too.

The crowd is now up on their feet, and we all chant *"Bul-gae! Bul-gae! Bul-gae!"* as the fire dog dives headfirst into the first tunnel as if he's jumping into a water slide. He slides right through the coil and shoots straight into the second one, hurtling into Charles, who is squealing at the top of his (high-pitched) lungs.

The timer beeps down to zero as the last tunnel ignites orange with fire, and the bulgae comes running toward me. He jumps onto my chest and licks my face. And without thinking, I hug him tight. Thanks to my ample cloud coverage, I'm protected from the flames. And instead, I'm warmed, right into the tiny crevices of my heart.

"You were amazing, Charlie!" Maru commends as Charles flies toward her, panting heavily.

"You did amazing!" I murmur at the same time into the bulgae's ear. "You were spectacular!"

The fire dog barks in joy and runs a few circles or four around me. But the fifth time around, he doesn't reappear.

When I spin around to see where he's gone, I realize that he's not the one that's disappeared.

I have.

I am no longer at the cloud rink.

Instead, as my hair whips at my face, it dawns on me that I am moving.

And I'm not standing on ground anymore.

I am sitting on a hurtling train.

18.
Commitment-Phobes
Need Not Apply

 OKAY, IT'S GENEROUS TO CALL THIS a train. It's more like a wobbly wooden cart—the type you see in mining caves during the gold rush days. But this one is moving. *Fast*. It's so small it only fits me inside, and I grip hard to its sides.

"Congratulations, moon rabbit! You are one of only three people that managed to successfully pass the Command round!" the (unnecessarily loud) voice announces from somewhere overhead, echoing slightly. It's talking slower than before, laboring each word. "You have now made it to the last and final round. The Commitment round!"

There is a deafening roar of thunder—so loud I have to cover my ears—and when I look up, there are countless sets of gigantic eyes attached to equally gigantic bodies looking down at me, screaming and cheering me on. Each person seems as tall as a skyscraper, and each head is so big that when one moves, it blocks the light from reaching me. If I didn't know any better, I'd say I'd either been shrunk, or they'd somehow been blown up. Either way, I am currently on a rail track built over a valley of jagged rocks, moving at hurtling speeds. And these giants are watching me, as if I'm some miniature Christmas train display at Macy's.

"The Commitment round is all about whether you have what it takes to be a great leader. Whether you can make the tough calls needed for the sake of the greater good. Do *you* have what it takes to lead people into a new era? Do *you* have the commitment required to make the hard decisions—the *right* decisions—when it really counts?"

The crowd roars again, making the world tremble. And I realize this right here is the million-dollar question. This is the final round to prove to myself that I *can* be a real leader. That I can win Mago's Fire fair and square so Dahl and I can unlock our true potential and lead the world into the new era—the Age of the Final Eclipse. And honestly, after the last two rounds, I am feeling quietly confident. I can do this. I have a real shot at winning this.

I grip on harder to the cart and clench my jaw.

I will not give up.

"The rules of this round are simple. And they will be illustrated via an initial lightning round. So listen closely. Up ahead, there is a fork in the track, fast approaching."

I strain my eyes to see, and indeed, it looks like the track splits in two.

"If you use the lever to turn left, you will hit and kill one person, kindly represented by a slime-filled dummy designed to look just like you."

"What lever?" I ask out loud just as a wooden stick appears

between my legs. It appears I can only move it one of two ways—left or right.

"What if I turn it right?" I call out nervously as the fork looms closer.

"If you use the lever to turn right, you will hit and kill five people, also kindly represented by slime-filled dummies designed to look just like you. You must choose a direction and move the lever before you reach the fork, or else both sets of dummies will be killed."

My heart starts to pump at triple speed. I know they're just slime-filled dummies, but they want me to choose who gets to live and who gets to die? Also, why have they been made to look like me? Way to take meta weirdness to a whole new level.

"But I don't want any of them to die?" I shout. My palms start to sweat as I grip the lever, making it sticky to the touch.

"These are the rules of the game," the voice concludes. "The fork will approach in ten seconds. Good luck!"

I sit there frozen as the sheer speed of the cart makes clumps of my sweat-drenched hair pelt me on the face. What do I do? What do I do? *What do I do?*

"Five seconds remaining," the voice calls out.

Up ahead, I can see more clearly now the one figure on the left track, and the five huddled together on the right diverging track. They are all clones of me, dressed in the same ripped jeans and T-shirt, singed with fire marks from the bulgae's flames. They're all wearing the same white mask that Sahm let me use, decorated with his two black feathers. All with the two pointy moon rabbit ears, jabbing into the sky.

I think fast.

If I don't do anything, all six of the figures will be de-slimed. If I go right, five of them will be demolished. And if I go left, one of them will be no more. The voice said the point of the round was about making the tough calls to benefit the greater good. The aim of the game is to preserve the most amount of lives.

Surely, I need to go left . . . ?!

The fork is imminent, and I tug the clammy lever to the left. The wheels underneath me screech as the cart veers left, but it doesn't slow down. If anything, we speed up as we hurtle toward the moon rabbit—toward *me*.

I close my eyes as the cart collides with the dummy with a great *pop!* and its skin bursts like an overfilled balloon. Cold, sticky liquid explodes everywhere, all over my hair and my skin. And when I look down at myself (the living, breathing, still-intact version), I am covered with bright crimson slime. *Urgh*. Did they have to make it so *red*?

"Well done!" the voice cries excitedly as the crowd cheers. "That was the correct decision. You can now proceed to the round proper!"

A giant hand, the size of a truck, reaches down and plucks the cart—with me still in it—off the tracks.

"Arghhh!" I scream as the cart wobbles all over the place. I dare not look down at the valley of rocks. Then the hand places me on a new set of tracks and pushes me forward and back, then forward and back, like a kid playing with a toy train.

"This is the final stage of the Commitment round. Much like the previous exercise, you will need to make a decision.

However, this time, the track is preprogrammed to veer right *unless* you turn left. There is also a pause button, which will allow you to stop the cart for ten seconds."

I look down to see a big red pedal appear between my feet.

"But you may only use this button once, after which the cart will resume its journey. Those are the rules." A pause. "Oh, and we may have employed proprietary divine magic to recruit some *special* personalities for this task. You will recognize them when you see them."

The cart is given a good, solid push. And just like that, I am off.

"Wheee!" the voice calls out gleefully. "Good luck!"

This time, I'm composed. I've done this before, and apart from the red slime still oozing down my head, which is seriously gross, I feel relatively calm. I know how this game works. They want me to ensure the smallest number of casualties as a result of my actions.

And it's funny, really. Because against all odds, I am starting to wonder if the goddesses aren't that different from us, after all. Sure, the people they want to protect aren't necessarily the same people I want to protect. And sure, they blatantly lie and spread false propaganda to achieve their ends, which isn't exactly the way I'd go about things . . . But they, too, seem to believe in the greater good. They also appear to believe that if there is a way to preserve the most amount of lives, that they *should*. Isn't that why my family, friends, and I are preparing for the army, too? To protect mortalkind from the chaos and danger that the goddesses want to bring upon us?

As the realization sets in, my cart gets closer to the fork in the track. The dummies are farther away this time, and I can't see clearly, but I'm pretty sure there are again, five figures at the end of the right track, and one lone figure at the end of the left. The voice explained that the track was already prepro- grammed to veer right, so I take the initiative to turn the lever now to the left. One versus five. It's an obvious choice, which was the correct choice earlier. I might as well lock it in now.

"You have selected left!" the booming voice cries over the roar of the crowd.

The fork looms mere seconds ahead, and that's when I finally get a closer look at the dummies.

My blood curdles.

Without a second thought, I pump my foot on the pause button. The cart screeches to a halt, literally inches from the fork.

I lean forward in the cart, straining my eyes, making sure I'm not imagining it.

On the right, there are five people—five *real* people— huddled together on a small wooden platform. And I recognize them. . . . It's the moon rabbit with the SNACKS ARE LIFE T-shirt from Tokki Pharmaceuticals, the tiger-tailed Lucha Libre man who told me about Moral Compasses, the two-tailed fox lady who got a hole in one from round one, and the two cheolli- mas from Charles's wedding that had the unfurling-fern GIFs on their back.

Their faces are bloated full of fear—that much is clear even from here. But they can't move or scream because they're tied up and gagged with rope, propped up like bowling pins wait- ing to be bowled over.

"No. Freaking. Way," I breathe, borrowing Hattie's term. I think of how the cart pulverized that dummy clone upon impact. The stakes are real. If I turn the lever back to the right, I will lose all five of them. The next time the cart reaches its destination, it won't be slime on my hands. It will be *blood*.

But if I don't turn the lever and continue going left, I will kill...

"*Nooo!*" I wail as I finally dare to look at who is stranded on the left.

The familiar uniform of black on black. Those newly broadened shoulders on that extra head of height. The strong arms plastered to the sides of his body bound tightly. The mouth trying to shout my name through the rope gagging it.

Memories of Emmett's burning body rush back to me as he hung from the crown of the Spiritrealm's Statue of Eternity, almost being expunged off Mago's Jokbo and from all existence. My heart wrenches. "I can't do this again! I can't! I won't!"

"Your time is running out," the voice calls out excitedly. "You have turned your lever to the left. Will you lock in your decision? Or will you change it? You have four seconds before the cart will resume its path."

Hiccups erupt from my throat, and tears spring to my eyes. *I can't. I can't. I can't.* I know the "right" decision they want me to take is to go left—to choose the loss of one life over five. To uphold the greater good. But Emmett is not just one life. He is my *best friend*. He is the boy who has been through hell and back for me. The boy who has grown and changed over the summer, and has started to make me feel things I didn't know I could feel.

"THREE!"

Trembling all over, I pull out my Moral Compass, my heart in my throat. I can't give up. I need to find a way to save him. There is no way I will let him die.

But the compass is still as it was in the previous round, showing me a simple mirror. I shake it and tilt it to make it do something—anything—but all I see is my own face reflected back at me. I'm as pale as makgeolli, my jaw clenched tight, with fear spelled as loud as day in my red-rimmed eyes. But there's also something else. Something vulnerable, open, and expectant. And I realize in that moment, in the most inopportune of moments, something I should have figured out months ago.

I like Emmett.

Not in a BFF kind of way. And not like a sibling, the way I care about Hattie or Dahl. But *like* like him. Like a boy. Like a boy I might want to hold hands with, and even maybe kiss. *That's* why I've been acting so weird around him. Because our relationship has changed, *we* have changed, and change is unsettling. Scary, even.

As the new emotion settles into my chest like a warm hug, the answer screams at me like a banshee. I will not risk Emmett's life. And if I want to save him, I need to stop this cart. I need to take it off the tracks entirely.

Without a second thought, I throw my entire body into the right wall of the cart. This thing is so wobbly already, surely it won't take much for it to topple. Sure enough, the impact of my body hitting the wall shakes the wooden car, making its wheels shake dangerously on its tracks.

"TWO!" the voice yells.

Triumphant, I repeat the action again. The cart keels a little more aggressively to the right. One more push and I think I can get it off the tracks. I throw my body again, and the two left wheels lift up, the entire cart leaning to the right, giving me a good look at the sharp boulders I'd be falling into.

"ONE! And you're off!"

The cart screeches back into action and immediately forks off into the left set of tracks. The movement throws the cart back down onto the tracks, thwarting my plans to derail it completely.

"NO!" I cry.

"*Caw-caw!*"

"Areum?" I gasp, her name getting caught in my throat. "Areum, is that you?"

As the cart picks up momentum toward Emmett, I shoot my hands up in the air and scream at the top of my lungs, "AREUM, PICK ME UP. NOW!"

My loyal inmyeonjo squawks loudly before shooting down to hook me up out of the cart by the shoulders.

"Toward Emmett!" I cry.

She flaps her powerful wings with everything she has, and we fly toward my best friend. But still the cart hurtles at equally dizzying speeds. We fly to the right of it, neck and neck like two race cars battling to the finish line. But there is a downward incline in the track, and the cart picks up momentum faster than Areum can fly. As we near the small rickety platform, I realize with certainty that we aren't going to win this race. The cart is going to hit Emmett.

It's going to *kill* my Emmett.

Before I know what I'm doing, I jerk my body to the left, hard. Areum squawks in alarm above me but doesn't let me go. Instead, like a parachute, she has no choice but to follow my lead, and her entire body keels to the left.

That's when I do it. I clench my core, lift my legs, and kick the side of the wooden cart as hard as I can.

CRACK!

Somehow, the mix of the cart's forward momentum and the adrenaline behind my well-timed kick is enough to topple the cart to its left. It flings off the tracks in a dramatic fashion and flies into the jagged boulders below, splintering into smithereens.

Areum reroutes us toward Emmett, and I try to wrap my arms and legs around his body to pick him up off the platform. But pain shoots up my left leg, making me scream out in pain. The wooden cart is not what I heard cracking before.

Wincing through the pain, I wrap my good leg and my two arms around Emmett, fastening myself to him like a magnet. He's still tied up, unable to move his arms, but I pull down on his gag, and his broken voice calling out my name says it all.

"Rye," he whispers hoarsely. *"Riley."*

"I've got him! Lift us up!" I shout as Areum pumps her wings.

My inmyeonjo propels us into the sky, and I bury my head into Emmett's neck.

"I'll protect you, Em," I cry into his ear. "No matter what, I will protect you."

19.
Prize-Giving Ceremonies
Can Be So Dramatic

"YOU DID IT, MOON RABBIT!" the adjudicator's voice cries triumphantly as my feet touch the ground. I yelp as my left foot makes contact with the hard surface, and pain ripples up my leg. *Ouch.* Definitely broken.

Somehow, in the time it took for Areum to pick us up and put us back down, the scenery has changed again. We are no longer in the weird miniature-train-set world, surrounded by giants looking down at us. We're back at Hungry Holes Mini Golf, standing on a platform of sorts. It's the size of a real stage, not dissimilar to the one at the Galaxy Convention Center where Dahl was giving his impassioned speech, except that it seems to be floating in the air, hovering high above the golf course.

I turn to Emmett and Areum, to check they're both okay. But they're gone. It's only when I hear people calling my name that I hobble (very painfully) over to one side of the floating platform and look over the edge. In the middle of a huge crowd below, my inmyeonjo and best friend wave anxiously from near the counter where I grabbed my golf club and ball. They're far away enough that I can't read their expressions, but I can *feel* their worry radiating from them. I give them a thumbs-up, just to let them know I'm okay. To my relief, Emmett seems to have been unbound, and neither of them look injured. Phew.

Confident they're safe, I turn my attention to the other people on the stage. The goddesses' chariot is parked on the platform, using it like a helipad, its wings tucked into its sides. Three of the goddesses are still sitting inside, watching me expectantly. But the Three-Legged Crow Goddess is standing in the center of the stage next to a pedestal covered by a gold dome.

I can't see what's housed inside the dome, but Sahm's left feather on my mask tugs strongly in that direction, while the right feather is pulling in the vicinity of the Nine-Tailed Fox Goddess. The fidget spinner and key of all keys must be here.

The Three-Legged Crow Goddess approaches me, clapping her hands together. "Loyal divine citizen, our most fervent congratulations! The closest other competitor killed one life to save the five, following the guidelines afforded to them. But your solution to the problem was unconventional—you utilized outside-the-box thinking to save *all* the lives."

The goddess's third leg scratches the floor of the stage, and a shiver runs up my spine. I am not enjoying being this close to a goddess in the slightest. Taggy tickles my earlobe ever so gently as if to give me strength, but for some reason, they seem a little more sluggish than usual.

"While some may see your action as having provided you an unfair advantage," the goddess continues, "it is our shared opinion that strategy is a key skill for head of the realm, and you have proven today that you possess this important ability. So, well done, moon rabbit," the goddess announces, oblivious (or just downright unconcerned) to my pain. "These are the reasons we have deemed you the winner of the tournament. Should you choose to accept, it would bring us great honor to knight you as the inaugural prime minister of the MegaRealm. Congratulations!"

The goddess's voice is clearly being broadcast to the crowd below, because there is a thunderous roar of applause that rises up from the ground to meet us. *"Moon Rabbit, Moon Rabbit, Moon Rabbit,"* the crowd cheers.

My leg is throbbing, and I adjust my standing posture, only for more pain to shoot up my leg. Impatiently, I glance toward the pedestal, where my left feather is still tugging persistently. "Will I be knighted now?" I ask, putting on a fake high-pitched voice.

The Three-Legged Crow Goddess cackles as if I just cracked a hilarious joke. "And she has a sense of humor, too!" She wipes a tear from her beady bird eyes with the tip of her wing. "Of course we won't be holding the knighting ceremony here at a *mini golf*!" Hearty laughter bubbles up from the crowds. "For that we'll move to a much more sacred location and hold a private ceremony. There, we will bless you with the Key to the Final Eclipse, and kick-start the birth of the MegaRealm with a big *bang*!"

I gulp, realizing that this means as soon as I am knighted,

the goddesses are expecting me to destroy the world as we know it.

The goddess takes a step closer to me. "Now, before we conclude the tournament, moon rabbit, please take off your mask and tell us your name. Let the realm know who you are so we can celebrate your success."

I freeze. As soon as they see my face or hear my name, it's over. I realize we never figured out what would happen *after* I won the tournament. Panicked, my mind races to come up with a plan.

Just then, the goddess points to my head. "What the—"

Instinctively, my hand shoots up, only for my fingers to close on nothing but air. *Oh no.* The gummy must finally have worn off. My moon rabbit ears have gone.

"I can explain—" I start.

"Who *are* you?" the goddess demands, her three talons digging into the stage floor, making a horrible screechy sound. The other three goddesses rise from their seats on the chariot, as the Three-Legged Crow rips the mask off my face, throwing it off the stage, along with Sahm's two feathers.

"*Gold-destroyer,*" she seethes, taking me in.

She swipes at me with her muscular wing, and I'm swept right off my feet. I fall with a loud *thwack* on the stage floor, but gritting through the pain, I try desperately to crawl toward the pedestal.

"Catch her!" the Mountain Tiger Goddess roars from the parked chariot.

The Three-Legged Crow Goddess is hot on my tail and takes another swipe at me—this time with her third talon, as sharp as a knife, just as the Moon Rabbit Goddess removes the dome and snatches the fidget spinner from its stand.

"*No!*" I cry from the ground, my leg radiating pain in all directions.

"Glamour the stage from the divine citizens," the Mountain Tiger Goddess commands the Nine-Tailed Fox. "Quickly!"

As the Fox Goddess obeys, the Crow Goddess plucks me off the floor by the back of my T-shirt, and she sneers into my ear, her expression changing. "How thoughtful of you to drop by. We were just on our way to collect you."

I scream and fight as she carries me toward the chariot, whose wings have fluttered to life. "Let me go! Let me *go!*"

But the goddess just laughs, as if everything is going to plan. "But you're a special guest to our private ceremony, *Prime Minister*," she jeers.

"The kid said to *let her go!*" a familiar voice shouts from overhead.

I look up in time to see Dahl riding a large bonghwang, flying straight at us. It looks nothing like the fake dull brown phoenixes back at the hotel canals. It's breathtakingly beautiful with a long tail of iridescent multicolored ribbons streaming behind it.

"Argh!" the Crow Goddess shrieks as Dahl and the phoenix bulldoze into her and I fall through her grasp. Their flying momentum pushes her right to the other side of the floating stage until she careens off the edge and down into the crowd of divine citizens.

"Dahl!" I shout, unbelievably relieved to see my soul brother. "You're on a bonghwang!"

He grins as the divine bird does an impossibly elegant figure eight in the air with him on board. "Ticked another thing
off my bucket list, kid. This is Eugene—a new friend I met at
Persimmon!"

"This is Eubin!" Taeyo announces as he zooms past on his
very own bonghwang.

"And this is Eurim!" Noah yells from the back of his stunning ribbon-tailed phoenix, with a blue dragon scooter strapped
to his back. Boris must've been left behind at Persimmon when
Emmett got magicked into my tournament.

"They're brothers from the software-development team,"
Hattie explains as she and Namjoon arrive onstage on the
back of Sahm of the Sisterhood. "Triplets, actually."

The winged chariot is flapping harder now, hovering over
the floating stage, with the Mountain Tiger, Nine-Tailed Fox,
and Moon Rabbit Goddesses sitting inside, preparing to fly
away. With the key of all keys and fidget spinner both on
board, getting to their "private ceremony" seems a higher pri-
ority to them.

As if knowing we need backup, Emmett flies up from the
ground on Areum to join Dahl, Taeyo, and Noah in encircling
the goddesses' chariot.

In the meantime, Sahm and Namjoon stand guard around
me as Hattie rubs her wrists and chants a familiar bone-setting
spell on my leg. Golden light streams from her hands and seeps
down through my skin and into my bone. It's comforting to
know that despite the Horangi biochips being defunct in the
Godrealm, Saint Heo Jun is still out down in the Spiritrealm,
powering the clan of Gom healers.

Noah throws Boris to Emmett, who catches his beloved dragon scooter with care. "Missed ya, buddy," Emmett says, hugging him tight.

"The Fox has the key of all keys!" I call out to our friends as I recover, panting, from the floor of the stage. "And the Rabbit has the fidget spinner!"

"Got it, kid!" Dahl responds as he directs the bonghwang triplets and my inmyeonjo to keep pressure on the trapped gourd chariot.

"You guys keep circling them," Noah says, breaking away from the formation and driving Eurim toward the Nine-Tailed Fox Goddess. "I'll go for the Key."

"And I'll go for the fidget spinner," Hattie shouts, jumping on Sahm's back and heading for the Moon Rabbit Goddess.

Catching on to what's happening, the Nine-Tailed Fox Goddess puts a glamour on the key of all keys in her hand, making it vanish from sight. And the Mountain Tiger Goddess uses her divine powers to create a protective orb over the gourd so no one can penetrate its layer. But before the orb is sealed, Hattie manages to swoop over the Moon Rabbit's head, and Sahm's sharp third talon pierces the goddess's left ear.

"Argh!" she cries as she reaches for her wound.

The fidget spinner drops from her hands and clatters down onto the hard floor of the floating stage.

"I've got it!" I yell, belly-gliding over to snatch the small sensory toy from the ground. "I've got Mago's Fire!"

"And I've got *him*!" the Three-Legged Crow Goddess screeches.

She must've recovered from her fall off the edge of the

stage, because the Crow Goddess has now returned, flapping her ominous black wings, with Dahl hanging precariously from her talons.

"One more move, and I'll drop him!" she shrieks.

"You wouldn't dare," Hattie challenges from next to me.

"You test me, mortal?" the Crow Goddess sneers, releasing her grip from Dahl's arms.

My soul twin's head and shoulders flop down like a rag doll with the talon's release, making him hang like a pendulum by the legs from the goddess's two other claws.

"Argh!" Dahl cries, his moon-colored hair flapping from side to side. "This is most definitely *not* on my bucket list!"

Fear grips me all over like a rash. "Fine, *fine!*" I yell at the goddess, still gripping the fidget spinner tightly in my hand. "You . . . You can have the Fire." I extend my open palm up to her. "But please. *Please*, let Dahl go."

Without hesitation, the Crow Goddess flaps her wings toward me and seizes Mago's Fire from my trembling hand. "Now there's a good little star." She smirks.

She swings Dahl toward me, and I reach my arms out to soften his fall. But at the last minute, the goddess does a talon switcheroo, using her far-right claw to hold Dahl's weight, her middle to carry the fidget spinner and her left to grab *me*.

"No!" I scream as I'm whisked up into the air. "You said you'd let him go!"

The goddess cackles. "And you trusted me? Oh, naive child, you have much to learn."

I thrash and kick while Hattie commands Namjoon to bite the goddess, but the Crow's wings are strong. She spreads her wings wide to take us even higher, when suddenly a gust of wind blows in from beside us and a floating door materializes in the air.

"I've got you!" a regal man dressed in a red-and-yellow silk hanbok cries triumphantly as he leaps through the door portal with his arms outstretched.

"Mayor Yeomra?" I yelp. "Is that you?"

He manages to grab Dahl briefly, but he's overshot the mark, and my brother slips through his grasp. He does, however, take hold of my legs and grips on for dear life. Screeching, the Crow Goddess propels higher into the air with her precious cargo in her talons. But with the added weight of the mayor now attached to my legs, I slip through the goddess's grip and drop with a heavy *thud* onto the stage, the mayor falling beside me.

"They've got Dahl!" I cry as my brother is flown away. His phone falls from his pocket onto the ground, and the screen cracks.

For a moment, the goddess looks back at me with her beady eyes, and I think she's going to return for me again. But the Mountain Tiger Goddess calls out from the orb-protected chariot.

"Leave her! We have what we need. Let's go!"

My friends on their winged companions try to chase the chariot, but the Tiger Goddess creates an ball of energy in her hands and releases it swiftly toward us. An invisible force explodes and throws us back, leaving us winded and gasping for air.

By the time we recover and look up, the chariot is nowhere

to be seen. And Mago's Fire, the key of all keys, and my soul twin have disappeared with them.

"*No,*" I cry again, searching the endless ceiling of the mini golf venue with frustration. "Where did they go?!"

"She said it was a sacred location, didn't they?" Emmett says, recalling the Crow Goddess's comment from earlier. He frowns. "Somewhere they can hold the private ceremony to birth the MegaRealm with a big bang, she said."

"But why would they take Dahl?" Hattie asks. "What does he have to do with anything?"

The mayor shakes his head, picking up Dahl's phone and passing it to me. The cracked screen is frozen on a partial screenshot of his bucket list. "I don't know, and I'm sorry, Riley. I tried, but I wasn't able to save both of you."

He looks devastated, and I shake my head. "No, it's okay. If it wasn't for you, they'd have taken me, too."

I glance back up at the air where the door portal had appeared out of thin air. "How did you do that anyway?"

"When I found one of the torn gateways from the Spiritrealm to the Godrealm, I went straight to Persimmon's offices to offer my assistance. And while I was there, the heavenborn gave this back to me." He takes out the mun-pen he'd gifted Dahl out from his pocket and sighs. "The boy said he didn't want it anymore after what it'd done to the fabric between the realms. Who knew it had such terrible power." His face lightens a little. "On the bright side, it appears when you use it here, it creates shortcuts within the Godrealm just like it does in the Spiritrealm. It brought me straight to you!"

"Well, it's nice to have you with us, Mayor," I say. "Because right now, we need all the help we can get."

I turn to my friends, who have all gathered on the stage. "We need to figure out where this so-called 'private ceremony' is going to be held so we can save Dahl and stop the goddesses from using the Key to destroy the world."

As everyone starts throwing out ideas, I quickly check my ear to see if Taggy is still alive. With great relief, I find that somehow, my little wakerpillar has made it unscathed through the whole fiasco. In fact, they seem to have made themself a cocoon and are hanging from my right earlobe like a dangly earring.

I turn to join the brainstorming session, when a hand pulls me by my forearm.

Emmett.

"Hey," he says, leading me as far away from our friends as possible. "Can I talk to you for a second?" He sounds kind of pissed.

"Um, hey," I echo.

He is frowning up a *storm*, and as I look up into his face, that wave of emotion washes over me again. The same ones that made me want to tip the hurtling cart over. The ones that made me realize that the feelings I have for Emmett Harrison have grown into something altogether new and scary, yet familiar and comforting.

"What the literal hells, Rye! You almost killed yourself trying to save me before."

It's a statement, not a question, and I'm not sure how to respond.

"Okay . . . ?"

"Not okay!" His newer, deeper voice rises, and the crease between his brows furrows even deeper. "It's *not* okay, Rye. Do you hear me? If it wasn't for Areum and Hattie, you might not be walking anymore. You might not even be *alive*. Never again will you *ever* put yourself in danger because of me. Do you understand?"

When I don't respond, he exhales deeply. "Swear it, Riley Oh. Right now. Promise that you'll never do anything so shamelessly stupid again for me. Say it."

I bite my lip. "I'm sorry, but I don't think I can promise that."

He puts his hands on his hips. He looks severely annoyed. "And why the hells not?"

Oh gods.

The gazillion-dollar question.

"Because I . . . I . . . Well, the truth is, Em, I . . ."

My face goes hot. You'd think this would be the least appropriate time to make such a confession—because, oh, you know, your soul twin has been kidnapped and you're on a floating stage at a divine mini golf with your friends trying to fight against time and a bunch of evil goddesses to stop the world from imploding. . . .

But also, that's *exactly* why I need to say it. Because after seeing him almost get pummeled into dust, I don't want to risk not letting him know how I feel before it's too late. What if this is it, and I don't ever get the chance again?

"The thing is," I mumble, fighting to spit the words out, "I . . . Well, look, it's because well, I, I li— Em, I lik—"

I take a big breath and basically scream so I don't chicken out. "BECAUSE EMMETT HARRISON, I LIKE Y—"

Emmett's lips cover my mouth before I can say the last word.

You.

His lips are soft, so unbelievably soft. All tender and fleeting like a gentle feather skimming my skin. Almost like cotton candy—its lingering sweetness making my lips tingle. For a moment, I think I imagined it. Surely, we didn't just . . .

But when I look into his dark honeyed eyes and see the vulnerability spelled out in loud, glistening sparkles inside his irises, I know it happened.

EMMETT HARRISON KISSED ME.

"*Holy shirtballs,*" I whisper.

"*Holy shirtballs,*" he whispers at the same time.

Wolf whistles fly in from our friends, but we don't even care.

"So yeah," Emmett murmurs, cupping the back of his neck. "I know—"

I hiccup.

"What you were gonna say."

I hiccup once more.

"Because I do, too."

I look down at my toes. If I look into his face, his eyes might burn a hole right through to my spleen.

"Like you, I mean."

A pause.

"A *lot.*"

I continue to stare at my feet, as if the off-white laces are the most exciting things I've ever seen in my life. When really, I want to be jumping up and down screaming *Emmett Harrison likes me, too!* at the top of my lungs.

"Cool," I say coolly.

"Cool," he repeats.

"Cool," I say again, because that's the extent of my vocabulary right now.

His frown finally melts into a grin. He grabs my hand and turns it palm-side up.

"Here. This is for you."

He places a red bracelet on my open hand. It looks like it was made with the seaweed from the Tree of Fate that Emmett and I got covered in when we fell into the Trevi Fountain. Except the stringy strands have been braided together to form a strong, tidy red band.

"What is it?" I ask.

"A friendship bracelet." He pauses, then says shyly. "Or maybe a more-than-friendship bracelet."

I pretend my face isn't about to burn right off. "Can you put it on for me?" I manage.

He wraps the strip around my wrist and then ties the ends together. "The Tree of Fate binds people's destinies together, right?"

I nod.

"Well, this is me telling you that, no matter what, I will always be at your side."

I don't tell him that he and I actually need to be tied *together* for that to work. Because that would probably ruin the moment. But the sentiment has been received, loud and clear. Emmett and I have always been there for each other. But we've just unlocked a whole new level in the game of relation-ships today, and it feels so . . . *right.*

He interlinks his fingers with mine, and as we walk hand in hand toward our friends, who are in a heated discussion about where we need to go, I realize that the war isn't over. Because it hasn't even *started.*

Together, with old friends and new, we *will* find Dahl, and we *will* stop the goddesses from destroying the world. Because as soon as that fidget spinner is in our hands, Dahl and I will activate our true potential, and we *will* reign victorious.

I squeeze Emmett's hand. And it will all be possible. Because we have each other.

20.
Car? Tick! Fuel? Tick! But Do You Have Your License?

 THE DISCUSSION ABOUT WHERE we need to go to find Dahl rages strong. The bonghwang triplets and Sahm—as our resident Godrealm experts— are spouting out potential locations the goddesses might deem sacred enough to hold their private (read: world-destroying) ceremony, while Hattie, Areum, Emmett, and Mayor Yeomra try to rank them in order of likelihood.

Taeyo is busy on his laptop trying to see if his reverse-engineered mortal GPS tracker could work for a heavenborn like Dahl (so far, no luck). And Noah is busy on his phone responding to Phoebe and the RilOh Fan Club's text updates from the Mortalrealm. Turns out the saram population of Vegas is getting increasingly perturbed about why the production company hasn't turned "the sun back on," and things are starting to get rather tense on the ground.

I, on the other hand, am doing none of the helpful things my friends are busy with. I am sitting in one corner of the floating stage above Hungry Holes Mini Golf, staring nervously at Dahl's bucket list, peeking through his cracked phone screen. The Three-Legged Crow Goddess had ominously said I was a "special guest" to their private ceremony. And then when she'd caught Dahl, the Mountain Tiger Goddess had told her sister to not bother with me, since they had what they needed. So what *is* it that they need us for?

I try to scroll up and down on Dahl's screen and, when that doesn't work, try to do a hard reset on it. I don't know why I'm trying to fix his phone when I should be brainstorming with my friends, but it's like I'm stuck in a loop and I can't move on until the phone's functional again. The side buttons won't even work though (ugh, typical), which means even a hard reset is off the cards. And as my tears of frustration build, I take out my Moral Compass. Maybe that will tell me how to fix this darn piece of technology.

As fate would have it, though, the only thing the compass does is point its slender gold arm at the very phone I'm losing my mind over.

"*Arghhh!*" I yell, throwing the phone on the ground. Unsurprisingly, more of the screen splinters, which makes me feel even more defeated. "We're running out of time! Where in the broken realms are we supposed to *go*?!"

Honestly, I'm not sure, kid, but it sure reminds me of Appa's chewing gum.

I freeze. "Did you guys hear that?" I ask out loud.

My friends stop their tasks to glance over at me.

"Hear what?" Emmett asks, looking concerned.

I bite my lip and shake my head. "Nothing," I murmur. I must be losing my mind, imagining that Dahl is here, talking to me.

They've covered my eyes so I can't see. But I'm telling you—it's like the air is full of that Acacia chewing gum that Appa loves. You know the one I mean, kid? The one that smells like flowers?

I leap up to my feet and yelp. "It's Dahl!" I exclaim, sure of it this time. "I can hear him. It's *him*!"

My friends come and crowd around me.

"Maybe it's the telepathic link you guys had that one time," Hattie asks hopefully. "Maybe it's come back!"

I hold my hand up to silence her, worried Dahl's voice will disappear.

Is that you, Dahl? I ask in my head. *Is that really you?*

Yeah, it's me, kid, Dahl's voice responds promptly, as clear as day. *You have no idea how happy I am to hear your voice in my head. Bada bing, bada boom! Soul twins for the win!*

I swallow the lump in my throat. *Are you . . . are you okay? Have they hurt you? Also, where are you? We're coming to get you!*

Honestly, kid, I'm fine! You know me—act it until you exact it! We're outdoors somewhere, and we've been walking uphill for a while. I tried to get them talking in case they reveal anything, you know? But all they said is that they need my help, and I haven't figured out why they need m—

He abruptly stops, as if he's just figured something out.

Dahl? I demand. *You still there?*

A pause.

You know what, kid? I don't think it's a good idea you come here. There's a weird tone in his voice, as if he knows something I don't. As if he's hiding something from me. *Definitely don't come here, you hear me? Swear it on my pomade. STAY AWAY.*

"What are you talking about?!" I demand out loud, too disturbed to only say it in my head. "Why would we not come to rescue you?"

My friends eyes widen, as they crowd closer, trying to piece together the conversation I'm having with my soul twin.

In fact, I don't think we're outdoors at all. I think we're in some kind of, uh, mall. Yeah, that's right. A mall. Or maybe it's a casino. Yeah, a casino! Anyway, talk to you soon, okay, kid? Later!

And just like that, the link ends, as if he just hung up on me. Rudely.

"Why doesn't he want us to find him?" Yeomra asks in concern.

"What have the goddesses done to our brother?" Hattie asks as she clutches Namjoon, anger flaring in her eyes.

"Maybe the moon rabbits at Tokki Pharmaceuticals finally perfected the formula," Taeyo says ominously.

Noah nods. "Maybe he's been gummy brainwashed."

I shake my head, determined. "It doesn't matter what he said. We're going to find him." I turn to Sahm and the bonghwang triplets. "What sacred location is outside, hilly, and smells like Acacia chewing gum?"

Sahm shakes his little wing stub excitedly. "Hey, isn't there that famous forest of acacia trees near the summit of Mount Baekdu?"

"There is!" Eugene responds, his ribboned tail swimming elegantly behind him in unison with that of his brothers.

"And it's flowering season," Eubin adds.

"Mount Baekdu?" Hattie repeats. "As in where Mago's Fire used to be kept before the Water Dragon Goddess stole it?"

Eurim nods. "Right at the peak—where the Tree of Life sits."

"The Tree of Life!" Emmett says. "That's the red seaweed forest Riley and I got tangled in when we fell into the fountain."

Mayor Yeomra shakes his head. "The red seaweed was from the Tree of *Fate*, which grows in my realm down under. The Tree of Life belongs in the Godrealm."

"It's what Mago's Jokbo is made out of," Hattie says quietly, as if remembering our recent journey to the Spiritrealm. I gulp.

Down in the afterlife, we learned that expungement was the process of being erased from the genealogy book for all humanity, which was made from the Tree of Life. Mago Halmi had used her own blood and sweat to inscribe the names of every soul she brought into the world on it.

"*That's* where we need to go," I conclude. "If that's where Mago Halmi gave birth to life itself, I bet the goddesses will deem it the most sacred place to give birth to their new realm."

"Are you sure?" the mayor asks. "If they're already there, we don't have much time. This will be our one chance to stop them."

The star compass is still open in my hand, and its golden arm is still pointing to Dahl's phone, which I threw away in my frustration. I go to pick it up, which, no thanks to me, is now well and truly shattered. But through the splinters and cracks, Dahl's bucket list is still frozen on the screen. And right there, in between the broken shards, I see it.

Bucket list #27: Visit the Sky Beam shooting out of pyramid at Luxor Hotel (*they say you can even see the sky beam from space?!*)

I remember walking down the Strip with Dahl, noticing how the Luxor pyramid would morph into a majestic mountain before returning back to its original Mortalrealm form.

The Acacia gum scent. The Tree of Life. The bucket list. This is no coincidence.

"I'm sure," I announce, as certain as can be. "Strap yourselves in, team. Looks like we're finally going to war. And it's going to happen at the place it—no, the place *we*—all began."

I task Sahm and Eugene to drop by Tokki Pharmaceuticals to make sure David, Jennie, and Cosette are okay. Now that the tournament is over, the scientists may be returning to work, and the last thing we want is for Eureka or any of the other moon rabbits to find our friends experimenting in their labs.

As we fly over the main drag of Vegas, it's evident the flickering between realms has finally settled. The replica of the Statue of Liberty has now solidified permanently into the Spiritrealm's version of Lady Eternity, complete with her hanbok and chalice in hand. The fake volcano in front of the Mirage hotel now seems to be a fully functioning, fully *real* volcano, bubbling lava out of its mouth. The sky is still dark and devoid of light—no sun or moon or stars in sight—but using the neon lights of the city, it's easy to see the winged creatures of varying shapes and sizes occupying the vast stretch of sky. No wonder the saram are starting to freak out. Even they can feel the chaos of the three realms merging together.

As we near Luxor Hotel, it's clear the pyramid has disappeared and has now been replaced by an impossibly lush, much larger, and almost-reverent mountain. *Mount Baekdu.*

"This is as far as we can fly without being seen by the goddesses," Areum announces as she lowers me and Emmett down onto the side of the mountain. The grass that is *so* viridescent that every shade of green I've witnessed before this moment was just a fake knockoff. "We'll have to walk from here."

On land, we take a look around to reorient ourselves. It's like all the colors and textures here are in ultra-uber-extra-HD. The vibrancy of the patch of hibiscus flowers to our right is so intense, I almost shield my eyes. Nature here is so real that it's unreal.

Eugene nods his head up the incline, where a gravel path leads. "That's the way to the summit, where the Tree of Life is."

To war.

"Are we ready?" I ask quietly.

For a moment, we all stand there, staring at the path, unmoving. We are deadly silent.

"Wanna ride Boris?" Emmett eventually offers, pushing his scaly blue scooter toward me. "It might be quite a walk up, and your leg was broken only a little while ago."

I shake my head and tap my left thigh. "It's all good. Hattie fixed me up."

Emmett nods and goes to grab Boris again, but Namjoon beats him to it. He sniffs curiously at Boris's tail and then, as if approving of his status, gives the scooter a friendly wet lick over his ear. I guess they're kind of related now.

Hattie smiles and gives Boris a tickle on his other ear. "Welcome to the extended yong fambam, Boris. Maybe I'll introduce you to the rest of my imugi posse one day?"

Boris wags his tail excitedly.

Hattie's stalling. We all are. No one wants to start making our way up to our likely doom.

Mayor Yeomra clears his throat, looking decidedly nervous. "Not to be the one to say it, but are we sure we want to do this? Sometimes, a war avoided is a war won. There's no shame in turning away."

Hattie and Emmett look to me for direction, and I bite my lip. I'm the last one to willingly walk into a fight. But we don't have a choice. If we don't act now, what will happen to Dahl? To our parents and the rest of the adult wax army? To kids who'll be brainwashed by gummies? Mortalkind will lose our free will. And who knows what they'll do to the Spiritrealm. . . .

I clench my fists. "We can't let everyone down. We owe it to everyone—to ourselves—to at least *try*."

There's a moment of pause before everyone starts nodding.

"We've got this," Hattie says with her unwavering optimism.

"You know I'm with you," Emmett says with his undying loyalty.

Seeing my friends bursting with courage, something comes over me. Perhaps winning the tournament has filled me with false confidence. Maybe I'm finally learning to overcome imposter syndrome. Or perhaps it's Dreamer Dahl's influence rubbing off on me. But my soul twin's motto, *Act it until you exact it*, suddenly rings true in my mind.

I am feeling the furthest from a hero than I've ever felt before. But I find myself opening my mouth to tell a white lie. Not because it's true, but because I know it will make them feel better. And right now, that is all I can do to help them.

"As soon as I have the fidget spinner in my hand, I know what to do," I assure them as steadily as I can muster. "Just keep out of harm's way until then, and I'll make sure you're okay." I turn to look at them each, one by one. "I'll make sure you're *all* okay."

Taeyo's eyes widen as he adjusts his bow tie. "Wait, have you figured out how Mago's Fire will awaken your true potential?"

Noah grins, patting his bonghwang companion. "It was on the flight over here, wasn't it? I'm telling you, the best thinking is done in the air. I'm convinced of it."

I push down the voice in my throat trying to scream, *I'm lying, I'm lying!* And instead, I nod firmly. "Yep, I've figured it out. I know exactly what I need to do."

We divvy up who will go after which goddess, and our friends high-five one another, their entire postures changing. They stand taller. Their heads held higher. And with conviction in their step, they start walking up the gravel path.

"Let's get this party on the road, then," Hattie says, almost excitedly.

Is a small part of me guilty for lying?

Yes.

Am I glad I can give them a little bit of comfort for the uncertain times to come?

Also yes.

The mayor puts his hand on my shoulders before I can follow them up the path. "Thank you," he says quietly. "And I'm sorry."

"For what?" I ask.

"For being a useless ally. You'd think the ex-king of the land of the dead may have some more tricks up his sleeve, eh?"

"You're helping us save the world," I say honestly. "What more could we ask for?"

He nods humbly.

We make our way up the gravel path toward the summit. We walk for what feels like eons, but eventually, we reach the forest of acacia trees, the scent reminding me of snuggling with Appa as he chewed on his fragrant gum. We walk farther, up and up, until finally, in the distance, we see the tree.

It's a gigantic Korean red pine. It's so big, its strong trunk soars into the skies as if it's reaching for the stars. Puffs of green pine needles are gathered at the ends of the branches, looking like tufts of cotton candy. And the tree stretches and creaks every few seconds, as if it's breathing. As if it's *alive.*

"The Tree of Life," Hattie whispers as we hide behind some thick shrubs at the base of the summit. There's another patch of too-vibrant hibiscus flowers next to us.

"And the goddesses," Yeomra says nervously, pointing at the four formidable deities under the canopy of the tree.

"And Dahl," I whisper, seeing my soul twin tied and bound to a chair beside the goddesses. He doesn't seem to be injured, and luckily, his blindfold has been removed. But his head hangs low, his overpomaded hair is sticking out at all angles, looking like he's been struck by lightning. There's even a big tear in his black leather jacket, which would make popping his collar impossible. For some reason, that makes a lump form in my throat.

We're pretty far away, but the wind seems to be on our side, because we catch snippets of the goddesses' conversation flowing over on the breeze.

"All things need to die to be reborn again, Moon Rabbit sister," the Mountain Tiger Goddess says. "Do not forget that. It is the circle of life and reincarnation. Things die, they live, they die again, they live again."

The Three-Legged Crow Goddess nods. *"Indeed. Like the winter before the spring. There are seasons of death and revival, and it is a virtuous cycle, because one cannot exist without the other."*

The Nine-Tailed Fox Goddess pats the Moon Rabbit Goddess on her shoulder, as if to assure her. *"So do not preoccupy yourself with the lives of the few, sister. There are bigger things to worry about. Bigger than us, even."*

The whole conversation makes a shiver run up my spine. Because it's eerily familiar. As if I've heard it somewhere before . . .

"Who's there?!" the Moon Rabbit Goddess squeals as Namjoon lets out an unhelpfully loud burp from behind the shrubs.

All four goddesses' heads snap in our direction.

"Oh no," I breathe. "They've seen us."

Dahl's eyes widen as he sees us manifesting from behind

the shrubs. He starts struggling against his restraints, his eyes wild. "I told you not to come!" he yells, looking like he's about to pop a vein. "Turn around and leave! The lot of you. Please! I've got everything sorted here!"

"Like hells you do!" I shout back.

I've never seen Dahl look so unhinged, and unease brews painfully in my gut. I try speaking to him in my mind voice, but it's like he's turned off his telepathic phone. Why is he trying to push us away when he needs us the most?

"Take your positions," I call out to my friends, not taking my eyes off Dahl. "It's time."

Areum, Taeyo, and Eubin start creeping toward the Mountain Tiger Goddess as Hattie and Namjoon start making their way toward the Nine-Tailed Fox Goddess. Emmett jumps on Boris and slowly approaches the Moon Rabbit Goddess with Noah and Eurim, while the mayor inches toward Dahl to release him from the chair.

You'd think by this point the goddesses would spring to action or attack . . . or *something*. But they just stand there and watch us with curiosity, as if they're at the zoo, waiting for the monkeys to finally do something interesting. The Moon Rabbit seems to be the only one even remotely jumpy at our arrival.

I glance over at the mayor, who's struggling to release Dahl's restraints, and I fill my chest with as much courage as I can muster.

"We're here for Dahl and the Key," I announce, steeling my voice so the trembles don't leak through. "And we're not leaving without them."

Looking between the four goddesses, I wish I still had Sahm's feathers with me. It's not immediately obvious who has the fidget spinner or our Key.

"I'm afraid you can't have the Key," the Nine-Tailed Fox Goddess states matter-of-factly, not batting an eyelid at Hattie, Namjoon, or the mayor, who have now encircled her. "I stole that fair and square from our sister." She preens the foxy red fur on her stomach, as if remembering the Key that I thought I'd driven into her gut. "I deserve an Oscar for my performance, really."

"However, if it is your wish, you may have the last fallen moon," the Mountain Tiger Goddess offers, surrounded by Taeyo, Eubin, and Areum. "But only for a price."

"Don't listen to them, kid!" Dahl begs as the mayor manages to loosen the rope around one of his arms. "Please!"

"I'm listening," I say instead, not taking my eyes off the Mountain Tiger.

She smiles, and it's a seething, squirming thing. "Are you familiar with cars?"

I splutter, confused at the sudden change of subject. "Excuse me?"

"She's probably too young to drive," the Moon Rabbit Goddess reminds her sister, looking a bit unsure about this entire reunion.

The Mountain Tiger flicks her strong tail, as if she couldn't care less. "The fact of the matter is that we must drive our way to our beloved MegaRealm, and we have already acquired our vehicle."

"The Key to the Final Eclipse," the Three-Legged Crow Goddess calls out, her birdy eyes sparkling.

"Indeed. The so-called key of all keys," the Mountain Tiger confirms, "for which we owe you our gratitude. But every vehicle requires fuel. For what use is a car that cannot drive."

The Crow Goddess squawks excitedly, as if she wishes *she* were the one giving this speech. "Mago's Fire! It's the perfect fuel for our Key. The most powerful, the most destructive power in all existence."

I feel my friends tense in unison. We were right. The goddesses need Mago's Fire to fuel the Key and use it to put an end to the world as we know it.

"But that's not all," the Crow Goddess interrupts, obviously unable to take the backseat in this presentation. "A car—even one full of fuel—cannot be started without switching on the ignition. In the same way, we must switch on the Key's ignition for it to start."

A terrible feeling creeps up my neck, but still—I ask the question. Because I need to know. For sure.

"And how do you switch on the ignition?" I ask quietly.

"Thought you'd never ask," the Fox Goddess says giddily, her nine tails shivering behind her. "To do that, we need a special type of *soul.*"

The four goddesses smile, and it's officially the creepiest thing I've ever seen in my thirteen years on Earth. All the hairs on my body reach tall, and suddenly, I realize what Dahl has been keeping from me this entire time.

This is a trap.

"Hurry it up, Mayor!" Dahl demands as Yeomra finally releases the last ropes keeping Dahl's torso trapped on the chair. To me, he shouts, "Kid, I tried to tell you! You need to get outta here right n—"

His insistence is interrupted by the Fox Goddess, who narrows her sly yellow eyes and screams.

"What are you waiting for, sister! DO IT!"

Before I can react, the Moon Rabbit throws the fidget spinner out of her paws as if it's a hot potato. It flies across our heads until it lands with precision into the hands of . . . the regal man in the hanbok.

Our ally in the Spiritrealm.

Mayor Yeomra.

Without delay, the mayor spins the toy to life, the intense purple fire exploding into flame above the spinning blades. Then, out of his hanbok, he unsheathes a familiar-looking relic—a binyeo hairpiece attached to a round stone, one half onyx, and one half ivory. He douses it in the violet flames, fueling it with the most destructive energy in the universe. And the key of all keys drinks it up—devouring Mago's Fire until it is fat with power, and the fidget spinner is no more than a flimsy piece of plastic flung across the floor.

The goddesses shriek with joy, and with a glint in his eye, Yeomra holds out the weapon, the sharp end pointed outward like a dagger. Then he advances. Toward *me.*

Confusion and clarity rush through me at once.

The mayor is trying to kill me.

The mayor planned this with the goddesses.

The mayor is a TRAITOR.

And everything begins to move in slow motion.

Areum shrieks. A drawn-out, bloodcurdling sound. Hattie jumps on Namjoon and gallops over to me. Emmett's eyes widen into saucers, and he speeds over on Boris, beating Hattie and leaping off his dragon scooter and onto the mayor's back. But Yeomra slips out of Emmett's grip like a slippery eel. The goddesses laugh. An empty, tinny sound. I try to move, but I'm stuck. Because I have the sudden thought:

I am going to die.

But I don't close my eyes. I need to see how this ends.

As the former king of the underworld comes for me with the Key to the Final Eclipse in his hand, someone with a shock of moon-colored hair lunges between us like a human shield.

My soul twin.

I am helpless as the traitor drives the weapon straight into my brother's heart.

21.
The Tree Giveth, the Tree Taketh

MAGO HALMI DOES NOT EXIST.

That's what I'm thinking as I watch the mayor rip the Key to the Final Eclipse out of Dahl's chest. It's dripping with blood.

Mago Halmi is a lie.

If she were real, this would not be happening. The Mago I know wouldn't let my brother bleed out on the summit of Mount Baekdu—the place she began creating the world. Not when we're supposed to be the two people prophesied to lead the world into the new era of the Age of the Final Eclipse. Not when she knows how much he is loved. Not when she knows how desperately he wants to *live*.

Hattie and Taeyo come to their senses faster than I do. They run to Dahl and fall at his side. Hattie immediately rubs her wrists and starts chanting, covering the weeping wound with her hands.

"Stay with us, please," Taeyo pleads, not knowing what to do with his hands. He ends up adjusting and readjusting his crooked bow tie. "I've never had a bestie before. I don't want to lose you."

Areum and Emmett surround me protectively, while the others watch the goddesses like hawks.

I find myself floating out of my body, disassociating with the scene. I refuse to believe this is real. I'm not really here. This is a figment of my imagination.

"It's not working!" Hattie cries, rubbing her wrists and trying a different incantation. "Why is it not working?"

"Because he's already dead," the mayor responds simply.

Dahl is dead.

"But I don't know how to bring back the dead!" Hattie cries, bursting into tears. "What do I do? Rye, what do I do?!"

Hattie's frenzied question is what pulls me back into my body, reminding me this sordid scene *is* real life. I run and fall on the grass next to Hattie and push my hands over hers, trying helplessly to stop the life from gushing out of Dahl's chest.

"There's nothing you can do for him now. I got him through the heart," the mayor points out. "And now his soul is here." He holds up the bloody weapon, still dripping crimson liquid onto the too-green-to-be-real grass of this mountain.

The key of all keys looks different now. Shape-wise, it hasn't changed. But there's a pearly violet aura around it that didn't use to be there that's glowing in a steady rhythm. Almost like it's pulsating with an energy. With a *soul*.

The curtain of death never lingers far from you and your kin, the Water Dragon Goddess's omen rings in my ear like a missed bell. *You must be careful. You must be vigilant.*

She had warned me. And I didn't heed her words. It was

supposed to be *me*, not him. But then Dahl came to save me at the tournament. And then again when he stepped in front of me to take my blade.

The injustice explodes out of me like a living, seething thing. "You *killed* him!" I shriek, wanting to claw at the mayor's face but equally unable to leave Dahl's side. Hattie's and my hands are still plastered above Dahl's broken heart, pushing down into his chest as if we could push the life back into him somehow.

"You *killed* the boy who wanted to live more than anyone else in the world! Do you know how many things he had on his bucket list? And because of you, he'll *never* be able to tick any of those things off. *Ever!*" Hot tears pour down my face, leaving streaks of fury and grief in their path.

The mayor holds up his hands. "I'm not the one to blame, child. You were the one who was so eager to bring us up to the summit, remember. I tried to remind you that sometimes a war avoided is a war won. I told you there was no shame in turning away."

And yet, I'd even lied to my friends so we'd willingly walk into this trap. And for what? For the greater good of the world? Isn't that the exact same thing the goddesses are purporting to uphold? I am just like them.

"Besides, don't be too hard on yourself," the mayor says flippantly. "It was obvious the heavenborn knew what fate awaited him. That's why he was so intent on keeping you away."

"To save *me*," I whisper.

My body shudders involuntarily, and I would honestly puke

if I had anything in my stomach. Dahl's insistence that we don't come find him. Him not answering his telepathy phone. He figured out what the goddesses were planning, and he knew they wouldn't give up. So he was going to offer himself up so I would be spared.

In that moment, the little ounce of confidence I had gained from journeying into the Spiritrealm and winning the Godrealm's tournament fades away into the puddle of blood pooling under my soul twin's body.

I killed him.

I slump over Dahl's body and begin to sob uncontrollably. It might have been the mayor's hand that drove the Key into Dahl's heart, but it was only possible because of me. My worst fears have come true. I am not a hero. I am a villain. One that leads her people into destruction and despair.

Emmett runs over to hold me tight, leaving Boris propped up against the bushes. And Hattie's fury alights.

"But you were supposed to be helping us!" she yells to the mayor, her eyes on fire. Namjoon stands by her side, baring his teeth. "You were our *ally*! After everything we went through. We helped you solve the mystery of your poisoned River of Reincarnation. We helped you become a better mayor. How could you have used us like this?"

The mayor shrugs, and a realization hits me like a gut punch. All the wind leaves my lungs.

The eavesdropped conversation the goddesses were having before about the seasons of change and how things had to die to be reborn...I remember where I've heard those words. It was down in the land of the dead. When I'd asked the mayor if there were seasons in the food forest, he had said that death was essential—virtuous, even—because without it, there'd be no growth. It was the circle of life and reincarnation.

"You knew about the poisoned river, didn't you?" I demand, the pieces falling together like a disturbing, gory puzzle. "You knew your CEOs were disgruntled, and so you used it to your advantage. You worked with the Mountain Tiger Goddess to poison the river so you could take control of your citizens. To use them as your *army*. And you made it look like the CEOs were the power-hungry, evil ones!"

The mayor's eyes flare. "And it was a *brilliant* plan, if I say so myself. Until you petulant children came and ruined it all." He tightens his grip on the glowing Key. "Luckily, we have found ourselves a new army of mortals, which the Three-Legged Crow Goddess will be awakening forthwith."

The idea of my parents and all the adults being used as the mayor's toy soldiers gives me goose bumps. I glare at him, in disbelief that someone could have planned something so dark, so complex, and kept up the ruse for so *long*.

"And *that's* why you gave Dahl your mun-pen," Hattie says quietly. "I thought it was weird you'd give your most prized possession to a kid you hardly knew. But it was because you *needed* him to have it. You wanted him to open the doors between the land of the living and the dead, because you knew eventually it would deteriorate the fabric between the realms."

Hattie looks to me, guilt spelled out across her features.

"And I made him use it all the time," I murmur.

"To come see me," she finishes with a pained expression on her face.

Namjoon makes weird gurgly growling sounds, while Areum squawks and Emmett holds me tighter. The image of Emmett's, Jennie's, and David's limp bodies hanging off the crown of the Statue of Eternity rushes back to me. To think the mayor was behind all that, too.

Something breaks inside me, like a delicate vase dropped on concrete. And I don't think I'll ever be able to put myself back together again. Too much has gone wrong. And this—*all* of this—can't be turned back. History can't be erased.

"But *why*?" Emmett asks, still holding me close to him. "Why did you do this, Yeomra? Why do the goddesses' bidding? What's in it for you?"

The mayor sighs. "I don't expect mortal children to understand the woes of someone of my age and stature, having done the same job for millennia. But put simply, I did what I had to do to survive. I knew the goddesses would stop at nothing to bring the world into the Age of the Final Eclipse—to awaken the MegaRealm. And I wanted to guarantee myself a job in the biggest restructuring known to the three realms."

"Because you wanted to become prime minister of the MegaRealm," Emmett surmises. "The tournament was just a PR stunt, wasn't it? You would've found a reason to replace whoever was rightfully voted in. Everything you've ever said to us has been a downright lie. Just a big ploy to get your big promotion."

Yeomra shrugs as if his actions are totally reasonable. "When the world's changing, you either change with it or get left behind. That's a lesson for you kids if you want to get ahead in life. Nothing personal."

Namjoon's growling has turned into full howls now. And when I turn to look at him, I realize why. The goddesses, who until now were watching this conversation with mild interest, have now become impatient.

"Do it now, Yeomra," the Mountain Tiger Goddess commands as she lowers her head and her tail swishes behind her. "Enough small talk. You have the activated Key. Get the job done."

The mayor nods obediently and makes for the Tree of Life, his kingly hanbok swishing behind him. "Yes, Goddess. Consider it done."

He approaches the tree. The green tufts of hair sitting atop the branches begin to frizz up, as if sensing something terrible is about to happen.

For the second time today, Yeomra grabs the Key to the Final Eclipse, now pulsating with the slain life of Dahl, and wields it in front of him like the deadly weapon that it is.

"It is time!" Yeomra shouts. "With the power vested in me as the *true* prime minister of the new era, I now deem the three-realm system obsolete. May the MegaRealm be BORN!"

"The tree giveth!" the four goddesses chant as one. "And the tree taketh!"

Yeomra drives the blood-covered Key into the trunk of the first tree to have ever existed in this universe, unlocking a door that should never be opened. The tree wails, and it's truly the most horrifying and sorrowful sound. The pain grates my ears and travels down into my toes, and I find myself weeping right along with it.

As Yeomra yanks the weapon out of the trunk, the tree screeches for mercy. White sappy blood gushes out of the gaping wound, before the trunk splits down the middle with a roaring crack. The green tufts turn into smoke and evaporate into the air, and then, bark by bark, the tree severs into two separate parts, keeling left and right as if it's been struck by lightning.

The mountain begins to tremble.

"The old realms are finally falling, sisters!" the Crow Goddess announces, sounding euphoric. "We have done the impossible!"

"We will start anew and succeed where the Mother failed!" the Fox Goddess sings.

I thought the sky had fallen today. But it seems the entire universe is about to fall with it. And when it rains, it pours.

The too-green grasses wilt and shrivel under us, and the earth starts cracking and opening up under our feet. Together, the goddesses chant an ancient language, and glimmery threads shoot out from their chests. It entraps my friends in its spidery divine web, and they all thrash and kick for life.

"Riley Oh!" Areum screeches as her wings get stuck in the strands. "I cannot help you, Riley Oh!"

The more they struggle, the deeper my friends find themselves caught in the goddesses' net. And I kneel beside Dahl's body, torn between leaving him alone and deciding who to go help first.

"Let them go!" I shriek.

But before I can even stand up, the Mountain Tiger Goddess is behind my back, stamping me down with her large front paw. My jaw hits the hard, already-scorched soil underneath, and my mouth fills with the taste of metal.

"This is personal payback for slaying my favorite sister," the goddess snarls as she releases the claws on her paw, digging the sharp spikes into the flesh of my back.

"*Argh!*" I scream, blinded by pain.

"Riley!" Emmett and Hattie both scream from their entangled web.

I see Emmett's eyes darting about, searching for any metal he can animate. Noah tries to rub his wrists. But even if their elemental magic could work in the Godrealm, there's nothing but smoke and ruin here. Areum flaps her wings so violently she cocoons herself completely into the sticky strands of the net. And Hattie tries to untangle Namjoon so he can help me, but the harder she tries, the more immobile he becomes.

There is a loud whimpering that travels over the sound of cracking earth, and Emmett cries, "Boris!"

The dragon-on-wheels is still propped up against the bush where Emmett left him.

In desperation, Hattie calls out to the scooter, "Just fly, Boris! You're as much a yong as I am. So use those wings! FLY!"

Perhaps it's because the Water Dragon Goddess's essence remains in Hattie's system, allowing her to tap into a well of divine power. Perhaps it's because the world is falling apart and all rules of physics and possibility have been thrown out the window. Or perhaps Boris had it in him all along. Whatever the reason, Boris explodes in a blue cloud of dust, only to emerge from the ashes a whole new creature. He's as big as a crocodile, covered with shiny blue scales, a long white beard falling down the sides of his jowls, and *wings*.

"Holy shirtballs, Boris!" Emmett cries. "You're a freaking dragon! A *real* yong!"

For a moment, as Boris spreads his wings and launches into the sky, hope seeps into the cracks of my shattered chest. Boris is going to save us. The dragon-scooter turned real dragon is going to save us all!

"They're creating an escape route," Noah yells as the Moon Rabbit Goddess flicks her ears, creating a weird burrow-like whirlpool underneath the canopy of the Tree of Life. The Mountain Tiger Goddess turns her attention away from me and joins her Fox and Crow sisters as they start to pull in the net of my trapped friends, as if they're fisherpeople hauling in their catch.

"You need to get the Key from the mayor!" Taeyo calls to me, his face flushed.

Hattie shouts from inside the moving net, "He's right, Rye. Don't worry about us! Mago's Fire is the only way to awaken your true potential and stop all of this!"

The mayor is already making his way toward the whirlpool portal, too. But Boris has seen him. He flaps his strong blue wings as if he's done this his whole life, and he flies over our heads toward the traitor. Yeomra was not expecting this, and in a stunned moment, Boris bowls him over with his new-and-improved muscular tail. The Key tumbles out of the mayor's hand and rolls away from him.

Boris quickly changes direction to go save our friends. But as he torpedoes toward Emmett, the same tail that caught the mayor unawares now catches in the web. It pulls him down, and he uses his right wing to unstick himself. Fatal mistake. The mysterious netting pulls at his wing until his body keels to the side, embroiling his left wing, until, eventually, his entire body spins like a coil right into the mess of bodies. He bellows in frustration. Whatever that web is made of, it puts Peter Parker to shame.

"Rye, get the Key!" Hattie screams at me. "Get it now!"

"It's there!" Emmett calls out, nodding through a gap in the web. It's close. I could get it if I ran, and the mayor is still on his hands and knees, disorientated from Boris's hit.

Ignoring the pain in my back and spitting the blood from my mouth, I run for it. The mayor pulls himself up onto his feet, though, and I only make it a second before him. I snatch the weapon with my trembling hands and point the tip of the blade at him.

"Don't you dare come any closer!" I sob, jabbing the Key aimlessly his way. Tears are streaming down my face, and I feel wild. The prophecy pegged its bets on the wrong horse, and there is nothing I can do to change the fate of the world. My friends believe a lie—I don't know how to unleash my true potential, even with this Fire-laden weapon in my hand.

"Let my friends go, or I'll use this!" I shriek as the goddesses lead my trapped sister and friends to the whirlpool portal. "I swear, I *will* use this on you, Yeomra, you lying, betraying scumbag!"

For a moment, his eyes betray a spark of fear. But as quickly as it came, the panic disappears and is replaced by a challenging stare.

"I don't believe you, child," he states confidently. "I have watched you now for many months. And I don't believe that you will harm me. Because you don't have it in you. You are weak."

"I'm not weak!" I argue back. "I won that tournament. Out of everyone there, I came out on top, fair and square!"

"You mean those childish games the goddesses put on?" He snorts. "You are much too weak to make the tough, difficult decisions that a true leader must. At some point, you must face the facts, Riley Oh. You will never be a *real* hero."

I sob harder, because he's right.

As the most powerful weapon in the known world falls out of my hand and clatters at my feet, I know I cannot end this soul's life—as evil and terrible as he is. Because that isn't me. I wasn't taught to maim and harm. I was raised to heal and serve. The entire world is falling apart, yes. But that doesn't mean I should help it along. I refuse to play even a small role in the play of this destruction. And if that makes me a poor leader, then so be it. Maybe I was never supposed to be great or a hero. Maybe I was just supposed to be *me*.

"I *choose* not to kill you!" I declare to Yeomra, the cocktail of anger and grief and helplessness building into a twister inside me. "My sister always said choice is paramount, and I refuse to be like you or the goddesses. I will not let myself be part of the death of the world!"

Yeomra sneers. "Like I said, you'll never be strong enough, last fallen star. Mark my words. *This* will be your downfall."

The Fox Goddess's white-tipped bushy tails are the last thing I see as my friends are taken prisoner into the underground portal by the goddesses. Hattie's, Areum's, and Emmett's screams for me are the last things I hear.

The mountain gives a final big heave before the earth cracks open, just as the Tree of Life did. The ground beneath me splits into two, one side with the whirlpool portal, getting farther and farther away from me. And the side I'm on, where rocks and shriveled plants are falling over the edge into the unknown.

I fall backward onto my butt, and I crab-walk to avoid falling in. I am no different from this dying mountain. I am crumbling. Falling apart. Unspooling. And things could not possibly get any worse.

But somehow, they do.

I bump into Dahl's body as I scramble back, and when I crawl over him, my soul twin's limp, unbreathing form gets swallowed by the chasm. He drops off the cliff and falls into the black abyss.

I wail.

I. CAN'T. TAKE. ANY. MORE. OF. THIS.

I must have said that out loud, because I hear Yeomra's voice behind me, empty and cold. "Truth be told, I can't, either."

Then he pushes me into the darkness below.

"I told you this would be your downfall," his voice echoes after me.

My sobs catch on gravity, and for a moment, my despair suspends into nothingness.

I'm just falling,

falling,

falling,

seemingly forever. It's like the gulf is endless, a black hole into the center of the earth and then even farther. And in some ways, the feeling is not unfamiliar. I recall the faintest memories of falling from the sky as a piece of the Godrealm's dark sun, and becoming the Mortalrealm's last fallen star. Maybe I could just keep falling for the rest of time.

But then I'm not falling anymore.

I'm *flying.*

Because I'm no longer alone.

I'm being carried on the back of a gigantic creature with a hide like heated marble, and a clear, sweet bell ringing around its neck.

The *Haetae.*

22.
For Future Reference, Canyons Are Good Places to Think

 I WONDER IF THIS IS WHAT dying is like.

Is death like falling until you're flying?

Is death where the wind streams through your hair as you soar through the empty black skies forever?

"You're not dying," the Haetae assures me as we touch ground.

The uni-horned lion beast, and Mago Halmi's loyal guardian, carefully rolls me off his back.

"Please do not be mistaken, last fallen star. You are very much alive."

The only light is coming from the Haetae's bioluminescent scales, softly illuminating our surroundings. We seem to be in some kind of slot canyon with tall, winding walls made of reddish sandstone, undulating like waves.

It reminds me of a place on Dahl's bucket list—the Antelope Canyon—which he explained had a Navajo name: Tsé bighánílíní, meaning "the place where water runs through rocks." He was amazed at how something as gentle as water could make the toughest, strongest rocks wield under its soft but persistent touch.

I think of my slain soul twin and my kidnapped sister and friends, and what little is left unbroken finally shatters into sand, no different than the powder under our feet.

"Haetae!" I sob, burying my head in his mane. "I failed! I let everyone down. And I tried; I really did. I *tried* to be the hero you said I was—that everyone kept saying I could be. But they were wrong. The prophecy was all wrong. I wasn't good enough. I wasn't strong enough. And now Dahl is gone, and everyone else is taken prisoner, and the world has broken. For all I know, the entire world and everyone I've ever known could already be gone!"

My chest shudders as the weight of my failures threaten to drown me whole.

The Haetae's bell rings softly around his neck, and for some reason, that sets me off. My grief flips on its head and becomes a fiery ball of fury.

"Mago Halmi is a *myth*!" I yell. "She is a lie! A fake! No mother would allow her children to fight and hurt one another like this. Tell me I'm wrong, Haetae. Tell me that Mago actually exists!"

The lion beast purrs and rubs his mane against my wet, swollen face. "But Mago has never left your side, last fallen star. She has always been with you."

I glare at the Haetae with all the darkest emotions I can muster. "LIES! How could you say that with a straight face? After everything we've had to endure?"

"Do you remember when you believed the Horangi clan to be wicked?"

The question comes from left field, and perhaps it's because I'm exhausted beyond anything I've ever imagined, but I find myself answering earnestly, "Yes."

"And what did you learn?"

"That they were merely misunderstood," I answer with a sigh. I recall how Emmett and I had traveled to Horangi HQ, hidden in the canopies of the Angeles National Forest, and how we discovered through meeting Sora, Austin, and Taeyo that there are always two sides to every story. History is told by the victor, but in war, there is never a true winner.

"And what about in your travels to the Spiritrealm?" he prods.

"What about them?"

"What did you learn?"

I frown. "What is this, Saturday School? Why are you trying to teach me lessons when the world is literally falling apart, Haetae? Didn't you hear me? I *failed*. What do we do now? How do I save my family and friends?!"

The Haetae pauses, then looks to the empty sky, which is devoid of stars, the sun, or the moon.

"Did you know that when Mago Halmi created the world, she shed a tear for the life she created?"

Now I'm really angry. I'm pretty sure there's smoke coming out my ears. "YES, Haetae. *Of course* I know. There was the big bang, she was exhausted from creating the world, so she shed a tear, and it caught flame. What do you think we've been looking for this entire time?! We've been trying to get our hands on Mago's Fire so Dahl and I could awaken our true potential! And then he got *killed*. Did you hear me? MURDERED."

The Haetae ignores my outburst.

"I find it interesting that people upon hearing that story interpret its meaning in such different ways."

"For the life of mortals, *please*, Haetae, for once in your long divine life, can you please just say what you're trying to say? No more riddles. No more weird, twisted ways to teach me a lesson. Just. Spit. It. Out."

The Haetae chuckles. "Fair point, last fallen star, so out with it, I will." He shakes his mane, and his bell rings crystal clear into the sandstone walls, the sound fragmenting and echoing back manyfold. "The Mother's first teardrop holds within it the most powerful fire in all of existence—an energy so true and so pure that it can never be extinguished. Many choose to focus on its power for destruction, but what they so easily forget is that the tear was shed in *love* for the world she created."

"Um . . . okay?"

"The tear was shed in joy for the sheer beauty of her children. For the life and light that was born unto this world. Because just like stories, or war, or mortals, even teardrops have within them the capacity for light and dark. For good and bad. It's what they are used *for* that makes all the difference."

I let myself digest that. "What are you saying?"

"What I'm saying, last fallen star, is that the *true* power of the Mother's teardrop was not for destruction. It was for *creation*."

Something flickers in the empty vastness of the sky,

sparking at the edge of my vision. But I don't look up. Because slowly, a small glimmer of understanding alights in my mind like a small, erratic firefly. And I can't lose focus of it or else it might fly away.

"Are you saying that the Key to the Final Eclipse can be used to put things back together?" I ask quietly.

"It can be used to create whatever you desire."

The little light inside me dims slightly as I think of Yeomra's words. "But I'm weak, Haetae. I'm so scared. And I'm so *angry*. I don't know if I have what it takes to put the world back together again."

The Haetae looks deeply into my eyes. "The only thing stronger than fear is courage. The only thing greater than ignorance is compassion. And the only thing more powerful than hate is love. Ultimately, it's up to you, last fallen star, to decide which path you take."

The flickering intensifies in my periphery, until it's so bright I can't ignore it anymore. I turn my attention away from the flickering firefly within and focus on the shower of light from above.

"What the—"

A warm pearly globe has reappeared in the dark expanse of sky. And through the gap in the reddish sandstone walls, its warm, humble light shines right down into the canyon, reflecting off the gentle slopes of the gorge and filling the space with hope.

"The moon," I gasp. "It's back! But how?"

And that's when I hear it.

His voice.

This is gonna sound super weird, kid, but heyyy, I'm back!

A whimper escapes my lips. "Dahl?" I whisper, tears brimming, "Is that you?"

Bada bing, bada boom! It's me, all right! And you thought you could get rid of me so easy!

"But how?" I demand, searching the wavy walls of the canyon for a glimpse of my ivory-haired brother. "Where are you? I hear you, but I don't see you."

Well, as it turns out, when we die, we return to where we came from. For us, that's the sky. So I'm talking to you from—wait for it, wait for it, taa-daa—the moon! No wonder I didn't have my true soul form on my Spiritrealm citizen ID card. I'd like to see immigration try to capture all of THIS in a photo, ha!

I stare up at the hunk of the natural satellite floating in space with awe and disbelief. "You're kidding me. You're literally *in* the moon?!"

Come on, kid. Give me more credit than that! I'm not in the moon. I am the moon!

For the first time since I met my soul twin in the underworld, I have the sudden realization that his name—Dahl—is the Korean word for "moon."

I laugh then. Because I don't know what else to do. I laugh so hard that my belly aches, and Taggy (who's still hanging from my earlobe in the cocoon) sways and trembles with my movement. I keep laughing until I cry, and I cry until I'm laughing again. When I couldn't possibly laugh or cry anymore, I fall to the dusty floor of the canyon. I lie back with my hands behind my head, gazing up at the newly born moon in the broken world's sky. The Haetae comes to sit by my side. He purrs.

"Are you okay up there?" I ask quietly. "Are you hurting? Are you...*different*, somehow?"

There is a pause.

I feel...I feel like I'm home.

"But don't you wish you were here? Ticking off your annoying bucket list?"

He chuckles, and I can almost see him popping his collar.

It's hard to explain, but I'm still there. And here. Everywhere the moon touches, I exist. They may have taken my corporeal form, but my soul still shines. I still live on, and I am all around you.

Another bout of tears floods down my face. "But I'll never get to see you again," I whisper.

You don't need to see me to know I am with you, kid. But you already knew that.

I sniffle and wipe my face with the back of my hand. It's hard to stop the tears because, well, because I'm me and crying is what I do best. But I believe him. I know that Dahl will always be a part of me. Forever.

Thank you for being my sister, kid. For giving me a chance at a mortal life. For helping me out of the Spiritrealm, for putting up with my bucket lists, for all my vain preening, for taking up all your bathroom space with my pots of pomade. Oh, and for introducing me to boba tea! If I had another shot at mortality, I wouldn't change one tiny thing.

There are too many turbulent waves of emotion ebbing and flowing inside me to return the sentiment in kind. There are too many things to say, and words don't seem a sufficient method in which to deliver them. So I stay silent.

And in true Dahl fashion, he's the one who still has something to say.

So you're gonna go save our family and friends, right, kid? You're not going to give up so easily?

I don't answer. That little firefly from before has grown into a greater light of realization deep inside my gut. But I still can't comprehend it completely. I still don't see how I'm going to get the Key drenched in Mago's Fire back in my hands, or how I'm going to put the world back together.

There's still a piece missing.

Something small. But crucial.

Oh, and by the way, Taggy's waking up.

My ear tickles as the cocoon cracks. I hear it rustling near my ear, and then I feel the slightest of movement—like a feather—hatching out of their home.

Even amid a crumbling world, the smallest of creatures—my little wakerpillar friend from the Spiritrealm—spreads their wings for the very first time and takes their virgin flight.

"Oh my Mago," I breathe, "Did Taggy just become a butterfly?!"

"Oh my Mago, indeed," the Haetae chuckles.

The lion beast, who has been quietly sitting by my side, now stands, and bows deeply to the tiny winged creature.

"It has been much too long, Mago Halmi. I am overjoyed to see you once more."

23.
When a Butterfly Flaps
Its Wings...

"WAIT, WHAT?!"

I look to the Haetae for answers. I look to the moon for answers. I look to the butterfly themself—*herself*—for answers.

"You mean to say that Taggy is Mago?"

No one responds.

"Mago Halmi, aka the mother of all creation, was hiding as a wakerpillar from the Memory Archives on my neck this *entire* time?!"

Still, no one says anything.

"Can someone please TALK TO ME?!" I yell, my face feeling like it might burst at any second.

The Haetae and Dahl laugh heartily, and the butterfly—aka Mago—flutters toward me.

Let's get one thing straight. This is no ordinary butterfly. Her wings are a kaleidoscope of colors that I don't know the names of. They shimmer and reflect emotions that can only come from a mother's embrace, because with every flap of her wings, I feel my shattered heart piece itself back together, shard by shard.

She nears, and my entire existence sings like a choir. She lands on my open palm, and I know, in that instant, that I am loved. I am drowning in her love for me. It's like jumping into the deep end of a heated pool and being engulfed by its warmth.

The water embraces me. It tells me I am worthy. Because I am her creation. And she did not create me to fail. She created me in complexity—with light and dark, with pride and vulnerability, with pain and joy, with *free will.*

And even though she does not say a single word, I understand her completely. The little firefly inside me alights into the biggest pit of fire inside my gut, and I know that these flames will burn so bright that all my fears and demons will be turned to ash.

Why?

Because the prophecy was right. My true potential needed to be awakened, but it wasn't really about Mago's teardrop at all. It was hidden in the tiny moments as I hungered for magic, when Hattie helped me summon the Cave Bear Goddess, and as I learned through discovering my hidden heritage that true belonging must begin from inside. It was peeking out of the shadows as I journeyed down to the Spiritrealm hoping to fix all I'd broken, only to learn that I was the sum of all those I chose to stand with, and that was what really mattered. The real potential was inside me all along.

You see, it seems so clear now—as crystal as the ring of the Haetae's bell. Heroes don't have to be confident or know what to say to woo the crowds. They don't have to be the best fighters, or the ones quickest to draw their swords. Heroes can be the ones that empower others to be their *own* heroes. The quiet leaders in the background who enable, and nurture, and *care*. Whose unwavering service and dogged empathy can give way to a beautiful new era.

Someone like *me*.

Mago takes flight once more, and this time she flies right into me. Into my chest, nestling into the deepest depths of me. As her wings dissolve, she forms an unbreakable, impenetrable shield around me, and I know she's not gone. She hasn't left me, but she has become a part of me. Just as I am a part of her. Because I finally understand that the ultimate power of the universe is not destruction or strength.

It is *love*.

The Elvis impersonator at Charles's and Maru's wedding was right. *True love doesn't shout—it whispers. True love doesn't fight—it nurtures.* He'd told us to remember that when you love, you should *give with all that you have, and all that you are.*

And that's when I know exactly how I'm going to save the world.

24.
Who Wants a Triple-Realm Sundae, Extra Sprinkles?

"Take me to my loved ones," I tell the Haetae, standing strong and proud and tall. I know I'm not invincible, but suddenly, I feel like I am. Because I am exactly where I need to be. And I am exactly who I need to be.

The Haetae throws his head back and lets out a resounding roar that shakes the walls of this desert canyon. "As you wish, fallen star."

We soar across the newly moonlit sky, over the desert and toward Las Vegas, which has become a cocktail of all three realms. There are jagged icy peaks of mountains sandwiched between casinos and hotels, reminding me of the Hell of Infinite Ice, the roaring of non-mortal creatures reverberating down into the streets. As we fly closer to the ground, deep ravines and dark valleys come into view, except they're tucked in between branches of Stairbucks and a large college campus called Mountain Tiger University of Knowledge and

Truth. There's even a new river that flows across the central city that was not there before, which my gut tells me is the River of Reincarnation from the Spiritrealm, leaking into this new MegaRealm.

It is chaos in its purest form. But sometimes, we need to know how things can go wrong before we can figure out how to put it right.

We fly over the Strip, where the Venetian and Madame Tussauds used to be. Except now, the buildings are mere rubble, replaced by multiple uncasked pits full of wax warriors, ripped open like a birthday present. There are too many of them to only be gifted adults, which means the Three-Legged Crow Goddess must've started enlisting the saram adults, too. As the Haetae flies us closer, it's clear this is the epicenter of the new era—there is a flurry of activity surrounding the wax army, and I immediately spot the goddesses in their formidable animal forms dotted among the throngs of people.

"Don't let them see us," I whisper to the Haetae. "Not yet."

We remain on the opposite side of the road where the mouth of the new river lies, and quietly, from on top of a huge shiny high-rise called Nine-Tailed Foxy Cosmetic Surgery, I get a lay of the land.

Across the river, I can see the goddesses and the mayor surrounded by a large, eclectic audience who are shouting and protesting, looking far from pleased with the new MegaRealm. Among them, I see cheollimas, bulgaes, multiple-tailed foxes, three-legged crows, inmyeonjos, and a whole host of divine creatures I can't identify. I even see the Lucha Libre mountain tiger that I met during the mini golf tournament. A line of waxlike soldiers separates the goddesses from the angry mob.

"This is false advertising!" a five-tailed fox shouts angrily.

"This isn't what you promised us!" an inmyeonjo a head shorter than Areum screeches. "This MegaRealm's a scam!"

"Yeah, bring back the old Godrealm!" Lucha Libre man shouts.

My eyes continue to scan the disgruntled citizens, and it becomes clear they don't all hail from the Godrealm. Dotted among the divine crowd, there are all sorts of souls in their animal forms. Looks like the Spiritrealm's citizens aren't happy with the upheaval to their world, either.

"We didn't even ask for this!" a panda shouts, his voice irate.

"I bet it won't rain mochi donuts the first Friday of every month here," a tricolored macaw laments. "And what's this talk of mandatory realmflation hikes? Everything was free in Cheondang!"

"And we didn't even have to work . . ." cries a spotted lynx.

The Mountain Tiger Goddess roars to get the crowd's attention. "New citizens of the MegaRealm, these are merely teething issues," she assures. "If you are patient, you *will* reap the rewards."

The Three-Legged Crow Goddess squawks in support of her sister's statement while commanding the wax warriors to close in on the protestors. One of the soldiers picks up a short inmyeonjo by the scruff of its neck feathers, jigging them like a pepper shaker.

"Heed my sister's words," the Crow Goddess screeches. "This is just the beginning of the new world—we *will* deliver on the vision we promised. Remain patient and your faith will be rewarded!"

As the protestors demand more answers from their new leaders, I turn my attention to the other side of the uncasked pit of wax warriors, where it's teeming with excitable energy. There seems to be large mobs of kids jumping up and down, trying to catch whatever it is the Moon Rabbit Goddess and Nine-Tailed Fox Goddess are throwing at them. The ones that manage to catch any are popping it in their mouths, groaning happily, before promptly being turned into blank-faced zombies.

The Haetae grumbles softly. "It appears the mind-controlling gummy has been perfected, fallen star."

I gasp. Not just because the goddesses and mayor have now figured out how to control all of mortalkind—young *and* old—but because I spot the much-too-familiar faces of my loved ones hidden among the sea of gummy-guzzling victims. Hattie, Emmett, Taeyo, and Noah are huddled together, trying not to give in to the irresistible pull of those green brain gummies. Areum, Namjoon, Eubin, and Eurim are crowding around them, trying to protect them from the onslaught of frenzied kids and gummy bullets. Boris is nowhere to be seen.

"It's time," I say to the Haetae. "Take me down to them."

The loyal lion beast lands me right at the center of the madness, close enough to the new leaders of the MegaRealm that I see the goddesses' eyes widen at our arrival.

"The Haetae?" the Fox and Moon Goddesses yelp in unison.

"What are you doing here, Mago's slave?" the Three-Legged Crow Goddess demands. If I'm not mistaken, she sounds somewhat nervous.

"I thought we got rid of you eons ago," the Mountain Tiger snarls.

"*You!*" Yeomra scoffs, more interested in my arrival than that of the Haetae. "I thought I got rid of you myself!" He clenches his fists, and I see the Key tucked into the belt of his hanbok. "I knew I should have finished you off properly."

He lunges for me, but I jump out of the way, one step ahead of him. "Give me the Key, Yeomra."

He pauses, studying me. "You have changed, child."

I let myself grin, because that's who I am now. I believe in the power of Mago, in the power of hope, and, most of all, in myself.

"I have, *Mayor*. Indeed, I have."

His eyes narrow. "I'm *prime minister* now. And it's too late for your antics. The MegaRealm has already been unlocked." He seizes the Key from his belt and holds it up, pointing its sharp blade at me. "Now it's time to finish you off, once and for all."

He lunges for me again, but I shift out of the way. I know it's coming, because if anything—Yeomra is predictable. His hate and hunger make him shortsighted.

"Come *here!*" he yells, his calm and collected veneer shattering under his frustration. "Come die by my hand!"

The Haetae roars at him, and the mayor cowers, running

to hide behind the Crow Goddess. She screeches and throws Yeomra a death glare over her shoulder. "You useless man, you can't even control one child. Step away. I will have my army tend to her."

She waves her wing ominously and mutters a weird ancient language under her breath, making the Key in the mayor's hand throb with violet light. Immediately, a block of wax adults from the closest pit raise their heads and start climbing up the ladders.

I bristle. *This* is why the Three-Legged Crow Goddess had waited to awaken the wax army. She needed to activate the power of the Key to take full control of the soldiers.

"Be prepared, fallen star," the Haetae warns from my side.

The brainwashed battalion start marching toward me like robots. I just need to avoid the army and get my hands on that Key. *I can do this.*

But it turns out I'm not prepared. Because two wax warriors step forward from the crowd, revealing their faces. And seeing them is enough to steal the wind from my lungs.

"Eomma?" I breathe. "Appa?"

If they hear me, they don't let it show. Instead, as the Crow Goddess chants more ancient words under her breath, they march forward. Toward me.

"Hey, it's me, it's Riley!" I call out, fear suddenly spiking my heart. Their eyes are empty, and I realize that if they're programmed to attack me, I will only have three options: Run. Be attacked. Or attack. And they're all options I'm not willing to take.

"Eomma, Appa, listen to me. You can shake this off," I

beg, my hands held out in front of me. "It's me, your daughter! Remember? It's *me*!"

Still, they proceed, until Eomma reaches me first. I should move. I really need to move, but I can't give up on them. I can't leave them.

With her empty eyes looking nowhere, my own mother splays out her hands and grasps for my neck.

"RILEY! FEED HER THIS!"

David Kim's usually quiet voice screaming so ear-piercingly loud makes me jump, moving just enough to avoid being strangled by my eomma.

I turn toward David's voice just in time to see him, Cosette, and Jennie landing on the ground and jumping off Eugene and Sahm.

"CATCH!" David shouts again as he throws a handful of bright red heart-shaped gummies my way.

I only manage to catch two, but that's enough. I quickly shove one each into the mouths of my parents and hold my breath.

The next few seconds take forever, but sure enough, the warm browns and clear whites return to my parents' eyes. And as they come to, they shake their heads and look around.

"What's happening?" Eomma asks, her voice shaking.

"Why are we here?" Appa says.

I let out a huge sigh of relief and count my lucky stars for the infusing genius of David Kim. "I'll explain everything later," I say. "But for now, I need you guys to help David feed those red heart gummies to all the wax warriors and all the brainwashed kids, too. Got it?"

My parents look confusedly at David, Jennie, and Cosette, who have already begun handing out the antidote gummies to all those who need it.

"Do you have enough?" I ask worriedly, glancing up at the mob of kids still excitedly catching green gummies from the Moon Rabbit and Tiger Goddesses.

Cosette grins and points at the doors of Nine-Tailed Foxy Cosmetic Surgery across the road, which bursts open to allow a huge colony of moon rabbit scientists dressed in lab coats and top hats to pour out its doors. They're each carrying a huge bag overflowing of red gummies, and I immediately recognize Eureka the scientist leading the charge.

"We made a few friends while we were at Tokki Pharmaceuticals, then found a shortcut over here through the Fox Goddess's cosmetic surgery chain," Jennie explains as she expertly dunks a red gummy three-pointer into two more adult soldiers' mouths. "Turns out David's quite the charmer."

David blushes. "We've got this, Riley. You go do what you need to do. We'll be right behind you."

"Our friends are hiding in the mob of kids," I explain in a rush. "They're trying hard to resist the gummies, but—"

"Like the boy says, we've got it under control," Jennie insists, pushing me away. "Now go save the world, star girl!"

I give them a grateful look before leaning over and whispering into the Haetae's ear.

"Come on, old friend. It's time. I need that Key."

Mago's lion beast roars with agreement, and I jump on his back.

The Rabbit and Crow Goddesses are still throwing out

brain gummies to the kids, not yet realizing the counterattack my friends are leading, while the Tiger Goddess is trying to keep the hordes of unhappy citizens at bay. Meanwhile, the Crow Goddess is busy reasserting control over her wax army, which is being released from her control quicker than she's able to brainwash them. And the mayor, the coward that he is, is still hiding behind the Crow Goddess, eyeing the Haetae's every move.

The lion beast flies me toward him, and the mayor flees, weaving his way through the wax-warrior battalion to get to the other side of the road.

"You know what your problem is?" I say as I jump off the Haetae to follow Yeomra. "It's that you're too stubborn to know that there are other ways of achieving greatness. You're too narrow-minded. *That* will be your downfall."

The mayor twirls around in the middle of the car-less road and stabs the Key toward me, despite me being much too far away. His eyes are flittering around, trying not to lose sight of the Haetae. "One step closer and I'll finish you," he warns, but the tremble in his voice is a dead giveaway.

As Yeomra's hand holding the weapon starts to shake, I send out a little SOS to my soul twin.

Hey, Dahl, a little hand here?

I hear a chuckle and a cracking of the knuckles in my head.

Geez, thought you'd never ask, kid! You know how good I am with a mop. Just wait until you see me with the moon!

There is an invisible but palpable force that moves over us, and a huge wave appears from the mouth of the river behind the mayor.

"The river!" Yeomra cries, turning and looking up at the curtain of water building above him. "It's . . . It's *alive?*"

The Crow Goddess pauses her attempts to re-control her army to point to the incoming wave, wide-eyed. "Sister, do you see?"

The Mountain Tiger Goddess looks up from her position as crowd control warden and gazes at the sky that is no longer empty of light. She frowns deeply. "The moon . . . The moon controls the tide."

She's got that right, kid! Dahl sings. *I control the tide, bada bing, bada boom! And speaking of Bada . . .*

I smile as two familiar ineo siblings appear through the curtain of water—Bada and Daeyang. They grin as the wave nears, and part of the river re-forms into a Dahl-shaped body of water, complete with popped-up collar and overstyled hair. He looks like a surfer riding the best wave of his life, surrounded by two old friends.

Surf's up! the watery Dahl calls out as he bowls himself into a screaming Yeomra. *I can finally tick surfing off my list now!*

The mayor turned prime minister is pummeled to the ground with the impact of the wave, and the Key clatters onto the pavement, the mun-pen rolling out of his hanbok with it.

Bada reaches a hand out of the water and slaps Yeomra across the face. It makes a satisfying wet clapping sound, and his cheek goes bright red.

"Hand-delivered on behalf of the underwater borough!" Daeyang says chirpily.

The wave subsides and is pulled back into the body of the river—surfer Dahl and the siblings along with it. The Haetae uses the opportunity to dive down toward the still-stunned Yeomra, who is clutching at his reddened cheek, and plucks him off the ground.

"Please, no!" the mayor groans, coughing and spluttering.

The Key! Dahl reminds me. *Grab it while you can!*

I turn for the weapon, ready to dive into the road for it. But while I was too busy watching the mayor get served, someone beat me to it.

"Good try, gold-destroyer," the Three-Legged Crow Goddess sneers as she waves the Key, which is grasped tightly in her right talon. Water drips from her plumage. "I'm impressed, but you'll need more than that to stop us."

With her middle talon, she picks up the mun-pen and swiftly draws a door in the air in front of her.

Then, before I can stop her, she leaps through the threshold, disappearing into the ether, taking the Key with her.

25.
War Is for Weaklings. Peace Is for the Powerful

GO AFTER HER! DAHL URGES from the moon. *Don't let that door close on you!*

I shove my foot in the door before it can shut completely and de-materialize. But I can't quite seem to make the full leap through the threshold.

"But what about all our friends?" I say out loud.

They've got everything under control, kid. You just need to get your hands on that Key!

I look over my shoulder at my friends and moon rabbits, still frantically delivering red heart gummies to all the brainwashed adults and kids. Hattie, Emmett, and Areum seem to have joined the task force throwing out gummies, so they must have gotten the antidote or held out until the end. And if I'm not mistaken, Cheol and Yeowu from the Spiritrealm protestors have joined the cause, too. At least now with the Crow Goddess gone with the Key, no one new can be brainwashed, which means it's only a matter of time before all the wax warriors and kid victims will be saved.

"Sisters, she's getting away!" the Mountain Tiger Goddess roars as she bounds toward me, her heavy four paws pounding the concrete. "Get her!"

The Fox and Moon Rabbit Goddesses drop their green brain gummies and chase after me, too.

"We're coming, sister!" they scream, although the Moon Rabbit sounds less sure.

I slip through the door, making sure to close it behind me, and am blasted with the smell of old cigarettes.

"*Urgh.*" I wince. "Gross!"

The door seems to have taken me to a casino, because I'm assaulted by a maze of slot machines with their flashing lights and constant whirr of spinning reels, jangly music, and occasional jittering of falling coins. It seems not all the saram population has been turned into wax warriors, because there's a good number of people sitting here, pulling the lever down and again and again, completely unaware of what's happening outside in the streets of Vegas.

Shiny black feathers catch my eye from the opposite end of the row, and I look up just in time to see the Three-Legged Crow Goddess disappear down the next aisle of slot machines. There's a glint of shiny binyeo reflecting off the lights, and a gleeful squawk floating over the beeping and chiming of the machines. She's enjoying this.

I speed after her, only to see her duck into the next row, gliding in the opposite direction. My Converses skid to a halt, trying not to lose her, and almost bowl into a large pullout banner advertising Olivia Rodrigo as their new singer in residence. Panting and grunting, I keep running after the goddess, but her three-taloned feet are fast, especially when paired with her flapping wings.

It's only when I chase her out of the maze of slot machines, across the lobby, down the hallway, and through a celebrity's greenroom leading straight to a dim stage overlooking an empty auditorium, that she finally turns to face me.

"Well, that's more exercise than I've had in a long time, gold-destroyer," she says, fluffing her feathers and holding up the Key and mun-pen in her wings. "Definitely clocked my ten thousand steps today!"

Then, using the mun-pen, she draws a portal and opens its door. "Welcome, sisters, please come in."

Through the threshold, the three other goddesses reveal themselves, the Moon Rabbit Goddess carrying in her hands a large stone mortar and pestle, big enough to fit an entire person inside.

"Just because we *prefer* others to do the work doesn't mean we won't get our hands dirty if we need to," the Mountain Tiger Goddess snarls, her voice frosty.

I remind myself of Mago's shield buried deep in my chest, and the one goal I have of getting the Key from the Crow Goddess's wing, as the four goddesses surround me like four points on a compass. North, east, south, west—they slowly close in on me.

"Admit your defeat now, and perhaps we can give you a new position in the realm," the Moon Rabbit Goddess offers hesitantly.

"Looks like you've proven yourself much more strategic

than that useless Yeomra, anyway," the Fox Goddess adds, her nine tails swimming behind her.

"I don't need a position in your realm," I say, feeling more confident and bold than I probably should. "Because I have bigger plans. *Much* bigger plans, in fact."

"Then so be it," the Tiger Goddess says, her patience snapping. "Moon Rabbit sister, pound her in your mortar. This insolent child has caused us enough trouble. It's time for us to end her, once and for all."

The Rabbit Goddess hesitates, pawing the stone pestle uncertainly in her grasp.

"It doesn't have to be this way, you know," I say seriously to the Moon Rabbit Goddess. "You are allowed to make your own decisions, independent from your sisters."

"Oh, sister, must you always be so timid!" The Fox Goddess, who is standing behind me, takes it upon herself to shove me into the mortar. I land unceremoniously into the groove of the stone bowl.

"Now, do it!" the Crow Goddess squawks. "Grind her to a paste!"

"Must we really do this?" the Moon Rabbit whines as she reluctantly goes to lift the pestle.

At the same time, a high-pitched British accent and a young, perky voice rings over the empty seats of the auditorium.

"Riley, my sugarplum mochi balls, never fear! We are heeere!"

"RilOh stans for liiife!"

I look up from my precarious spot inside the Moon Rabbit's

stone mortar to see Charles the cheollima and Phoebe from the RilOh Fan Club riding Maru's wide back, flying toward the stage. Next to them is one of the other RilOh stans covered head to toe in a white fluffy substance, riding a familiar fiery bulgae. And accompanying them is the final RilOh club member riding . . . *Boris*?

The newly transformed blue yong roars happily upon seeing me and nods his head back to the auditorium doors, which burst open to allow a murder of imugis to pile through. I'm pretty sure I recognize at least six of them from my time in the Spiritrealm, in less-than-ideal circumstances. But for now, I am elated to see them. Turns out Boris didn't need Hattie to introduce him to the imugis, after all.

"Now, just like we practiced, sweet puffy éclairs!" Charles calls out to his posse, like a seasoned school teacher. "And ready, steady, *go!*"

Boris roars the command, and the murder of imugis race up the steps to the stage, their acid-laced tails poised and ready to strike. The goddesses are struck before they know what's hit them, and they fall to the ground, momentarily stunned into inaction.

"*Argh!* My tails!" the Fox Goddess shrieks, pulling them into her chest protectively.

"*Argh!* My wing!" the Crow Goddess echoes.

The Tiger Goddess glances down at her singed coat. "*Argh!* My fur!"

The Moon Rabbit Goddess, however, does not cry out for herself. Instead, dragging her injured leg, she drags the stone pestle behind her, dropping it next to the mortar.

"You're right," she utters, her eyes big and wide. "It doesn't have to be this way. What we have done is wrong. I knew it from the start, but I was swayed by my sisters. This MegaRealm... it was a mistake!" She pushes the pestle toward me. "Please, have my mortar and pestle—my greatest possessions. It is yours. I hope you can find it in yourself to forgive me and my sisters."

Coming to their senses, the three sisters yell and scream.

"Are you mad, sister?!"

"Have you lost your mind?!"

"What do you think you're doing?!"

And that's when I see my chance.

As the sisters berate their Moon Rabbit sibling, I leap toward the Crow Goddess, seizing the Key from her feathers.

You've got it! Dahl exclaims in my head. *You did it, kid!*

The auditorium's doors swing open again, and this time it's the Haetae that soars in, with the mayor trapped like a bone in a dog's jowls, howling for his life. Behind him flies Areum and Sahm side by side, and Emmett, Taeyo, and Noah on their bonghwang companions. If that isn't enough, Hattie and Namjoon come bounding in after them, followed by David, Jennie, and Cosette with my parents, Auntie Okja, and my Horangi guardians. It's the biggest family-and-friends reunion ever, and I'm all for it.

"You won't get away with this," the Mountain Tiger Goddess snarls, regaining her composure as the Crow and Fox Goddesses eye the mortar and pestle, more than ready to pound me to my doom.

But here's the thing.

I'm not scared. Because as the Haetae said, *The only thing stronger than fear is courage. The only thing greater than igno-rance is compassion. And the only thing more powerful than hate is love.*

And ultimately, it's up to *me* to decide which path I take.

With a smile on my face, I hurl the Key of the Final Eclipse into the Moon Rabbit Goddess's mortar at the same time as I reach over to snatch the pestle from the ground. Then, with every muscle activated in my body, I pound that stone bat against the mortar, pulverizing the powerful relic with the might of Mago.

And the truth is, I wasn't sure if it would work, but the proof is in the pudding.

The Key shatters into tiny little pieces, the purple flame of Mago's teardrop and Dahl's sacrifice binding themselves onto each shard, creating a powerful cocktail only I could concoct. And then I let it all go.

I throw my arms up wide and unbridle my beating chest, unleashing the invisible colors of Mago's butterfly wings into the auditorium. Because a power as great as the Key of the Final Eclipse should never be trapped inside a relic, or taken into one mere being's possession. A love *this* monumental deserves to be shared, and to live *inside* us—in each *one* of us.

The tiny fragments of the broken Key fly out of the mortar, and they fly to each and every one of the people I care about. To my parents, my auntie, to my Horangi guardians. To my old friends and new friends, to Areum, to my sister, to my Emmett. The shards pierce them in their hearts, and their bodies con-vulse as the splinters engulf them in a brilliant purply moonlit glow. And I know that through this act, I have ensured that a piece of me, a fragment of Dahl, and a sliver of Mago's divine power, will live in them for eternity.

Surprisingly, pieces of the broken Key are shot into the hearts of the goddesses as well, puncturing a hole for their darkness to seep out. Because compassion isn't only for your friends—it's for your enemies, too.

As the force hits them, the goddesses shrink, as if the full force of Mago's love has humbled them into smaller versions of themselves. They're still in their animal forms, but it's like time has turned backward, transforming them into infants. They circle around one another nervously, sniffing the mortar and whining, trying to figure out what has happened to their greatness.

The Haetae drops the mayor to the floor of the auditorium stage and keeps him pinned under his colossal paw as Hattie, Namjoon, Boris and the murder of imugis approach him.

"Hey, guys, do you think Yeomra would make a good janitor down in the underworld?" Hattie asks with a mischievous gleam in her eye.

Yeomra starts screaming, "No, not that! Please, no! I'd rather you just end me right here and now!"

Namjoon gurgles a gleeful, phlegmy sound, and Boris howls happily.

Noah joins Hattie's side and squeezes her hand, happy to be by her side again. He grins. "I'd say for this man, it'd be a fate worse than death."

And as for the goddesses, well, what can I say? Emmett has always been an animal person.

He closes in on the four shrunken goddesses and calms

their erratic circling with soft shushes. "You guys are *much* cuter when you're not destroying the world," he coos gently. "Shhh, yes, that's right. Very cute, indeed."

Taeyo, Cosette, Jennie, and David come to join him, and they each pick up a goddess carefully in their arms. Taeyo holds the tiger cub, Cosette the fox pup, Jennie the crow chick, and David the bunny kit, and there's a weird full circle moment seeing the young witches holding their ex-patron goddess in their arms. Almost like a changing of the guards—out with the old, and in with the new. Because unlike the mayor or the goddesses, my friends know compassion, and they have no intention of using this opportunity to bring more destruction into their lives, or ours.

Nobody needs an epic final battle when you have humanity.

War is for weaklings. Peace is for the powerful.

There is a moment of silence—a moment of reflection. And my friends look to me for guidance as the adults come to join us, too.

"What happens now?" Hattie asks quietly. "The Key was the only thing that could put the world back together. Now what do we do?"

I look to the Haetae, considering Hattie's question. But I already know what I need to do. The truth is, I just want to take a moment to enjoy this moment, because there will be no more like it.

"I need you all to know that I love you," I manage. "More than life itself."

I think I know how that rabbit felt now, jumping into the fire for the beggar. Love can make us do the unspeakable.

Because true love trumps the pain of saying good-bye. In some ways, the mayor wasn't totally wrong. There is some merit to the idea of seasons of change. Sometimes, things must end for new things to begin.

As if sensing the change in the air, everyone comes to stand with me. We form a circle of united souls who have gone through so much for one another, with one another.

"Why does this feel like good-bye?" Hattie asks, trying not to cry. "Are you . . . ? Are you *leaving* us?"

Areum *caw-caws* sadly, and Emmett reaches out to squeeze my hand. "Please don't leave, Rye. *Please.*"

My parents don't say anything. They just hold each other and weep silently.

"I will never be gone," I explain, remembering what Dahl told me. "Every morning when the sun rises, know that I am there. Every ray of sunshine, every ounce of warmth that kisses your skin, know that I am shining for you. And for me. And for everyone. I will always be here."

We are a puddle of emotions, huddled tightly together.

"But, sweetheart," Appa whispers, his voice breaking. "Why do you have to go? Why can't we figure it out together, like we've always done?"

"Because it's time for my final eclipse," I say. "The mayor and the goddesses broke the world as we knew it. And Mago's Fire can no longer be returned to Mount Baekdu because it lives inside all of you—as it should. The old world is gone, and we can't turn back that clock."

"But where will you go?" Eomma warbles, her chest full of turbulence.

"I'm the last fallen star. A piece of the dark sun that fell from the Godrealm's sky. I'm going home."

"But how will that help, Riley Oh?" Areum screeches sadly as Sahm comes to console her. "I do not understand how this will fix the world."

"Mago's first teardrop exploded the world into being with a big bang. When I return to the sky as the rising sun of the new era, there will be another beautiful explosion. One so powerful and so dazzling that it will kick-start a whole new world—one where love reigns supreme. It's my destiny." I pause, looking over at my sister. "No, it is my *choice*."

Phoebe and the RilOh stans are the first to come over, clutching to the bulgae and the newly wed cheollimas, sniffling as a choir.

"RilOh stans forever!" Phoebe cries.

"We'll name our firstborn after you, sugarplum donuts," Charles promises.

Sora and Austin find me next, with Auntie Okja in tow. "You unlocked your potential," Sora says proudly.

"We *knew* you would," Auntie Okja says.

"Thank you for believing in me," I whisper hoarsely to them all. "Even when I didn't. *Especially* when I didn't."

My dear friends Taeyo, Noah, David, Jennie, and Cosette are next in line, and they envelop me in a group hug so big I can't figure out where one person starts and another ends. Our new bonghwang friends pile on, too, and soon we're a heap of crying, spluttering teenagers covered in rainbow phoenix feathers.

"Riley, my aegi-ya!" Eomma weeps, rushing over and

stealing me from the mountain of friends, unable to wait any longer. "I will look up at the sun every day and think of you. We are so unbelievably proud of you."

Appa follows behind her, joining her in our embrace, sobbing together. Appa doesn't say anything, but he doesn't need to. Because I am a product of his love, and that's truer than any words that can be uttered.

Areum flies over to envelop all three of us in her wings, and she lets out a warm, chattering sound. "It has been the greatest pleasure of my life to serve and protect you, Riley Oh." Sahm softly coos beside her. "Thank you for showing me my worth."

My sister, the one who's normally the strong, certain leader, hides out in the dark wings of the stage, unwilling to bid me farewell. Namjoon and the rest of the imugis surround her protectively, making strange gurgly sounds, and Noah goes to stroke her back.

"Hat," I say softly, approaching her. "Remember how you could create storms down in the Spiritrealm? Do you still have those weather-manipulation skills?"

She sniffles and wipes her nose. "You mean like this?"

She snaps her fingers, and thunder cracks in the sky outside the auditorium, shaking the walls. The imugis' white scales shine a brilliant white, as if feeling the spirit of the yong in Hattie.

I chuckle. "Just like that." I pull her into a Hattie hug—the type that makes you feel like your eyes are about to pop out of your head. "Once it happens, you need to make it rain, okay?"

She nods, pulling me even tighter. "If I could do life again, I would choose you as my sister. Every single time."

"Ditto, Hat," I murmur, hiccup-weeping (it's a thing). "You know that."

Then, finally, I turn to Emmett, who frowns deeply—his frowniest frown ever.

"Emotions give you wrinkles, you know," I murmur through my tears.

He pulls me into his arms and doesn't let me go. "I'd trade a face full of wrinkles for more time with you." Boris roars mournfully by his side.

I think I'm on the brink of dying from overcrying. Which would be a waste of my big plans to become the sun.

So I find the will to pull away from him and raise my wrist. I'm so choked up, I can hardly talk. "Em, would you mind if I used your bracelet?"

He nods, his Adam's apple bobbing with the effort. "Bracelet or no bracelet, you know I'll always be with you."

So I untie the threads of the Tree of Fate that Emmett braided together. And I unravel it to form one very long string. And with the help of everyone I have ever loved, I tie myself to the goddesses, binding our fates together. Because if we're going to create some fireworks in the sky, I'm going to need all the divine power I can get. We're *all* going home.

With the four baby animals tied to me, I utter my final words.

"If you need me, just look up," I say.

"Always," Hattie responds.

"Forever," Emmett echoes.

And with that, I pull away from my kaleidoscope of people, my brightest, proudest mosaic of love. I jump on the Haetae with the goddesses anchored to me, and with one final look at my loved ones, I shed two final tears—one in grief for the world I leave behind and one in hope for the world we wish to create.

"Fly me as high as you can," I say to the Haetae. "As close to the extinguished sun as you can manage. It's time for us to finally get this party started."

He drives us into the stratosphere and into the empty expanse of space. And when we reach the sun with its lights turned off, I utter into the empty void with peace in my heart.

"And thus was born the Age of the Final Eclipse!"

The Haetae drives me as close as he can toward the dark celestial body, and I leap off the lion beast's back and into the star, clutching the four goddesses close to me. I feel the most at home I have ever felt in my existence.

We explode into a dazzling spectacle of light. Some might say this was our end, our final moment of life as many know it. But others would say that we gave birth to the first day of a new era. I don't know about you, but I'd hardly call that a death.

The explosion reshapes the world, putting the three realms back together. The River of Reincarnation subsides back down into the Spiritrealm, the Godrealm's creatures fly back into the sky world, and the Mortalrealm re-forms stronger than it was before.

Except one thing has changed.

As I asked of my sister, Hattie makes it rain. And as remnants of the explosion shower down onto the skin of every mortal on Earth, its divine power blesses them with the promise of magic. Because magic should live in each of us. And it should belong to all those who choose to wield it.

You see, my name is Riley Oh.

By now, you may know me by many other names. But the only thing you really need to know is that I am the brightest star in all the skies.

Every time you wake to my rising sun and feel my rays warm your shoulders, just remember—divine light flows in the very fabric of my existence.

That means every day you step out into the world, you are awash with the power of magic.

You are filled with *endless* possibilities.

And you, like me, were born into this world to SHINE.

Epilogue: One Year Later

Being the sun is way cooler than you think.

No, really. You get to live up in the sky, where the air is *way* sweeter, there's no traffic, and you get to check in on all your loved ones whenever you want. You don't even need a phone! You can just shine down on whoever you choose, give them a little bit of sun, and remind them that you're there.

But aren't you lonely up there? you ask. *Don't you wish you could be living a normal life in the Mortalrealm with everyone else?*

Well, firstly, can I just point out that Dahl doesn't *let* me be lonely. Nope, never. Seriously, he never stops talking. During the day, he's always being nosy, asking what I can see, what everyone's doing down below, and generally being a run-of-the-mill brotherly pain in the butt. Then, at night, he's going on about all the cool stuff he's seeing, telling me how I'm "totally missing out, kid!" and won't let me sleep. If I had a star for every time he's screamed "bada bing, bada boom!" I'd probably own the entire sky. Honestly, I need to invest in some heavy-duty lunar-proof noise-canceling headphones that work on telepathic links. Because, a girl's gotta get her beauty sleep, amirite?!

Secondly, being the cool creature that she is—Areum comes

to visit me often to tell me funny stories about what's happening down below. As an inmyeonjo, she's always been able to travel between the Mortalrealm and Godrealm at choice, so it's easy enough for her to fly up and come see me. She tells me she and Sahm have moved in together, and that they might even consider having little mini inmyeonjo-samjogo hybrid babies soon. Gahhh, can you imagine?! I better be a godmother, that's all I'm saying.

The Haetae comes to visit me now and again, too. I wish I could tell you that his days of only turning up when he wants to and only communicating in confusing riddles are long gone. But they haven't. He's just as bad. Perhaps, even worse? The one great thing is that he always brings Mong, our family Samoyed, with him each time he comes to visit, which means I get to play with our big white furball just like I used to back home. The Haetae is actually training Mong to be his protégé. Can you imagine Mong with wings?! #DogGoals. Billy the Bulgae often joins us, too, when he's not busy killing it at the canine agility competition reality TV shows. You're welcome.

Speaking of the golden realm, the place was in dire need of new leadership after the mishap with the major goddesses and the failed MegaRealm. Luckily, Charles and Maru paired up with the Lucha Libre tiger man (his actual name is Pyo Beom, by the way) to step up to the plate. Last I heard, they're trialing a new form of United Nations–style leadership model where each divine creature species gets a seat at the table, and they make decisions democratically as a realm. Good for them.

As for my sister, Hattie—well, what can I say? I always thought she'd make a fine president. But I don't think I had my scopes set high enough. Or should I say, down low enough. It turns out that with Yeomra now officially employed (for infinity) as a janitor in the H-Mart's toilets, there was a gap for the new ruler of the Spiritrealm. As a natural hellbeast whisperer, and with the essence of the Water Dragon Goddess still flowing in her veins (which turns out, not only allows her to control the weather, but also lets her breathe underwater!), she was already quite a contender for the role. She definitely had the underwater borough's vote in the bag. But in true Hattie fashion, she campaigned like a boss and ended up winning by a landslide (waterslide?).

The only people that were saddened by her success were our parents, who having already lost me and Dahl were understandably distraught at the thought of losing Hattie, too. Luckily, Hattie managed to negotiate a jobshare deal with Cheol (her ex-tour guide from her visits to the underworld) and Yeowu (our gorgeous fox-red Labrador puppy friend), which was a realm first, and a huge achievement for the future of HR practices. Essentially, Cheol and Yeowu look after the underworld on school days, while Hattie goes down to assume her throne on the weekends and the occasional school night. Eomma and Appa seem to be happy with the arrangement.

Speaking of my parents, I won't lie—I miss them. A *lot*. After all, I may have saved the world, but I'm still a thirteen-year-old kid, you know? After a while, it just wasn't enough watching them from up in my nice perch in the sky, so Mago Halmi threw me (and Dahl) a bone. As a respite from our duties as the sun and moon, Mago lets us visit the Mortalrealm every year on vacation! (And yes, thanks to this nice little arrangement, Dahl has been ticking off a whole lot of things from his ever-growing bucket list.)

While I'm Earthside, I get to spend my days eating all the things with Eomma and Appa and Auntie Okja, visiting Sora and Austin at Horangi HQ, and hanging out with Hattie, Noah (Oh-Noh! Haha, that will never get old!), Taeyo, Jennie, Cosette, and David. Noraebang is one of our favorite places to hang. As well as having bulgogi tacos at David's parents' restaurant, Seoulful Tacos. As well as mini golf. Yes, you have permission to call me Hole-in-One Riley, don't wear it out. I even make time to give motivational talks to the RilOh Fan Club, would you believe? Phoebe's pretty awesome, actually. She might even start a fashion line of Riley-related merch. What a Boss!

And what of Emmett, you ask? Well . . . *blushes* Don't tell anyone else, but he's probably the highlight of my visits down below. He bakes me my favorite salted-caramel cookies (with an *E+R* stamped in the middle) and those delicious Nutella–cream cheese donuts I love so much, and we talk about everything and anything under the sun (LOL that me!). Sometimes we talk about the future, but mostly we focus on the moments we're together, because like Charles the cheollima once said, tomorrow's not guaranteed, and the now is a gift, which is why we call it the present. Truth be told, Emmett still frowns a lot, but he's stopped wearing his all-black uniform (when the sun shines on you so brightly, wearing black makes for very hot days ☺. He still dreams of opening a bakery one day, though, and he said he's going to call it When Boy Met Star. I can't wait!

So I guess what I'm trying to say is that sacrificing myself to save the world and to become the sun was the best decision I ever made. And I have zero regrets. In fact, I wear it like a badge of pride. Turns out I'm not such a bad hero. Go figure!

But the coolest thing about all this?

Well, remember when Hattie made it rain, and divine power literally fell down onto the shoulders of all of mortalkind? Well, it just so happens, that in doing so, we turned magic into a free resource for everyone to access. Even without their patron goddesses, the gifted clans found that both their clan and elemental magic came back, and stronger than ever. Not only that, it seems all witches can now do all six types of clan magics at their will. How cool is that?!

If that wasn't mind-blowing enough, I've been seeing other miraculous happenings of late. Like, the other day, I saw a four-year-old saram girl smile at a tiny daisy growing in a meadow. Then, in front of her very eyes, the daisy grew. It kept growing and growing until the daisy's face was bigger than the girl's. You should have seen them both. They were amazed at each other, grinning like they were magic. And the thing is, they *are*.

Magic is all around us, and new magics are forming every day—even among the saram. This is a new era. An entirely new world of possibility and wonder. In fact, my friends (led by Taeyo and Emmett) have decided to start a new initiative to teach people how to use their magic. If there's a whole new generation of people experiencing the power of magic for the first time, they want to be the ones to help guide them. Because open-source magic is great, but there is always potential for darkness in everyone, even in the best of us. Education is key, and they want to be part of that picture. I'm so proud of them for that.

So there you go. One year into the Age of the Final Eclipse, and we've already come a long way!

But here's the *real* million-dollar question.

Where to from here?

(This is where you come in.)

Thanks to us—you're welcome!—magic is all around you. It's inside you. It shines down on you in the day and warms you in the night.

But how will *you* make use of it?

How will *you* live your best magical life?

Take your time. Think about it. And when you're ready, give me a shout. Inquiring minds must know. After all, you know where I live! Just look up and wave.

I'll be here.

Author's Note

There are so many stories, both shared orally via my parents and Halmeoni as well as those I learned in my research of Korean mythology that have made their way into the Gifted Clans trilogy. Some I preserved in their traditional forms—like the origin story of the first Korean woman who used to be a bear, or the rabbit who jumped into the fire for the beggar's meal. Others have seeped in more subtly through the texture and backdrop of Riley's journey.

However, there is one story I wanted to share with you here. Because interestingly, this is one that I didn't know I was telling until Riley told me (quite definitively!) that this is how her story would end.

It's called "Haewa Dari Doen Onui," which translates to "The Sister and Brother Who Became the Sun and Moon." Unsurprisingly, it tells the origin story of the sun and the moon.

Once upon a time, back when tigers used to smoke, there lived a sister and a brother. They had no father, but their mother, who raised them on her own, spent her days working for a rich yangban's family on the other side of the village. The yangban was demanding, and often their mother came home late, long after the sun had set over the horizon.

One evening, as the tired mother was returning home, a tiger appeared, as hungry as ever. The woman pleaded for her life, for she had children to feed. But the tiger's belly was growling, and no sooner had she finished begging than he gobbled her up whole. But still, he remained hungry. So he decided he would eat her children, too.

The tiger dressed in the mother's clothes and went to the home where the son and daughter were waiting. The brother and sister were astute, however, and they saw the tiger for what he was. Fearing for their lives, they ran out the back door and clambered up the nearest tree. The tiger climbed after them, looking forward to his meal.

Trapped in the canopy of the tree, the brother and sister called to the heavens for help, and heeding their prayers, the heavens sent down a rope. Grateful for the lifeline, the brother and sister began to climb. They climbed and climbed until they had reached the sky kingdom, where the brother became the sun and the sister became the moon.

The tiger also prayed, but the heavens sent down a rotten rope. And when the tiger began his ascent, it snapped. Screaming, the tiger fell onto a sorghum field and met his death, coloring the seeds with his blood and giving them their reddish tinge.

Living in the sky, the brother and sister rejoiced, for the heavens had taken pity on them. And life in the sky kingdom was good. But soon, the sister found that she was afraid of the dark. So the brother switched places with her, thus becoming the moon. And

*the sister spent her days as the sun, illuminating the world with
her most radiant light.*

Riley's story across all three books—*The Last Fallen Star, The
Last Fallen Moon,* and *The Last Fallen Realm*—seems to have
been working up to retell this one specific folktale.

But here's the thing.

I had never heard the tale of "Haewa Dari Doen Onui." It
was only *after* I'd drafted the third manuscript that I randomly
stumbled across it.

And it made me wonder: What is that we storytellers do,
exactly? Do we merely craft plotlines to be printed and sold
as books? Or is there more happening to us—*in* us—than we
know?

Maybe there's a mysterious energy, floating in the ether,
that seeps through our fingers and onto the page. Maybe we
are the sum of all writers who came before us, and it's their
legacy that fuels our pens. Maybe we are empowered by the
spirits of our ancestors, who fill our hearts and minds with
endless possibilities.

I don't know.

One thing I do know is that we are in the business of
magic. And that without our readers, our magic has no home.

So thank you, dear reader, for coming on this journey with
Riley Oh, and with me. I am so grateful you are here, and I
can't *wait* to share more of my stories with you. I hope you're
ready for even greater adventures ahead.

Shine Your Light,

Graci x

Glossary

aegi-ya (EH-ghee-yah) What my eomma calls me when she's about to deliver bad news. *Aegi* is Korean for *baby*, and the *ya* on the end is what you add when you're calling out to someone.

appa (AH-bbah) Korean for *dad*

annyeong haseyo (AHN-yong hah-say-yo) the Korean word for *hello* and also for *good-bye* (the formal, polite version you use for adults or people you don't know)

binyeo (BEE-nyo) a traditional Korean hairpin that kind of looks like a fat needle with an ornament on one end that's used to keep your bun in place

bonghwang (BONG-hwahng) a Korean phoenix. A benevolent creature from the Godrealm.

bulgae (BOOL-geh) Literally "fire-dog." The dogs of the Godrealm, who are covered in flames. Extremely intelligent but notoriously difficult to train.

cheollima (CHOL-lee-mah) winged horses that are the preferred mode of transport for the goddesses in the Godrealm. Cheollimas are known for being too big, too swift, and too majestic to be mounted by any mortal being. Interesting fact:

Ages ago, a cheollima who lost his wings and fell from the Godrealm became the first horse on Earth.

Dalgyal Gwisin (DAHL-gyahl GWEE-sheen) literally *egg ghost* in Korean. A scary, featureless ghost who haunts poor, unassuming kids. Honestly, don't look this up.

dokkaebi (DOH-ggeh-bee) really scary goblins that enter your dreams and make you live out your worst fears so they can eat them (literally).

eomma (OM-mah) Korean for *mom*. Pronounced with the "o" sound from *octopus* with a "mah"

Haetae (HEH-teh) a uni-horned lion-like beast, and Mago Halmi's guardian pet. He's known for his incredible loyalty, and his ability to manipulate time.

imugi (EE-moo-ghee) a creature that is part snake, part yong. The original imugi was a snake who failed Mago Halmi's assignment to become a yong (aka dragon), and then got stuck as a weird snake-yong hybrid for the rest of its days.

ineo (EE-noh) a creature that is half human, half fish. They are the Korean cousins of the Western merpeople, but they prefer the term ineo.

inmyeonjo (EEN-myon-joh) a wild creature with the body of a bird and the head of a woman. They can fly between the Godrealm and the Mortalrealm at will, and are obsessed with destroying mirrors because they hate their own reflections.

Jokbo (JOCK-boh) the genealogy book for all humanity, made from the Tree of Life. Mago Halmi used her own blood and sweat to inscribe the names of every soul she brought into the world on it. It's also the word used for individual family's genealogy books in Korean culture.

key of all keys a prophesied relic created by combining Mago's binyeo, Dahl's moonstone, and my onyx teardrop stone

Mago Halmi (MAH-goh-HAHL-mee) the mother of the three realms, mother of the six goddesses, mother of mortalkind, and mother of all creation. Basically, the head honcho who made the world.

Mago's Fire the first fire ever created that's kept on the summit of Mount Baekdu. The most powerful energy source in the entire universe, and the origin of all light.

Mount Baekdu the reverent mountain in the Godrealm where Mago's Fire is kept. (Also a beautiful mountain in North Korea!)

mun-pen a special pen that Mayor Yeomra gifted Dahl, which allows the creation of shortcuts and portals

Red Strings of Fate string made from the fibres of the Tree of Fate (aka red seaweed) that when used to tie people together, binds their destinies

salmosa a divine tiger serpent created by the Mountain Tiger Goddess, using her own arm. Its poison is so lethal, it has been known to wipe out entire civilizations. It's also the name of one of the most venomous snakes in South Korea.

saram (SAH-rahm) the word we use for people who aren't gifted with magic

saranghaeyo (SAH-rahng-heh-yoh) Korean for *I love you*

Spring of Eternal Life the liquid of life that flows into the River of Reincarnation and allows for the cycle of rebirth. It powers the current in the river that leads up to the Mortalrealm, but it's also used to make the Soup of Forgetting, and has powerful medicinal properties that, if prepared and consumed in the right way, can cure suffering—completely and forever. Powerful stuff.

Tree of Fate a red seaweed forest found in the oceans of the Spiritrealm whose fibers are used to create the Red Strings of Fate

Tree of Life a tree on Mount Baekdu in the Godrealm, whose wood pulp was used to create Mago's Jokbo (aka geneology book) for all of humankind

wakerpillar small caterpillars who work in the Memory Archives down in the Spiritrealm. They watch visitors in case anyone gets too lost in the memory books and can't get out. They release a special gas that wakes them up from the REM-ing process.

yeo-ui-ju (YO-ee-joo) the pearl of wisdom that some believe can grant immortality, or carry the knowledge of the universe. It's the stuff of legend though, because we mortals have never had it in our possession to know for sure.

yong a Korean dragon

Yongwang (YONG-wahng) the Dragon King, the ruler of the rivers and seas

Acknowledgments

I'm not gonna lie—this book was *hard* to write. Not because I didn't know what needed to happen in Riley's story, but because I didn't want to say good-bye to the characters I'd grown to love. That's the thing about a finite series, I guess. By virtue of it being a trilogy, the third book is inherently a final adventure, a last hurrah, and also a farewell.

It's therefore with bittersweet gratitude that I thank for the last time all the people that made this book and the series possible. Without each and every one of you, I couldn't have given Riley Oh and the Gifted Clans the send-off they deserve.

Firstly, a huge thank you to my amazing team at Rick Riordan Presents, Disney Hyperion, starting with my indefatigable and unflappable editor, Rebecca Kuss. You're a full-on hype team hiding in one body, and I am so indebted to your encouragement, support, and brain power. GK ♡ RK FOREVER. The hugest of Hattie's signature eye-popping hugs also to Stephanie Lurie, Rick Riordan, and Becky Riordan. Becky—I so appreciate all your Twitter love!

A special thank you to Jess Brigman for being such a champion for these books, and to Ashley Fields for being my angel of administration. To Kieran Viola, Ann Day, Crystal McCoy,

Emi Battaglia, the Core Four Media team, Sara Liebling, Guy Cunningham, Jacqueline Hornberger, Joann Hill, Andie Olivares, Marybeth Tregarthen, Jerry Gonzalez, Dina Sherman, Matt Schweitzer, Holly Nagel, Danielle DiMartino, Jordan Lurie, and Monique Diman. If I've forgotten anyone from the (seventh) Disney clan, or have not yet met you at the time of writing this, please know that I am sending you my gratitude.

A big shout out to Jodi Reamer, and also to Carrie Pestritto, who made these books possible. My excitable gratitude to the publishing teams in Germany, Italy, Poland, and Turkey for making my translation dreams come true. To Hachette Aotearoa New Zealand for being my publishing home at home.

A special thank you to all those incredible people who took my (creepy?) face cutout to their local Barnes and Noble stores to celebrate *The Last Fallen Star* being the Monthly Young Reader Pick for May 2022. I'm looking at you, amazing readers and booksellers! Thanks to you, the book hit the *New York Times* best-seller list just as I was facing developmental edits for *The Last Fallen Realm*. Talk about the best incentive to get cracking.

My utmost gratitude to everyone in New Zealand who voted these books into the Whitcoulls Kids Top 50 for 2022/23, and those that voted me as Best New Talent in the 2022 Sir Julius Vogel Awards. A huge thank you to all the bookstores and libraries who have hosted me for talks and events with open arms, and who recommend my books to new readers every day.

Big hugs to Xiran Jay Zhao for being my launch buddy for *The Last Fallen Moon*; to Julie Abe for having the vision and generosity to send me book-labeled cookies; to Regina Jang imo (aka "Halmeoni Book") for the lemon waters and energetic playdates; to Arne Hilke for my amazing ergonomic kneeling rocking chair; to Madi, Vicki, and Dean Curtayne for your admin prowess; to Hayoung Yoon and her family for their assembly line magic; and to Jmejam for being my half orange, which is reason enough to get a shout-out in every book I'll ever write.

A heartfelt shout-out to two of the most influential teachers in my life: Marian Burns and Cara Bergin-Stuart. Without you two, I'd never have been brave enough to come out of my intermediate school shell. It was a full circle moment reconnecting with you recently. All my love.

An emotional thank you to the amazing HPELC staff in the Pepe Room and Teina Room, for putting my anxious heart at ease so I could get lost in my imaginary worlds. And an equally emotional group hug to my ever-constant, ever-eternal kimchingoos: Jessica Kim, Sarah Suk, Grace Shim, and Susan Lee. You know I wouldn't be here without you.

Of course, no acknowledgments would be complete without my profuse confession of love for my family. To my parents on both sides, my siblings on both sides, and all the other permutations of family I hold dear, born and found. I am who I am because of you. A particular mention to Smelly, Spudman, and Skye (S-triple threat?) for putting up with me and filling my many days with love and laughter. And to Joya for pushing me to step up my screen-monitor game—my eyes and body thank you!

Because of the magic that is the publishing machine, the

acknowledgments of a book must be written well in advance of the book's release. In fact, at the time of writing this, we are still almost a year out from the publication date of *The Last Fallen Realm*. This means that there are bound to be *heaps* of people I haven't even met yet that will be influential in this book's birth into the world. To all of you precious people, thank you, thank you, thank you from the past.

Finally, to all the readers I've met at school visits, festivals, conferences, via email, and via social media, thank you from the bottom of my heart for allowing me to live my best author life. Keep sending me your messages—I love hearing from you. Your support is the reason I get to live out my wildest dreams.

Thank you always.

Graci x

JUL 2023